GW01445173

Massacre Site

Blue Moon Boston - Book 2

Justin Herzog , Steve Higgs

Text Copyright © 2023 Justin Herzog & Steve Higgs

Publisher: Steve Higgs

The right of Justin Herzog and Steve Higgs to be identified as author of the Work has been asserted by him in accordance with the Copyright, Designs and Patents Act 1988

All rights reserved.

The book is copyright material and must not be copied, reproduced, transferred, distributed, leased, licensed or publicly performed or used in any way except as specifically permitted in writing by the publishers, as allowed under the terms and conditions under which it was purchased or as strictly permitted by applicable copyright law. Any unauthorised distribution or use of this text may be a direct infringement of the author's and publisher's rights and those responsible may be liable in law accordingly.

'Massacre Site' is a work of fiction. Names, characters, businesses, organisations, places, events, and incidents either are the product of the author's imagination or are used fictitiously. Any resemblance to actual persons, living, dead or undead, events or locations is entirely coincidental.

Contents

Foreword

Gold is a living god and rules, in scorn, all earthly things but virtue. —
Percy Bysshe Shelley

Gold and Brass. December 16th O942hrs

THE GOLD REVEALED ITS solemn nature in the candlelight.

Even before the phosphorus had seared itself across his vision, Halfcrown believed that to be true. There was power in the wax and the wick, one capable of casting away falsities and revealing fidelity in the length of shadow it cast. He savored the warm glow of the flame as it danced between the coins serrated edges, their circular bodies passing through his fingers and touching down on top of one another with a gentle *clink* that echoed through the air.

He'd separated his treasures into two piles on the desk. The first was cast from gold, stolen dreams melted down, reforged and re-stamped. The second was made of brass. Rounded cartridges arranged into neat little lines like soldiers standing at attention, their payloads eager to be spent.

Each pile kept to itself, content to allow their silence to convey their worth. For all their differences, they were more alike than not. Each carried the possibility of fortune, and each reserved the right to take life in that pursuit. There was an honesty in their silence, a purity of truth that set aside the pretenses of societal expectations and allowed itself to just be.

Life was simpler in the silence, but nothing could exist forever within a vacuum. Not even him.

A knock sounded at the door, punctuated by a long moment's hesitation before it swung inward. It opened softly, reluctantly, the groan of the hinges offering a whining resonance of the man who stepped inside.

"You in here, boss?"

Sixpence then. For a moment, Halfcrown couldn't help but wonder if they truly believed it mattered. If they had convinced themselves that he favored any one of them over the other. Ludicrous, and yet, people needed their illusions. Better to play to their preconceptions and allow them that faux sense of security.

"In here," Halfcrown said.

"I can't really see," Sixpence said.

Halfcrown allowed himself a brief smile as Sixpence hesitated, debating whether he should risk making his way deeper into the room or remain near the doorway, thereby allowing himself a quick exit if needed. In the end, he chose the latter.

"You wanted to see me?"

Halfcrown turned in his chair, the swiveled springs casting a shrill cry into the dark and causing Sixpence to flinch. "I understand you and the boys went carousing last night. Did you have a good time?"

Silence greeted his words, lasting several seconds before it was broken. "It was just a bit of fun. After how hard we worked, we figured we were due a night out."

"I understand. You needed to blow off some steam."

"Exactly," Sixpence said. "We had a couple of drinks and saw a show."

"By which you mean a live show, with live girls?"

It was a rhetorical question. Halfcrown already knew what time they'd left, what route they'd followed, what establishments they'd frequented and what time they'd returned. The only thing he didn't know for certain was the only thing that truly mattered.

"Uh, yeah. I guess there were a few of those."

"Did you talk to anyone?"

Sixpence cleared his throat. "Yeah. Lots of people."

Halfcrown didn't need to be close to know there were little beads of sweat appearing on Sixpence's forehead, or that perspiration was soaking through the underarms of his shirt as he shifted his feet. He let the man linger in uncertainty for several seconds before he spoke again.

"Did you *talk* to anyone, Sixpence?"

"No, boss. Not a word. Not about... that."

"You're certain?"

"Yes, boss."

Halfcrown made an acknowledging sound. "And how did you fund this night of frivolity?"

"What?"

"Money, Sixpence," Halfcrown said. "How did you pay for it?"

"W-we didn't take any, if that's what you're asking," he said. "Not like we could spend it, anyway."

"That's not really the point."

"No, of course not. We used cash, just like we talked about."

Halfcrown nodded and made a show of lifting one of the coins, allowing the flame to play over the curved bits of the seal as it cast its shadow along the wall. "You're sure about that?"

"Positive."

"Because I'm going to count it, Sixpence. I know how much is supposed to be there. Down to the very last ounce. And if you're lying to me, I'll know that too."

"We didn't take any. I swear on my mother, we didn't."

"I certainly hope not."

"C-can I go now?"

"In a moment," Halfcrown said. "First, answer me something. What are we?"

"Boss?"

"What are we, Sixpence?"

He drew in a breath. "Patriots."

"Not thieves?"

"No, not thieves."

"And why do we call ourselves patriots?"

"I'm not really sure."

"Pity," Halfcrown said. "Do you know the prevailing idea this country was founded on?"

"Freedom?"

"Close. It was brotherhood. It was the notion that a man should care more about the people beside him than some distant king they've never seen, much less spoken to. And when words gave way to treason, it was done with the full understanding that it would only be successful if the men and women rose up beside one another. Without their neighbor's support, there could be no victory. We've lost that connection, Sixpence. Or better said, it was stolen from us. Do you understand?"

"I guess."

"A woman was murdered last night."

"Uh, yeah, we heard about it from some of the dancers at the Slipper."

"Apparently, her body was mutilated and left to rot in a parking lot. No one noticed the murderer as he dragged her from the street. Even if they had, they wouldn't have bothered to intervene. There's a sickness in this city. A rot. You can see it on every street corner and hear it inside every coffee shop."

"Hear what, boss?"

"The silence," Halfcrown said. "People aren't listening anymore. We've stopped caring about one another. We're all so obsessed with ourselves that we don't even notice when our neighbors wind up homeless on the streets. We step over them without so much as a backward glance, and even if we were to recognize their plight, it would only be to thank our lucky stars that it's not us in their place."

"That's not right."

"No, it isn't," Halfcrown said. "The city is a shell of itself, Sixpence. It can't be allowed to continue. Benjamin Franklin said, *'Those who would give up essential liberty to purchase a little temporary safety, deserve neither liberty nor safety. True justice will not be served until those who are unaffected are just as outraged as those who are.'"* Halfcrown dropped the coin back onto its pile and abruptly rose from his chair. "It's time to wake this city up, Sixpence. Time to shine the mirror back and let its citizens see what monstrous creatures they've become. To open their eyes to the horror and the shame until the penitent ones come forth to begin anew." He turned his head. "Gather the others."

"Now?"

Halfcrown nodded. "Tell them to bring the gold and the brass. We'll need both before this is all over."

Federal Reserve Building. December 16th 1705hrs

WE DROVE STRAIGHT FROM the pier to the Federal Reserve, pausing only to pass through the drive-through of a nearby coffee joint. I ordered mine black, not because I liked it that way, but because after two days of minimal sleep, little food, and more fist fights than I could count, I needed the caffeine more than I needed the cream and sugar.

My name is Chloe Mayfield. Welcome to the show.

Three days ago, I was an upstanding member of Boston's finest. Assigned to the Neighborhood Watch division, I spent my days arranging meetings, organizing fundraisers and handling noise complaints. Then, while affecting the arrest of an underage street racer, I inadvertently stumbled upon the mayor in bed with her teenage lover.

News of the scandal spread like wildfire, and the resulting fallout ripped through City Hall like a runaway freight train. As a result of my involvement, I'd been blacklisted and reassigned to Boston's newly formed Blue Moon division.

The brainchild of famed paranormal investigator Tempest Michaels, our division was tasked with investigating the world of the supernatural, disproving ghosts, vampires, werewolves and all other manner of boogeymen that everyone knew didn't actually exist. It was our job to uncover the truth and to ensure it fit neatly onto one of the department's incident report forms.

It sounds respectable enough, at least on paper, but unofficially, we were outcasts. So much so that the brass had literally kicked us out of police headquarters and assigned us a three-room hobbit-hole inside the Government Parking Garage. We had no funding, and the rumors circulating throughout the department suggested we were nothing more than a convenient dumping ground for officers who'd screwed up so royally they couldn't be trusted with anything else.

I was one of those officers, although, to be fair, life in Blue Moon was turning out to be more interesting than I'd expected.

In the past forty-eight hours, I'd been kidnapped by bay-spurned cultists, set on fire by angry witches, and nearly strangled by a dirty cop whose body was currently on its way to the morgue. Not bad for my first week on the job. Especially if I was about to add hunting leprechauns to that list.

The Federal Reserve was located in the city's Financial District, just past the bridge overlooking the Fort Point Channel. Boasting thirty-two stories, it was the fifth tallest building in the city, and had a harsh, imposing look that made me think of a prison tower or military fortress. Yellow police tape was strewn about the building's entrance, and armed guards lingered about outside, loaded down with flak vests and gripping assault rifles.

Lieutenant Kermit parked along the curb, maneuvering his dark green Jaguar F-type with practiced precision. A former British naval officer who'd retired from service and become a Bobbie in East London, he was in his mid-sixties, with silver hair parted down the side and a respectable air about him. He'd come to Boston two decades prior as part of an officer exchange program and never left. Far as I knew, he was the only officer in the entire department who didn't carry a gun, preferring his wits in lieu of kinetic force. He was also my boss, and with Topher gone, it was just the two of us.

"So, leprechauns," I said from the passenger's seat. I had my cell phone balanced on my knee and was gripping my coffee cup with both hands.

Kermit nodded. "Leprechauns."

"Do we know anything about leprechauns?"

"Truthfully, not much. Most legends depict them as diminutive fairies of Irish descent with a penchant for mischief. They're said to be more tricksome than dangerous."

"Might want to rethink that last part," I said, and motioned toward my phone. "There's nothing diminutive or mischievous about those guns."

The phone's screen displayed a grainy black-and-white image taken off the surveillance camera that Lieutenant Kermit had shown me back at the pier. I'd only had a couple of minutes to study it on the drive over, but it showed four men, all dressed in dark combat fatigues. Two of the men bore assault rifles strapped across their backs, while the other two carried various tools and miscellaneous objects attached to their flak vests. All wore heavy rubber masks that reminded me more of a goblin than a leprechaun, with shoulder-length red hair hanging down from beneath scuffed top hats and Abraham Lincoln style beards.

"Fair point," Kermit said. "I don't suppose you've any experience in this arena?"

I shook my head. "Not unless you consider breakfast cereal ads or NBA mascots as reliable sources of information."

"We'll just have to learn as we go, then. On the bright side, it's said if you catch one, you can force it to tell you where their pot of gold is hidden."

"Good to know, because at the rate I'm going, I just might need it."

I glanced through the windshield, peering at my reflection in the glass. To say I was a mess was putting it lightly. Half my face was currently being held together by adhesive glue, and a large section of my hair had been burned away by a witch's makeshift fireball. That, combined with the lack of food and sleep, gave me a slightly unhinged look that even I had to admit was unbecoming of a sergeant within the department.

Then again, if they wanted someone respectable handling leprechaun bank robbers, they would have assigned it to another division.

"Here," Kermit said. He reached his arm across the inside of the vehicle and opened his glove box. Inside was a dark blue baseball cap with the Boston Police Department's shield logo stitched on the front. He drew it out and handed it over. "I reckon it's a bit dusty, but should serve you fine all the same."

I nodded my thanks and slid it overtop my head. It didn't necessarily make me look any less disheveled, but it served to hide the scorched ends of my hair, and cast a small shadow down onto the cut along my cheek.

We exited the vehicle, and I followed him up onto the sidewalk, trying hard not to shiver. Spending all day on the pier waiting for the Leviathan to appear had given the late-December winds ample time to dig their hooks inside of me, and while the car's heater and the coffee had provided some relief, the chilling winds struck back with vengeance, redoubling their efforts as we made our way toward the building.

As we walked, I couldn't help but note the hard-eyed stares the other officers cast our way, and it took a conscious effort of will not to shift or fidget under their gaze. My discomfort wasn't only a result of my injuries. I'd lost my Kevlar vest back at the airport, and the pistol holstered on my hip felt awkward, especially since it wasn't actually mine.

It belonged to Everett Mackleroy, the department's most notorious homicide detective, who'd taken three bullets to the chest only hours before. There'd been no official announcement regarding his condition, which made me think he'd survived the trip to Massachusetts General Hospital and was likely still in surgery. I made a mental note to swing by there and check on him later, even though I suspected my presence wouldn't be welcome.

Come to think of it, I also needed to check up on my sister. She's been getting over a bad breakup and had been staying at my place when the bay-spurned cultists attacked. They'd come looking for me, but had taken her instead, and even though she'd escaped unharmed, experience told me she wasn't about to let an opportunity like this pass her by. She was probably lingering about the hospital halls even now, hoping to meet a successful doctor in search of a wife.

Speaking of doctors, I needed to wrangle one up for myself. Not for marriage, although I wouldn't say no to a stroll through the Commons or a meal that didn't come served in Styrofoam, but because the adhesive glue holding the split ends of my face together was only meant to be a temporary solution. I needed stitches, sooner rather than later, or else I'd better get used to seeing a large scar every time I looked in the mirror. Before I could do that, though, I needed to see about unraveling the mystery behind the leprechauns who'd just robbed the Federal Reserve.

We made our way up the stairs to the front door, where a uniformed officer examined our credentials before motioning us inside. Half a dozen steps carried up through the doorway and into a second security station. This one contained a pair of metal detectors, similar to what you might expect to find in an airport. There were more guards stationed behind the security desk, and they double-checked our IDs before waving us through. On any normal day, all the extra security might have seemed like overkill, but given the current circumstances, I couldn't really blame them.

Once past the second checkpoint, the facade of orderly chaos began to deteriorate, breaking down into just the chaos. It happens like that sometimes, when multiple departments get involved on the same case. We passed uniform officers, as well as Federal Reserve officers, and several men and women wearing off-the-rack suits that smelled strongly of Quantico.

Most of the suited agents were on the phone, relaying updates to superiors, or else hustling back and forth through the hallways, moving with determined strides and dipping into open doorways. I tried to keep out of their way as much as possible, falling into step behind Kermit as the pair of us made our way deeper into the building. Eventually, we came to a small row of elevators being watched over by two armed guards and a tall, light-skinned woman in a smart pinstripe suit who was grimacing and looking like she wanted to bite someone.

"Is that our reporting party?" I asked, keeping my voice low.

Kermit nodded. "Her name is Maura Youngman. Chief financial officer of the Reserve."

I let out a low whistle. "Betcha she's having one heck of a bad day."

"I don't doubt it."

I placed Maura Youngman in her mid-forties, but, in the right circumstances, she could have passed for younger. Standing half a head taller than me, she was lean and fit, the curvature of her shoulders beneath her suit suggesting she'd been a rower in her youth, and had maintained the discipline into middle age. Her hair was more silver than white, and she had the type of eyes that changed color based on the outfit she was wearing.

Kermit made a beeline for her and introduced us, his voice never rising above a low whisper. Youngman shook his hand, then turned and said something to the guards that caused them to step aside and allowed us entry into the leftmost elevator. I followed the pair inside, and the doors came together with an airtight *hiss*.

We descended three floors before the elevator came to a halt and the doors slid open to reveal a long hallway similar to that of an airport loading bay. Heavy-duty trollies and push carts were arranged into neat lines, and yellow stripes adorned the dark gray floor, indicating the path we were meant to follow. Youngman led the way, and Kermit and I followed her past several large offices containing various machines used for cash transfer and currency sorting. Heavy pipes ran the length of the ceiling, their steady *hum* suggesting the Federal Reserve had gone to great lengths to control the temperature as well as the amount of moisture in the air, a practical necessity when housing large quantities of cash.

We followed the hallway down for a hundred feet or so before we rounded the corner and arrived at a final security checkpoint. This one was manned by four armed guards and half a dozen men in suits. Unlike the ones above, these didn't strike me as law enforcement types. More like accountants, auditors and custodians.

Youngman spoke with the guards, then led us through the final gate and into a barren room connected to three separate bank vaults. Each door contained a heavy locking mechanism and looked to be made of solid steel, probably weighing somewhere in the neighborhood of a metric ton apiece. The center vault doorway was already open, and Youngman led us inside. Lieutenant Kermit followed her and I came in last, drawing to a sudden halt after two steps.

"Whoa," I said, my voice coming out breathless.

The room was packed with gold bars. There had to have been... well, more than I'd ever thought to see in my lifetime, at any rate. It was stacked floor to ceiling, arranged into narrow alcoves built into the wall and safeguarded by heavy reinforced gates with barred doors containing multiple key locks. Each door had a steel plaque beside it containing an identifying serial number. There was a weighing station in the center of the room, a heavy duty, industrial balancing scale with a digital readout, as well as an upright storage bench containing multiple weighted plates for comparison.

"Amazing, isn't it?" Youngman said. "More than any king or emperor in history has ever owned, and it's all gathered here in this room."

"It's definitely something," I said. "Although, I guess you're used to it."

Youngman shook her head. "I'll let you in on a little secret. You never really get used to something like this. Twenty-two years I've been here, and the sight of it still puts a smile on my face. There's something about it that you just can't help but to love."

"Yeah," I said, and turned my attention to the final alcove along the left side. "I guess that's part of the problem."

The last alcove's doorway stood open, and the neatly lined bars of gold that should have been present were nowhere to be seen. Instead, there was a single bar laid out along the floor, surrounded by a ring of neatly clipped green foliage. Four leafed clovers unless I missed my guess. Cause, you know, leprechauns.

"Do we know how they got inside the vault?" I asked as I made a slow half-circle around the empty alcove.

Youngman grimaced. "We're working on that."

"I don't see any signs of forced entry."

She shook her head. "Each vault rests on a layer of reinforced bedrock, it's necessary in order to handle the weight of the gold, and is composed of ninety tons of hardened concrete and reinforced steel. You could fire a tank at it and not even make a dent."

"Let's assume for the moment our leprechauns didn't have a tank," I said. "I'm guessing it's not as simple as just swiping a key?"

"No," Youngman said. "Accessing any of our vault doors requires three keys, and the Reserve takes steps to ensure no one person is ever in possession of all three at once."

"Who has those keys now?" I asked.

"Two senior vault custodians, as well as our chief auditor. Police officers were dispatched to their homes as soon as the theft was discovered. They're currently being debriefed, but each is insisting their keys haven't left their possession."

"Meaning the leprechauns either had duplicates or found a way around them?"

"Stands to reason," Youngman said.

There was a sharp note to her voice, and it didn't take a genius to figure out why. Even a cursory examination of the vault door would have revealed if the kidnappers had tried to drill or blast their way inside. Instead, they looked to have just walked right in. Which suggested it was an inside job. My recent experience with discovering that someone I worked with wasn't who they claimed to be had left me intimately familiar with the raw emotions such a revelation can bring. I imagined Youngman was feeling much the same and decided not to push her on it. For the moment, it was best to assume that the leprechauns had found some way around the vault's security. The question was, how?

I glanced over at Lieutenant Kermit. "Don't suppose you know anything about lock picking a vault?"

Kermit shook his head. "Bit beyond my reach, I'm afraid."

"We'll have to find someone who does then." I considered it for a moment, then glanced back toward Youngman. "Do we know how they got inside the building?"

"Not at this time."

I frowned. "No other cameras picked them up?"

Youngman's teeth ground together, and she clenched her fist before answering. "The head of security reports that there appears to have been an anomaly with our automated security system."

"What kind of anomaly?"

"A malware program. One that caused all our cameras to begin updating their software at the exact same time. We don't know how they managed to penetrate our system, but the picture in your possession is the only image that was recorded before they switched off. My officers thought it was just a glitch, and by the time they realized what had happened, it was too late."

I grunted. "What about the actual officers guarding the vaults? Nobody saw anything?"

"The Federal Reserve employs round-the-clock security, but our people can't be everywhere at once, and we don't station anyone permanently near the vaults. Too much liability."

"What are the chances our leprechauns knew that?"

Youngman shot me a look that said she'd already considered that question and didn't like the answer. I nodded and turned my attention to the adjacent alcove, motioning toward the serial number on the plaque.

"Do we know who the gold belonged to?" I asked,

"I've not been authorized to reveal that," Youngman said.

"It will be common knowledge by tomorrow. Suppose you had to guess?"

Youngman's mouth tightened. "Avant-Garde Financial Securities. They're an international investment advising firm with ties to the World Trade Organization. Their headquarters is here in Boston."

"And how many gold bars were in their vault?"

"Fifty-one," Youngman said.

"What's that translate to in dollars?"

"It depends on the market," she said.

"Rough ball it."

"Each bar is valued at approximately five hundred thousand dollars," Youngman said. "Fifty bars would therefore be—"

"Twenty-five million," I said and shivered.

On the opposite side of the vault, Lieutenant Kermit glanced between the nearby alcoves, his mouth drawn into a pensive frown. It didn't take me long to realize why.

Proud and shining, aligned in perfectly symmetrical rows, there was no denying that the gold had a mesmerizing quality about it. It took a conscious effort of will to stop thinking about it as gold and treat it instead like merely pieces of a larger puzzle.

Twenty-five million dollars was a lot of money, but it also wasn't as much as our leprechauns could have gotten away with. Peering around the vault, it quickly became clear that not every alcove contained the same amount of gold. In fact, fifty bars placed this particular alcove on the lighter end. Which begged the question, why? If our leprechauns were smart enough to side-step the Federal Reserve's security system and make their way into the vault without need of hostages or explosives, why would they settle for one of the smallest lots?

"And why," I said aloud, "would they leave this lone bar behind?"

"Probably because they couldn't afford the extra weight," a man's voice said a moment before he stepped through the vault entrance.

He was maybe a decade my senior, placing him just shy of forty, dressed in a tailored suit with a plain dark tie. He had soft brown hair, a neatly trimmed beard, and intelligent eyes. There was a slight curve to his mouth that I suspected would transform into a boyish grin, given the right circumstances. His tan told me that he wasn't a local, and the uneven bits said he'd come across it the old-fashioned way, as opposed to being sprayed down in a salon.

"Who the hell are you?" Youngman demanded. "And how did you get past security?"

"I showed them my badge," the man said. "And as for the lady's question." He made his way across the room, side-stepping around the balancing scale and drawing to a halt beside the weight rack. He searched among them for a moment before selecting one and drawing it from the holder.

"Excuse me!" Youngman said. "Just what do you think—"

"Bear with me," the man said, as he made his way back. "This won't take but a second." He extended the weight out toward me. "If you would be so kind?"

I glanced over at Kermit, who shrugged, before I reached out and accepted the weight. I didn't groan, or gasp or anything, but it took both hands to hold it, and there was no way I could have moved quickly with it.

"Heavy?" the brown-haired man asked.

"Maybe a bit," I admitted.

"27.3 lbs., give or take an ounce," he said. "That's what each of those bars weigh. People don't realize just how dense gold is." He flashed a quick smile and turned back to Youngman. "In regard to your question, ma'am, my name is Special Agent Alexander Gordan, with the FBI. I'll be supervising this case from here on out. And, of course, I know who you are, Ms. Youngman, but as for you two, I'm afraid I'll need a proper introduction."

Lieutenant Kermit introduced himself first, the pair sharing a polite handshake before Agent Gordan turned to me. "And you?"

"Sergeant Chloe Mayfield," I said. "Boston PD."

"Pleasure to meet you, Sergeant, or at least it would be, if you weren't bleeding on my crime scene." Agent Gordan reached up and tapped his cheek. "Just a bit, right there."

My hand shot up, and a flush of embarrassment swept through me that I'm certain was reflected on my face. Even first-year officers knew better than to go around leaving their DNA at a crime scene. Especially in a case this high profile.

I started to turn away, then stopped after a moment and squared my shoulders. Maybe it was fatigue, or maybe it was just plain stubbornness born of a hard week, but I wasn't about to be bullied or made to feel less by anyone. Especially some fancy-pants federal agent. I'd like to see him take a fireball to the face and show up for work that same day. Besides which, something he said struck a chord inside of me.

"What do you mean, your crime scene?" I asked. "Last time I looked, it was *our* crime scene."

"Not anymore, I'm afraid," Agent Gordan said. "The Bureau will be taking the lead from here on out."

"That so?"

"It is," he said. "We will, of course, welcome any and all assistance from our friends at the Boston PD."

"I sense a big 'but' coming."

Agent Gordan dipped his head. "But we would appreciate if, for the time being, you would focus your efforts on determining the significance of the leprechaun persona our thieves adopted. My understanding is this type of thing is right up Blue Moon's alley, and since the calling card of four-leafed clovers suggests there's more to this than merely an aesthetic choice, any information you can uncover will only increase the likelihood of our catching them."

"Translation, you want us to focus on the little green men while you find the gold?"

"Precisely," he said.

"There might be more overlap than you think," I said. "It would probably go smoother if we all just agreed to share whatever information we find."

Agent Gordan offered me a tight-lipped smile. "Unfortunately, that might not be possible. The Bureau is more capable than most media outlets would prefer to believe. However, sharing information isn't our strong suit. Make no mistake, Sergeant, this is our case, and if you want to stay on it, you'll need to play by our rules."

"How about a show of good faith, then?"

"What did you have in mind?"

"You seem pretty confident you know why they didn't take more gold. Is it just a weight issue?"

"More of a logistical one, actually," he said. "Based on video footage taken from the surrounding neighborhoods, we're confident that our thieves departed this facility in an unmarked Ford cargo van with pilfered plates. A vehicle of that size is capable of holding approximately 3,300 lbs. Taking into account four men with an average weight of two-hundred and twenty-five pounds, plus another hundred pounds apiece in gear, and you're looking at approximately two thousand pounds of available weight. Fifty bars weighing in at—"

"1,365 lbs.," I said.

Agent Gordan frowned. "Precisely."

"They gave themselves a cushion of just over six-hundred pounds," I said.

He nodded. "Likely didn't want to risk blowing out their tires."

"Which means they're careful." I let out a sigh. "Which means it's going to be that much harder to catch them."

"Oh, I wouldn't worry about that," Agent Gordan said. "They might be careful, but they're also showmen. The computer virus, the costumes, and the gold. It all suggests a healthy dose of ego. A crime this brazen has a way of spreading. Our thieves won't be able to stop themselves. Mark my words, Sergeant. They're celebrating now, but we'll have the entire lot in handcuffs by Christmas."

A Long Cold Winter. March 15th 0930hrs

Despite Agent Gordan's assurances, Christmas came and went without any arrests, and in the wake of the new year, temperatures plummeted, heralding in one of the worst winters on record. Seven feet of snow descended on the city of Boston, laying siege to the downtown and forcing the residents to seek shelter indoors or underground within the subway tunnels.

The cargo van Agent Gordan had mentioned turned out to be a dead end. The pilfered plates belonged to an elderly woman who lived in the town of Braintree. It took about five minutes to clear her of any involvement, and when the cybersecurity technicians were unable to offer any insights into how our leprechaun thieves had circumvented the automated security system, the investigation ground to a stale halt. As the weeks passed, Agent Gordan's frustration grew, until he finally stopped communicating altogether. I eventually got word that the Bureau was shelving the investigation and diverting resources elsewhere until the snows cleared.

For my part, I took advantage of the winter respite to heal up, which included getting stitches along my face and arm. The doctor *tsked* as he worked, admonishing me for waiting so long to seek medical treatment. I tried explaining that I'd been busy battling bay-spurned cultists who believed a sea-monster was going to rise from the harbor and consume the city, but he just gave me a funny look and finished up quickly. I learned later that the story had already spread through the hospital, courtesy of my sister, except in the version she told, it sounded like she'd been the one saving me, rather than the other way around.

Once I was released from the hospital, I made my way back home and spent the next several weeks building a new routine. I would wake up, exercise as much as I could comfortably manage within the confines of my apartment, hit the shower and pack myself a sack lunch before donning my Winter-Walker snow shoes and heading off to the Boston Public Library.

Located across the street from the famed Trinity Church, the Boston Public Library was the third largest library in the United States, just behind the New York Public Library and the Library of Congress. A trio of tall archways flanked by heavy stones formed the main entrance, leading inside where residents could find research rooms, museum-worthy galleries, and rare, private collections held under lock and key. An open-air courtyard was located in the building's center, surrounded by exhibition rooms which the library used to host free public events, including author talks, local history lectures, concerts and art exhibits.

Most of the city buildings were shut down due to the winter storm, but the library had elected to stay open, its staff donating their time to ensure those less-fortunate citizens who were unable to find refuge within the subway tunnels and shelters had a place to escape from the storm, even if only for the daylight hours. In return, the transients kept the surrounding sidewalks and entryways clear, shoveling the snow out into the street every few hours, while also monitoring their own, ensuring that any who sought to steal extra food or sneak away into the aisles to get high were quickly shown the door.

I tried to help as best I could, slipping in through the front doors and shaking the snow from my shoes before dropping the day's offering onto the main desk. Usually, it was canned goods or bags of apples purchased from the nearby markets. It wasn't much, but every little bit helped. From there, I made my way upstairs to the non-fiction section, claiming a table near the mythology sub-section where I spent the rest of the day researching local legends connected to the northeast, including leprechauns.

I figured if I was going to be embracing my new role within Blue Moon division, then I'd better learn to do the job well, and that meant building up a base of knowledge, so I wasn't constantly having to learn on the go. Unfortunately, it wasn't as straightforward as you might think. So much of Boston's history was intertwined with English and Irish ancestry, not to mention the northeastern Native American tribes who'd been here long before the European settlers arrived. I couldn't take any books home with me, on account that they'd be ruined by the storm, so I settled in and spent hours reading through the heavy tomes.

I don't mind admitting that the first few weeks were a bit overwhelming. I didn't have a background in mythology or folklore literature, and so many of the legends were either built upon one another or convoluted to the point of being almost indecipherable. Luckily, one of the librarians noticed me struggling, and she directed me to a corner of the children's section, where I found old copies of Grimms' Fairy Tales, Classic Mythology and Native American Folklore.

Because they were intended for children, the authors had taken great care to simplify the material inside, and reading them provided me a base for some of the denser tomes back in the non-fiction section. I was by no means an expert by the time spring rolled around, but I wasn't entirely clueless anymore, either. More importantly, I'd made connections with the local librarians, who seemed downright amused when I told them my job, and who offered to help me as needed.

Which was kind of nice, if I was being honest. It felt good to have someone rooting for me. I just wished I could replicate that feeling within my own department.

Up until now, I'd spent my entire career assigned to the community policing division. I was used to being out and about, meeting with people both inside and outside the department on a regular basis. Being left on my own like this, utterly ignored by the rest of the department, save for the occasional check-in call from Lieutenant Kermit, was disheartening. It felt like I'd been fired, even though my paycheck still showed up in my account every other week. Outside of that lone electronic transfer, however, I'd been largely forgotten.

Which is why it came as a bit of a surprise when we got our first big break in the case.

It was two days shy of St. Patrick's Day, and I was seated at my usual table, dividing my attention between Legends of the Northeastern Native Americans and the Boston Globe Newspaper. The former had to do with the legends of the Kanontsistóntie's, disembodied flying heads with fiery eyes and long tangled hair that had allegedly terrorized the Iroquois Confederacy. The latter was reporting on the latest celebrity-endorsed crypto-currency scandal, a virtual ledger called Fidelitycoin that had only been in effect for three months before it seemingly vanished, taking millions of dollars with it. I didn't immediately recognize my cell phone's ringing chime, but once it finally dawned on me what I was hearing, I fished it out from my pocket, blowing dust off the screen before answering.

"Hello?" I asked.

"Sergeant Mayfield?" a woman asked. Her voice was crisp, proper, and to the point. I recognized the tone, if not the person. She was calling from our dispatch unit.

"Speaking," I said.

"We have a 10-25 request for you. I'm sending all details to your computer now."

I blinked. A 10-25 was a request to meet in person. Often times, it was used as a polite way of requesting assistance, or, in rarer cases, a formal method of requesting someone get their keister over to a crime scene right the heck now.

"A request from whom?" I asked.

"Lieutenant John Kermit."

I gave myself a shake, acknowledged that the message had been received, and that I was on my way. Then I hung up my phone, gathered my things, returned my books to their shelves (cause only a giant asshat would leave them on the table for someone else to put away) and made my way out into the street.

My apartment was only a mile from the library, and I traveled on foot, careful to avoid the last remnants of slush still clinging to the edges of the sidewalk. Most of the snow had melted away over the past week, hastened by the combination of street salting and the city's recent acquisition of three commercial snow melting trucks nicknamed the Snow Dragons. Attached to the back of heavy trucks, they were essentially enclosed engine rooms containing hot water baths and heater exchange tubes that could turn thick snow into boiling water, which was then sprayed back onto the surrounding ice.

As I crossed the street, the sun beamed down from overhead, casting its glare on the remaining slush even as it coaxed the first hints of green from the flat brown soil. Once I reached my apartment, I donned my Kevlar vest and jacket, then grabbed my tactical patrol bag, which contained my Massachusetts State Law book, a laminated map of the city, a fingerprint kit, extra pens, gloves, my flashlight, a multi-tool ki t, traffic flares, extra report forms and evidence bags, a first aid kit with an emergency tourniquet, and a couple bags of trail mix that were probably stale. I tossed it over my shoulder and made my way down to the street to where I'd parked my new Ford Crown Victoria.

I say new only in the loosest sense, because while it may have been new to me, the car had definitely seen better days. Back when I'd been in the department's good graces, I'd been assigned a Police Interceptor SUV. I'd loved that vehicle, but it had been firebombed during a fight with three rogue witches. Never in my wildest dreams did I believe the department would ever let me have another vehicle, but the Crown Victoria had shown up outside my apartment a few weeks ago, along with a stack of business cards containing my name and contact information on the passenger's seat.

A four-door sedan whose silver paint had faded to light gray, there were no decals or signs, and no light bar, which meant I'd had to purchase my own and attach it to the dashboard using a combination of Velcro and Duct Tape. The seats were worn, fraying along the edges, and the mileage counter had given up its ghost at just over three hundred thousand miles. To make matters worse, the entire thing had a stale, wet-cardboard aroma, and the first time I started up the engine I'd disturbed something that had been living inside, causing it to scream and howl before sliding down from the engine block and scampering away into the snow.

Bottom line, it was less than ideal, but I told myself that this was better than taking the subway.

I tossed my bag inside, then slipped into the driver's seat and inserted my department issued laptop into the mounting brace. I was a little surprised to see that my name and password still worked, but I quickly admonished myself not to think that way.

No matter how unconventional my role might be, I was still a member of the Boston Police Department, and, who knows? If this went well, other departments might follow suit. Given enough time, it might even become common practice to employ a paranormal division within each department. For all I knew, I was standing on the precipice of change, a pioneer in a new, emerging division within law enforcement agencies across the country.

I like that idea. Way better than the alternative, which suggested I was only here until the department found a convenient excuse to get rid of me.

Think positive, Chloe.

Regardless of what the future might hold, I wasn't going to be employed for long if I didn't answer my calls. I switched over to our dispatch system and found the 10-25 request. It was light on the details, offering little more than an address. I quickly typed it into the GPS and frowned when it came back to a place in Charlestown.

Located just north of the city, Charlestown drew its roots from Irish immigrants, hard-working, blue-collared types who occupied triple-decker homes with bars on practically every corner. It was home to several historical landmarks, including the Bunker Hill Monument and the USS Constitution battleship. Despite what certain movies might imply, not everyone in Charlestown was a professional bank robber eager to shoot it out with the police at the drop of a hat. That said, there was no denying that a large portion of career criminals got their start there, and that violent crimes statistics spiked the minute you crossed the river.

I loosened my gun in its holster and headed that way, passing through downtown and the North End before crossing over the Washington Street Bridge. As I drove, I took a moment to organize everything I knew regarding the investigation and the mythos surrounding the leprechaun.

Lieutenant Kermit had been right on point when he'd described them as mischievous fairies of Irish descent. Originally believed to be scions of the Fair Folk, the earliest legends suggested they were more partial to red than green, and affiliated them with cobblers and shoemakers. They were known to be sneaky, tricksome, apt to disappear if left un-supervised and vicious when angered. There were other tidbits, little stories or anecdotes found in literature and folklore that I'd earmarked over the past few weeks, but nothing that immediately stuck out to me as useful to our case.

Regarding the theft itself, I'd tried figuring out how our thieves had circumvented the vault's lock, but that turned out to be a dead-end, especially after the FBI denied me access to the vault's blueprints. I'd tried explaining my reasoning for the request, but had been firmly rebuffed and reminded that the robbery itself was not within my scope of the investigation. As a result, I was left with little more than guesswork, relying on a few books as well as half a dozen conversations with various high-grade locksmiths and security experts within the city, none of which were able to offer me much help.

From there, I'd spent some time looking into Avant-Garde Financial Securities. The company was based here in the city and had a fairly stellar track record dating back almost forty years. There were reports, mostly hearsay from old website forums and a few smaller newspapers, that they'd taken heavy losses during the Dot-Com crash, followed again by the Housing Crisis, but nothing definitive that I could see to make them a target.

In some ways, it felt like I was fumbling in the dark, but I reminded myself that most cases started out like this. It wasn't my job to pick and choose what facts I paid attention to, but to gather all the information I could and then examine each piece of evidence to see the picture it formed.

Preconceptions could be deadly for a detective, and going into a situation thinking you already know what you're going to find is a sure-fire way to ensure that killers, or in this case leprechauns, were allowed to walk free.

And I'd be damned if I was going to allow that to happen on my watch.

All That Glitters.
March 15th
O957hrs

THE ADDRESS LED ME to a green triple decker with faded yellow trim located a few blocks south of the Bunker Hill Burying Ground. Marked police cars had blocked off the street, and there was yellow tape strewn around the property. I parked along the curb, then made my way in on foot, flashing my badge to one of the uniforms who motioned me forward. I ducked under the yellow tape, then crossed the length of the sidewalk and went through the door.

They say it's not four walls that make a home, but the love a person feels upon entering. That may be true on some level, but your environment still counts for something, and stepping through the door, I didn't feel any warmth or love. All I saw was neglect and abandonment.

The floorboards were worn, warped and rising in places where water damage had set in. The furniture was all secondhand, stained yellow along the arms by sweat and God only knows what else. The drapes in the window were faded to resemble the color of tobacco smoke, the accompanying stink of which was buried into the house frame.

There were bugs in the kitchen, crawling between open canned goods left on the counter and dark brown beer bottles, the latter of which outnumbered the former by a significant margin. A lone little girl, maybe ten years old, sat in a rickety chair, crying, while a uniformed - officer stood awkwardly by. His nametag read: Bill Thompson, and his face lit up at the sight of me, likely hoping I was with the Department of Children and Families and here to relieve him of his charge. I shook my head and showed him my badge, earning me an annoyed frown before he flicked his chin towards the upstairs. I turned and headed that way, making my way up a narrow stairway bearing the imprint of countless footsteps worn into the wood. At the top of the landing, I caught wind of movement to my right, and I followed the noise down to a small bedroom.

It was a narrow room with worn paint along the walls and an unmade bed shoved into the corner. A lopsided dresser lay against the far wall, clothes bursting forth from half-open drawers to litter the floor. There was a guitar case in the corner, the edges so worn that they were peeling away like a battered old book spine, and a pile of little wheels that looked as if they would fit on a skateboard.

The corpse lay on the floor.

He was facedown, one arm splayed out above his head, the other bent behind his back. Dressed in loose jeans and a gray hooded sweater, I wasn't entirely confident calling him an adult, regardless of what the law might say. I thought back to the crying girl below and put two and two together, figuring him for her older brother. There were bloodstains along the back of his sweater, and the back of his skull was... I shuddered and looked away, turning my attention to the second figure in the room, who was kneeling above the corpse holding a large camera.

In his late forties, heavyset, with brown hair swept back, Jerry Gantenbein was dressed in khaki pants and a dark windbreaker jacket with the word "Forensics" stenciled on the back. He had a notepad open in front of him and was jotting down notes to coincide with his photos.

"Hey, Jerry," I said as I took up next to the doorway. "What's shaking?"

He snapped another photo, then lowered the camera and sighed. "My balls hurt."

I blinked. "Come again?"

"I'm sorry, Chloe. I don't mean to be crude, but I'm in pain, and the brochure said it helps to talk about it."

"Uh-huh," I said. "Okay, uh, what seems to be the problem?"

"It's my wife. Rosie."

"She hit you or something?"

"What? Oh, God, no," he said. "A few months ago, we were discussing whether to have any more children."

"I didn't know you had children."

He nodded. "Three. We were hoping for more, but time just sort of slipped away from us. Rosie's no good about taking the pill, so we talked to the doctor about other options. He said she could get her tubes tied, but it was easier for me to get snipped, so I started looking around for a doctor." He set his camera down beside his notepad. "My brother-in-law claimed he knew one. Said he came highly recommended. We had our consultation last week. Smaller man. Mild-mannered. He had tiny little hands. I thought that meant he would be better with the delicate stuff." He swallowed, and some of the color faded from his face. "I was wrong, Chloe. Once he had me up on that table, all I could hear was the *snip, snip, snip* of his scissors. You'd have thought he was giving me a haircut. I don't know what he did, but my boys are swollen up like grapefruits."

I tilted my head. "There does seem to be a bit of a bulge forming down there."

"The painkillers wore off hours ago. They're aching like anything."

"When did this happen?"

"This morning."

"This *morning*?" I asked. "Why aren't you home?"

"I'm saving up my sick days to take Rosie to Hawaii next summer," he said. "Plus, things have been so quiet lately around the office, I figured I could just slip in and out without anyone noticing." He shook his head. "The call came in when I was still on the table with that sadist's hands around my boys."

"Talk about bad timing."

"Tell me about it. I should be watching old hockey reruns with some frozen peas pressed against me. Instead, I'm here, crawling on all fours like a toddler."

"Maybe it would help to distract you from the pain if we just focused on work?"

"Worth a shot," Jerry said. "Lord knows, I'll try anything at this point."

I nodded toward the corpse. "What can you tell me about him?"

"Well, according to his ID, his name is Ricky Brannon." Jerry shifted his stance and motioned to the nearest wall, indicating the red splotches marring the faded paint. "I'll need a few days before my official report is ready, but based on the height of the blood splatter, it looks like our killer marched him up here, then forced him to kneel down before they shot him in the back of the head."

I exhaled and wiped my hands along the edge of my jacket. "Do we know if it was just one killer?"

"Impossible to say for certain," Jerry said. "More technicians are on their way. We'll need to process the scene completely. All I can tell you right now is that it looks like the first bullet entered through the right side of his skull and exited out the opposite end. You can see where the bullet impacted." He pointed toward a section of the wall, indicating where the bullet had imbedded itself. "Once he was down, the shooter put two more bullets into his back."

I grunted. "Guess whoever did this wanted to make sure he was good and dead. Which means it was probably personal."

"This is Boston," Jerry said. "All murders are personal."

"Fair point," I said. "Did we get anything from the girl downstairs?"

Jerry shook his head. "Nothing yet. We can't do a formal interview without her parents present, and we're having trouble locating them."

"Shocking," I said. "Did anyone think to try the nearest bar?"

Jerry gave a "*What can you do?*" shrug and raised his camera to resume shooting.

I drew in a long breath and let it out slow. "Three gunshots should be enough to draw attention. I assume we've got uniforms out canvasing the neighborhood to see if anyone saw anything?"

Jerry snapped a photo, then adjusted his angle. "Detective Mackleroy has them deployed in an eight-block radius."

My stomach dropped. "Mack's back?"

41

"Yeah, for a couple of weeks now," Jerry said. He glanced over, and his eyes widened when he saw my face. "Oh, Chloe, I'm sorry, I didn't realize."

"It's fine," I said.

"I wouldn't have said anything if I'd known—"

"It's fine, Jerry," I said, my voice firmer this time. "I don't suppose you've seen Lieutenant Kermit around, have you?"

"No, I don't think he's been here," Jerry said.

"Okay then," I said. "In that case, I should probably go. I'd appreciate it if you didn't mention that I was here."

"No worries, Chloe. No one will hear it from me. Unless you want me to, in which case I'll—"

"That's okay, Jerry," I said. "I'll catch up with you once things have settled."

I turned to leave, but a figure emerged from the stairs and stepped into the hallway, halting so close that I almost slammed into him. I gave a surprised start and caught myself, instinctively shying back as I caught my balance.

"Scutt," I said. "Er, I mean, Detective Ruscutt."

Detective Collum Ruscutt was in his late forties, with beady eyes, a broad nose, and hollow cheeks. His hairline was receding in tracks, separating his head into three distinct sections, and his face was pock-marked, craggy and troubled, lined with years of nicotine abuse that showed itself around his eyes and in the yellow tinge of his mustache. Raised in Charlestown, Scutt was the embodiment of blue-collar Boston, everything from his stance to the scars along the back of his hands identifying him as a workingman's man. He had fifteen years invested in the department, and his reputation was one of a steadfast, if unremarkable, detective.

"You alright there, Chloe?" Scutt asked. "You seem a bit shaken."

"Fine." I took another step back, taking a moment to adjust my jacket. I'd never felt entirely comfortable around Scutt. It wasn't just the lingering scent of nicotine coming through his pores, although that was pungent. It was his eyes. I'd seen the way they tracked the other female officers in the department, and felt them on me when I walked away. He'd never even cracked so much as an off-color joke, but there was something in him that set alarm bells ringing in my head. When you know, you just know, and when it came to Scutt, I knew.

"Can't be your first body," Scutt said. He shifted his feet in the hall, blocking the path to the stairway. "Can it?"

"Nope," I said. "Not even a close second."

"Ah, that's right," he said. "I forgot you had that architect fella last year. The one who was going to rebuild the South Waterfront. Guess that didn't happen, did it?"

"Not that I've noticed," I said.

"Course, then there was that little runt too, wasn't there? The Gopher."

"Topher," I said.

"That's right," Scutt said. "Broke his neck, didn't you?"

I had a flash of memory, Topher's body floating face-down in the water, and a shiver went down my spine. "Technically, the stairs did that. I was just trying not to get killed."

"Ah, don't be modest now, missy," he said. "Man tried to do you in, and he paid for it. Guess you're more dangerous than you look."

"If you say so." I glanced back over my shoulder. "Jerry, you'll let me know if anything comes up?"

"You mean with my..."

"The body, Jerry," I said.

"Oh, sure thing, Chloe," Jerry said.

Scutt frowned. "You're keeping an eye on things here? Did I miss a trick? Are you a homicide detective now?"

"Nope," I said. "Still in Blue Moon."

"Hunting down mothmen and unicorns?"

"No unicorns yet," I said. "But you never know. Today it's leprechauns."

"How's that connect to this boy's murder?"

"Afraid I can't say yet, but I'll be sure to let you know if anything pops up. Last thing I want to do is interfere in your investigation. Now, if you'll excuse me."

Scutt sidestepped, blocking my route. His face shifted, his pock-marked cheeks rising as his dried lips split apart into a wide smile, revealing yellow-stained teeth. "I appreciate the professional courtesy, but I'm afraid it's misplaced."

I squared my feet and purposefully kept my hands down at my sides. "How so?"

"This isn't my case."

I frowned. "Whose case is it?"

Scutt started to answer, but a noise rang out from the stairway, cutting him off. A trio of sounds, two footsteps followed by a wooden *thump*. I didn't realize what I was hearing at first, but then a figure appeared, and my heart sank.

Everett Mackleroy stood a few inches below average height, with a clean-shaven head and soft blue eyes that always seemed to see more than he let on. He was a living legend within the department, a throwback to old-school muscle who'd been kicking in the worst doors in Boston for the better part of twenty years. What he lacked in height, he made up for in brash ego, and he went about his work with tenacity and viciousness that didn't always stop short of being excessive.

I'd known him for the better part of four years, and had come to recognize his duplicitous nature. If not working for the department, he likely would have been involved with the mafia, carving out his own little kingdom within the city borders. Most of the officers who knew him thought we were lucky to have him on our side, and I used to agree with them. These days, however, I wasn't so sure.

He'd lost some weight since I'd seen him last, his clothes hanging looser than I remembered, and he moved with the aid of a cane, the slight hunch in his back suggesting that his chest and abdominal muscles were still healing. His gaze locked onto me, and there was nothing friendly in his smile.

"Well, well, look what we got here. Thought I heard a familiar voice. Our very own turncoat. What's a matter, Chloe? Cat got your tongue?"

"Mack...."

"Best give her a moment," Scutt said. "Poor girl looks like she's seen a ghost."

"Is that so?" Mack said. "I look like a ghost to you, Chloe?"

I swallowed and cleared my throat, trying to work some moisture back into my mouth. "I didn't realize you were back already. How are you?"

"What, you mean since you lured me into that little death-trap and nearly got me killed?"

"It was never my intention for you to get hurt."

"Course not," he said. "Or, at least, not unless you were the one doing the shooting, right?"

"Christ, Mack," I said. "I thought you were a murderer."

"Don't be so sure I'm not," he said. "Fact is, I can think of a few people I wouldn't mind finding face down in a gutter. Present company included."

Something tightened in my chest. "Nice, Mack," I said. "Real nice."

"Ah, drop the wounded bird act," Mack said. "We both know you've got some payback coming. It's why you've been hiding yourself away in the library for all these months."

"I haven't been hiding," I said. "I've been—"

My voice trailed off, and a small shiver passed through me. I hadn't told anyone where I was spending my days except Lieutenant Kermit, and he knew enough about Mack's nature, as well as our history, to keep quiet about it. I also couldn't recall seeing any other police officers inside the library during my time there, which meant he must have gotten his information from another source.

Instinctively, I started running through the library employees, mentally shuffling the faces of the librarians and custodial staff to see who might have been on Mack's payroll. Unfortunately, it quickly became clear that there were too many for me to sort through, and besides, it didn't necessarily have to be a member of the staff at all. Plenty of transients who'd been calling the library home had extensive criminal histories, most of which included drug charges. For years,

Mack had alternated between working homicide and narcotics as it suited him, and there was no telling how many spies he had around the city who might be willing to trade him information in exchange for a get-out-of-jail-free favor down the line.

"What's a matter, Chloe?" Mack said. "Nothing to say?"

I swallowed and shook my head. "I'm glad you're okay, Mack. Now, if you'll excuse me?"

"By all means," Mack said and stepped aside. "Friendly little warning, though. Watch your step out there. It's a dangerous city. You never know what's around the next corner."

I thought about trying to say something tough. A warning of my own, or maybe a not-so-subtle reminder of what happened to the last crooked officer who came after me, but honestly, I just didn't have the stomach for it.

I'd always known what Mack was, but I'd overlooked it because I'd been on his good side. That wasn't the case anymore, and there was a heavy feeling in my chest as I made my way down the stairs.

It wasn't just Mack's words that were weighing me down. It was everything. Or better said, everyone. Police work, at its core, is a brotherhood, a family, and like it or not, I'd been cast out of the tribe, exiled to the outskirts with only Lieutenant Kermit for company. And sure, I might have been warming to my new role, but it didn't change the fact that things were different. I missed having people that I could count on, men and women who I knew had my back. I missed having their support behind me.

I reached the bottom of the stairs and turned, glimpsing inside the kitchen, where the little girl had devolved into silent sobs, slowly rocking herself in the chair as Officer Thompson looked on. His previous awkwardness had shifted into outright annoyance, and I made a snap decision and stepped into the kitchen.

"Take a walk," I said. "I'll stay with her until DCF arrives."

Thompson hesitated, his desire to be rid of the weeping child not quite enough to override his sense of self-preservation. "Detective Mackleroy said we can't interview her until her parents are found."

"I'm not going to interview her," I said. "It's called common freaking decency. Now move."

Officer Thompson cast one last glance at the girl, then turned and made his way out of the kitchen, disappearing through the front door without a backward glance. I waited for him to leave, then I pulled up a second chair, sliding it across the floor until it stood adjacent to the little girl. I lowered myself down, then reached out and gently laid my hands on her arms.

People forget how hard it is to be a child. The world is a scary place, and everyone is so big. Monsters linger in every shadow, some imagined and some real, and emotions can hit so hard.

As soon as my hands touched her, she melted and fell forward in her chair. I caught her and brought her to me, letting her cry into my shoulder as I softly stroked her hair. There were lots of things that I wanted to say in that moment. I wanted to tell her how sorry I was, and how I was going to do everything I could to find her brother's murderer and bring them to justice. Those were all important things. Things she would need to hear in time. But not right now.

Instead, I just held her, gently rocking until the flow of tears eventually subsided and fatigue began to take hold. She'd worn herself out, and was lingering somewhere between consciousness and unconsciousness when her hand opened, and a small disk dropped from her palm, spinning twice before clattering down to the floor with a metallic *clink*.

My gaze instinctively followed it, noting the way it caught the afternoon sunlight streaming in through the hazy blinds, casting up a shining reflection that stood in stark contrast to the marred, dirt-stained floor. The little disc gleamed proudly, holding my gaze and demanding attention as it glittered.

Glittered like gold.

A Little Blackmail Among Friends. March 15th 1200hrs

THE LAST RESIDUES OF snow chilled the early spring air as it slid across my face, slipping beneath my collar and forcing me to pull my jacket tighter. From the opposite end of the street, I watched the pair of taillights disappear.

More than two hours had passed before DCF finally arrived and informed me they'd been unable to locate the victim's parents and would be taking the girl, whose name I still didn't know, to a foster care facility. She'd fallen all the way asleep by that point, and barely stirred as I'd carried her to the car, whimpering softly as I buckled her in and whispered a soft goodbye.

Once the taillights disappeared, I glanced back toward the green triple-decker, debating if I should return before eventually deciding against it. Nothing I said was going to make a difference when it came to Mack or Scutt, and trying to butt my nose into their investigation wasn't going to get me anywhere. Not without proof, at any rate.

I drew in a long breath, allowing the chill to sit in my lungs for a long moment before exhaling. I felt heavy inside, my arms tingling with the memory of the sleeping girl even as my ears resonated with her whispered confessions. The golden coin she'd dropped burned in my pocket as I made my way back down the street. I had my head down, a stupid choice given the neighborhood, but my mind was whirling, already working the angles.

It bothered me that Lieutenant Kermit had ordered me here and then not shown up, but I told myself to slow down and ponder why. Delegation was nothing new in police work. There were plenty of high-ranking officers who were more than happy to let their subordinates do all the work and then take credit for their achievements. Lieutenant Kermit had never struck me as one of those types, though. He enjoyed being out in the field, working the cases alongside the other officers. Fact is, he could retire tomorrow and no one would fight him on it. He continued to show up every day, even knowing he wasn't entirely welcomed by the upper brass, because he loved the work and wanted to be here.

Which kind of begged the question, why wasn't he here?

I thought about it for several minutes before concluding that the simplest answer was probably the right one. Somehow, he'd known, or at least strongly suspected, what I might find, and he wanted me to chase it down and draw my own conclusions.

There was probably a little more to it than that. A skilled psychologist might suggest that this was a test to see if I was ready to return to the field. After all, there's a reason why officer-involved shootings come with a mandatory administrative leave period. The after-effects of acute violence don't always show up right away, and giving the officers involved time to work through the consequences of their actions can be beneficial on multiple levels.

In my case, being exiled from the police station had turned out to be more than just a symbolic gesture. In the wake of Topher's death, none of the usual department shrinks had shown up asking if I wanted to talk. Not that I necessarily would have accepted it if they had. Lord knows, there are no department packets for working through the aftereffects of when your partner tries to kill you. And make no mistake. There were aftereffects.

Topher might have been in the ground, but his memory was still living rent-free in my head, usually appearing in the dead of night, when the world was quiet. I'd read online that nightmares were normal at this stage, but the knowledge didn't help much when I woke shaking and sweating.

What did help was building myself a new routine. I'd found solace in my workouts, and within the quiet peace of the library. It was assuaging, although, from an outsider's perspective, I suppose it could've been seen as merely hiding myself away.

Well, enough of that. I was done hiding. Done lowering my eyes in front of Mack and everyone else just like him. They could think what they liked, but at the end of the day I knew I was a darn good officer, and if the upper brass thought that I was some pawn they could sacrifice on the altar of political convenience, then they were going to learn the hard way that they were wrong.

Everyone else might view Blue Moon as a joke, but I refused to see it that way. I had an opportunity here, a chance to make a difference, and I was going to do just that, starting with finding the people responsible for Ricky Brannon's death and then following them to whoever had orchestrated the Federal Reserve heist. I was going to hunt the leprechauns, follow them across the rainbow to their pot of gold, and shove it right down the throats of the upper brass.

My lips peeled apart into a fierce grin, and I punched my fist into my opposite hand, feeling a ferocious warmth bloom in my chest. I reveled in the feeling for a long moment, so distracted with my newfound motivation that I didn't immediately notice the figure kneeling beside my car until he rose up in front of me.

"Top of the afternoon, Sergeant," he said.

My head snapped up, and I jerked back so hard that I slipped on a lingering patch of ice clinging to the sidewalk. My hands flailed, and the figure shot forward and seized my arms, holding me steady until I found my balance. Once I had my feet beneath me, I purposefully took a step back and smoothed my jacket sleeves before turning to regard him.

"Oh," I said. "It's you."

FBI Agent Alexander Gordan smiled. "Good to see you as well."

"What are you doing here?"

"Well, I should think it rather obvious," he said. "The snow is nearly melted and the first notes of spring are in the air. The Bureau felt it was time for me to resume my investigation. As of this morning, I've been officially reassigned to the Federal Reserve theft."

"Uh-huh," I said. "But what are you doing *here?*"

"Well, this seemed as good a place as any to rekindle our partnership."

"Partners," I said. "Is that how you see us?"

"Of course," he said. "Didn't you get the memo?"

"I must have missed it. Remind me, was it before or after you disappeared without so much as a word?"

"Oh, come now, Sergeant," he said. "Don't take it personally. The Bureau's policy of withholding information is in everyone's best interest. The fewer people who are privy to the intimate details of an investigation means less chance those details could find their way to potential suspects. And besides, the Bureau is willing to suspend that policy in select cases when deemed appropriate."

"Like when it's been three months since the heist and you have zero leads?"

"Precisely," Agent Gordan said. "I'm so glad you understand."

"Oh, I understand perfectly," I said. "But you've got another think coming if you think I'm going to let you tag along with me. I don't even know how you found me."

Agent Gordan frowned. "I'm not sure tag-along is the appropriate phrase, and I knew you were here because your lieutenant was kind enough to inform me."

"In that case, I'll be sure to take it up with him. In the meantime, I've got work to do." I stepped around him and made my way over to my car, withdrawing my key and sliding it into the door.

"Sergeant, perhaps I'm not being clear," Agent Gordan said. "It really is in your best interest to partner with me."

"Oh, and why's that?"

"Well, first, because working together will only increase our odds of catching these leprechaun thieves, which will no doubt satisfy your sense of civic duty, not to mention raise your standing within your department. Second, need I remind you that this is still the Bureau's case? If you're not willing to comply with our methods, then I'm afraid I'll have no choice but to put in an official request to have you removed."

"I'd like to see you try it," I said.

His mouth tightened. "No, you really wouldn't."

"Lieutenant Kermit—"

He held up his hand, cutting me off. "I've no doubt that your Lieutenant would stand in support of you, but this request would almost certainly go over his head. Fact is, given the gravity of the situation, your department would have little choice but to replace you with someone more amenable to the idea of department cooperation."

"So, you're blackmailing me now?"

"I was hoping it wouldn't prove necessary, but you're not leaving me any other choice," he said. "Cards on the table, these thieves are a bit more astute than I initially gave them credit for. My people have hit a wall. We're out of leads and running short of options."

"Poor baby," I said and brought my fingers together, miming as if I were playing a tiny violin.

Agent Gordan's mouth tightened. "Despite what you may think, Sergeant, you're not the only one who cares about their career. I don't relish the idea of spending the next twenty years digging little stuffed leprechauns out of my desk. They've already started calling me clover boy. As it stands, you're the only one in this entire investigation who's managed to make any headway." He smiled. "And that makes you my new best friend."

I frowned, then blinked. "Wait, did you seriously just quote Titanic to me?"

"Why not? It's a classic, not to mention the greatest love story of our time."

"I don't believe this."

He narrowed his eyes. "Kate Winslet's performance was nothing short of magnificent. In fact, I challenge you to—"

"Not her," I said and waved my hand. "This. All of *this.*"

"Oh, well, give it time. If it helps, you can think of it as a partnership born with reservations."

"How about a partnership born under duress?"

"Whichever you prefer," he said. "Just so long as you understand that we're either in this together or not at all."

I drew in a long breath, then let it out in a huff. On paper having an FBI agent working beside me could only help. I didn't know Agent Gordan all that well, but our brief interactions had revealed that he wasn't some witless thug. He was a thinking man's officer, and right now I could really use one of those. That didn't mean I had to love his smug attitude or the twinkle in his eye as he watched me weighing the pros and cons.

Despite my own personal misgivings, I reminded myself that there was a bigger picture here to think about. These leprechaun thieves had already robbed one of the most secure buildings in Boston, and while they might have done it without violence, it wasn't without consequence. The dead body in the house served as a grim reminder of just how high the stakes were, and the memory of that little girl's weight in my arms wouldn't allow me to just throw away any potential help out of pride.

Like it or not, Agent Gordan had a point. I wasn't positive I could solve this on my own, and if having him along, and by extension the federal resources he brought with him, meant the difference between finding another murder victim or finding these leprechauns and making sure they ended up behind bars, there was only one choice I could make.

"I'm driving," I said. "And don't touch my radio."

Breeding Hamsters with Aunt Shirley. March 15th 1300hrs

WE PILED INSIDE MY not-new Ford Crown Victoria, buckled our seatbelts and pulled away from the curb. Agent Gordan whistled softly in his seat, his smug grin lasting right up until the heater kicked on, and a pungent aroma that can only be described as a cross between burned fur and old shipping containers flooded the vehicle's interior.

"Christ on a pogo-stick," he said and wrinkled his nose. "Has someone been breeding hamsters in here?"

"Not that I'm aware of, but I wouldn't put anything past the night shift crew. They get bored easily."

He shook his head. "I'd heard rumors your division was under-funded, but this car is..."

"Unconventional?"

"I was going to say deplorable," he said. "Does your Lieutenant not like you or something?"

"On the contrary, I think he likes me very much. Otherwise, we would be taking the subway." I hesitated a moment before I added, "His boss, on the other hand, probably doesn't share that same sentiment."

"Why is that?"

"I had the audacity to actually show up and do my job."

A flash of understanding appeared in Agent Gordan's eyes. "Ah, always dangerous, that. Been there a time or two myself."

"How did it pan out?"

He shrugged and fiddled with his collar, massaging the skin beneath. "I'm still here, so not all bad. Might be I could have gotten a bit further ahead if I'd been more willing to play the game."

"You weren't?"

He made a soft growling sound, rubbing his fingers across his throat. "Let's just say I didn't always play it the way the chiefs would have preferred."

I made an acknowledging sound, and a soft silence settled over the vehicle as I changed lanes and headed back toward the bridge. I stayed just under the speed limit, careful to avoid the lingering ice patches and pools of slush gathered along the roadways, and most definitely not because I was enjoying watching Agent Gordan fidget in his seat. You'll have to trust me on that one.

"Merciful Mary," he said. "I haven't itched this much since that summer my parents sent me to stay with my Aunt Shirley."

"You're allergic to your Aunt Shirley?"

"Yes. I mean no. Not directly at any rate. She was a bit of an odd duck. No children, never married. A spinster." He glanced over at me. "You remind me of her."

I blinked and straightened. "Excuse me?"

He held up a hand in a pacifying gesture. "Shirley had a good heart, but her social skills were somewhat lacking. She would have been the quintessential cat lady, if not for the fact that she was allergic."

"That must have been hard."

"She compensated by breeding Syrian hamsters. Ugliest little things you've ever seen." He sniffed and wrinkled his nose. "I swear I can smell them clear as day."

I had a quick flash of memory back to when I'd first started the engine, and the sounds that had accompanied the previous occupants as they scurried away into the snow. "Nope, no hamsters here."

"Huh. Well, should you come across any, don't let their façade fool you. They may look innocent, but they're Satan's spawn."

"You think hamsters are in league with the devil?"

"Oh, I don't think. I *know.*" He glanced over and must have noted the disbelieving look on my face. "Their teeth can punch through metal as easily as flesh, and they urinate on absolutely everything. On the rare times my folks forced me to go visit, I'd wake in the middle of the night to find them standing on my chest, their black, beady eyes offering me a shadowed glimpse into their nonexistent souls."

"You're nursing quite the grudge," I said.

"I still have nightmares about them," he said. "Some nights, I swear I can feel their little toes scratching my skin."

"Why didn't you just ask your aunt to put you in another room?"

"I did," he said. "But at some point, the apartment became more their home than hers. At least until she was evicted."

"Because of the hamsters?"

He nodded, rubbing at the skin between his fingers. "Some of the more inventive ones figured out how to undo the cage locks. Once the others picked up on it, there was no stopping them. They chewed their way through the walls and began descending into the other apartments."

"Eww," I said, shivering at the mental image. "How many hamsters are we talking about here?"

"Pest control estimated it to be somewhere in the neighborhood of a thousand," he said. "They were eventually forced to condemn the building, and Aunt Shirley was given three months' probation and a court order barring her from housing any more pets. And, of course, once word got out, she wasn't able to rent anywhere within the city. She had to move back home with my grandma."

"Well, at least she's not alone anymore."

"This is true." He drew in a long breath and then let it out in a huff. "Jokes aside, I'm not sure how much more of this I can bear. Where are we headed?"

"Back to the city."

"And then?"

"We're going to hunt down a murderer."

He frowned. "Truly?"

"Yeah," I said. "How much did Lieutenant Kermit tell you?"

"Alarmingly little it appears," he said. "When I contacted him, he informed me where to find you and was kind enough to note that you'd had a break in the case. He didn't mention specifics." He shifted in his chair. "On principle, I'm not opposed to tracking down murderers, but would you mind explaining to me how this is connected to our case?"

"See for yourself." I reached into my pocket, drew out the gold coin and flipped it to him. He caught it in one hand, then opened his fingers and stared.

The coin itself was a shade smaller than a quarter. One side bore the image of men fighting in front of the Old State House. Soldiers wearing matching coats fired on civilians, with the date March 5th, 1770 displayed on the bottom. The other side bore the image of a broken crown, and two eyes, one of them with a jagged line running through it.

"Is this what I think it is?"

"Depends."

He drew in a long breath. "How do you know for sure?"

"I don't, but it's a heck of a coincidence otherwise." I flicked my turn signal and shifted lanes, passing around an antique Corvette. "You saw the little girl I brought out of the house?"

He nodded.

"Yesterday morning, she went snooping inside her brother's room and found a bag of gold coins hidden inside his guitar case. She thought they were candy, so she went out to share them with some of the other neighborhood kids."

Agent Gordan's face grew somber. "They weren't candy, were they?"

I shook my head. "Word spread, and two older boys showed up this morning."

"Did she know them?"

"Just the one. His name is Corwin Sullage. A small-time street hustler who's been known to recruit some of the younger kids to mule for him. He and an accomplice forced their way inside the house, and took her brother upstairs. The girl didn't see anything, but based on the available forensics, it looks like Sullage forced her brother to give up the bag and then killed him."

"The girl told you all this?"

"She was already pretty worn out by the time I got there, but I was able to piece it together based on her answers."

"Shouldn't you have informed the homicide detectives? I'm sure they'd want to speak with her."

My mouth tightened. "No."

"I don't understand."

"The lead detective and I are not on good terms. He's going to view anything I say with a heavy dose of suspicion, if not outright hostility. Plus, it's against the law to interview a minor without their custodial guardian present."

"But you did it anyway?"

I shook my head. "Technically, what I did wouldn't constitute an interview. I mostly just listened to her."

Agent Gordan made a low noise in his throat. "That's a dangerous game to play, Sergeant. Especially in a murder case."

"You see now why I didn't say anything? I know she's telling the truth, but any defense attorney worth their salt would argue that I'd violated her constitutional rights, and if the judge ruled their way, then any statements she made would be inadmissible. The entire case could fall apart before it even began." I was quiet for a long moment. "Plus, she's been through enough. I'm not going to force her to deal with Mack unless there's no other option."

"Mack?"

"Lead homicide detective. He's a bully and a narcissist who blames me for what happened to him last year."

"Be that as it may, if that girl can positively identify your killers, then her testimony might be necessary."

"Maybe," I said. "But there's a better option. If I can find our killer, then I can match the gun and let the homicide detectives use that to build their case, or, even better, draw out a confession."

"You don't think they'll be angry when they learn you've been with-holding information from them?"

"I think they'll be furious," I said. "But they can't realistically hate me any more than they do right now. And besides, it's the right thing to do."

"I suppose," Agent Gordan said. "But this may be bigger than you think." He held up the coin. "If we're right, then we still need to figure out where this gold came from. Charlestown has a reputation for high-profile heists. Your victim, as well as this young man, Sullage, may be involved in the Federal Reserve theft."

"I thought about that already, but it doesn't track."

"Why not?"

"Both our victim and his alleged killer are relatively small-time criminals. The Federal Reserve heist took cunning, patience, and discipline. Not really traits that either of them possesses. Plus, even if they were in on it, why would our victim still be here? I mean, let's face it, if you've got twenty-five million dollars worth of gold in your back pocket, would you really stay in Charlestown?"

"Could be he was worried about his sister. Familial responsibilities can be a powerful motivator."

"Not that powerful," I said. "And besides, he could have simply taken her with him."

"Maybe the other members of the crew wouldn't allow it," Gordan said. "There were four thieves involved, and you can be certain they made plans for how they would behave if their heist was successful. It's possible they agreed to continue going about their daily lives in order to keep up appearances. For all we know, our thieves have spent the last three months melting down those bars and turning them into something more transportable."

"Something like that?" I motioned to the coin.

"Quite possibly. If your victim decided to smuggle the coins out and the other members of the crew found out, they may have concluded they were better off without him."

"Two problems with that theory," I said. "First, even if they did kill him for stealing gold, why would they leave the body? They're smart enough to know that the cops will be involved, and if any traces of gold were found inside the residence, it could potentially lead them to the other thieves. Second, they know the girl saw them. If they were serious about tying up loose ends..."

"They wouldn't have left her behind," Agent Gordan finished. "Fair enough. In that case, what do you think happened?"

I shook my head. "We won't know until we find Sullage and his accomplice. For right now, let's assume our victim came by the coins some other way. Maybe through trade, or maybe just by sheer dumb luck."

Agent Gordan glanced at me. "Clearly, we have very different views on what constitutes luck."

"The girl I spoke to didn't know how many coins were in the bag. She thought maybe a dozen."

"Or sixteen?"

"Possibly. Is there some significance to that number?"

Gordan turned his arm over and bobbed the hand holding the coin up and down. "Based on the heft, I'd say this coin contains roughly an ounce of gold. Assuming they're melting down the bars and reforming them using molds, sixteen coins would make an even pound."

"What's that translate to in dollars?"

"Right around $19,000."

I let out a low whistle. "Lot of money for a kid from Charlestown. At least now we know where Sullage and his accomplice are going."

Agent Gordan frowned. "We do?"

"Sure," I said. "Think about it. Imagine you're a small-time Charlestown dealer, used to sleeping three families to a house, and all of a sudden you find yourself with a literal pot of gold at your feet? What's the first thing you'd do?"

Gordan pondered it for a moment, then winced. "Christ on a cookie. They're at the mall, aren't they?"

Prudential Center. March 15th 1332hrs

THERE ARE PLENTY OF places to spend money in Boston. Little Italy in the north is home to some of the most flavorful cuisine and wine anywhere in New England, and the shops along Boylston and Newbury Street cater to the finest, by which I mean most expensive, of tastes. Bottom line, if you've got cash to burn, then you could do a whole lot worse than Beantown.

That said, there's a difference between spending massive globs of money and being *seen* spending massive globs of money. If you're after the latter, then the Prudential Center is the only real choice.

An enclosed shopping center located in the Back Bay neighborhood, the Prudential Center was named as one of the top five shopping centers in the world by Women's Wear Daily, and is home to a vast array of high-end shops including fashion, jewelry, fragrance and footwear.

Dozens of restaurants and boutique eateries lined the halls, along with the headquarters of the Boston Duck Tours, a full-service post office, and even a Catholic Chapel. The Green Line Subway station connected to the lower floors, allowing for direct access to the Hynes Convention Center as well as the Sheraton Hotel.

I parked on Boylston Street, making use of the valet spots just outside of the First Republic Bank. No sooner had I killed the engine than one of the parking attendants came running over, but a quick flash of my badge and a few words sent him retreating back the way he'd come.

I'd never been one of those officers who delights in abusing my authority. The badge-heavy ones that can't resist flaunting their power to the civilian public. But these were special circumstances. The Prudential Center had its own parking garage, and while getting in was usually not a problem, getting out was another story. Depending on how long it took us to locate our shooters, we might need to leave in a hurry.

We exited the vehicle and made our way up onto the sidewalk, passing the aforementioned parking garage and crossing beneath the walkway bridge before entering through Saks Fifth Avenue. Agent Gordan held the door for me, and warm air flowed over me as I stepped inside, carrying the intermingling aroma of cashmere, Tom Ford perfume, and sharp Italian spices from the California Pizza Kitchen located next door. I breathed it all in, the combination of warm clothing, enticing scents and good food raising my spirits and serving as a pleasant reminder of why I loved this city.

We made our way down a long walkway aisle lined by headless mannequins with altars of neatly folded clothing and accompanying footwear at their base. Several of the sales associates gave me curious looks as I passed, and it wasn't too hard to figure out why. Blue Moon was a plain-clothes division, meaning there was nothing on my person that would readily identify me as a police officer. For those who made their living manipulating clothes to look enticing on the human form, the bulge of my Kevlar vest, not to mention my gun and handcuffs beneath my jacket, was, at best, a poor aesthetic choice, and, at worst, a fashion sin of the highest order. Luckily, none of the sales associates sought to rescue me from style purgatory. Whether it was simply too late in the day to be bothered or they merely dismissed me as a lost cause, I couldn't say, but we passed through the store unchallenged, and came out though the mall entrance.

"Oh, wow," Agent Gordan said. "This is... something."

He wasn't wrong.

Shops and restaurants stretched the length of the mall, the former stocking their entrances with decadent goods and colorful end tables designed to make shoppers pause and take notice, while the latter employed hostesses, usually in the form of young women wearing tight black attire, wielding menus and well-practiced smiles with equal skill.

Above the hustle and bustle, large skylights formed a dome-shaped ceiling along the mall's interior promenade, six-foot wide glass pane windows allowing for breathtaking views of the surrounding skyline and descending sun, its orange rays dancing between the buildings as it sank down along the western horizon.

"How are we ever going to find Sullage and his accomplice in all this?" Agent Gordan asked, spreading his hand to encompass the shopping crowd.

"What's the matter, Captain fancy-pants?" I asked. "You've never run target reconnaissance before?"

Agent Gordan hesitated, then reluctantly shook his head. "Not really."

"I thought you bureau guys were all about that cloak and dagger stuff?"

"You're thinking of the CIA. Our field agents do a bit of inter-department crossover work, but nothing that I've been a part of."

"Not your thing?"

He shook his head. "I'm assigned to the financial crimes unit."

"So, you're a numbers guy?"

He frowned. "I'll have you know, Sergeant, that stealing money is only half the battle. Criminals still have to be able to spend it. People can't usually haul around large quantities of cash without drawing suspicion, so they tend to set up dummy accounts either using off-shore banks or outright fake identities. Those banks require deposits upfront, and if you can positively identify them, then you can seize them outright, thereby allowing you to recover at least a portion, if not the entirety, of the stolen funds."

"So, you're a numbers guy."

His mouth tightened. "Can we please just focus on the task at hand?"

"Don't stress out," I said. "I can talk you through it." I slowed my walk, allowing my gaze to pass over the goods, focusing on a pair of discounted winter candles before moving on. "Reconnaissance 101. First step is to blend in with your surroundings. You want to avoid drawing attention to yourself at all costs. Take those two for instance." I nodded towards a pair of dark-haired young women lingering in front of a nearby storefront.

"What about them?"

"See how they're dressed?" I asked.

Agent Gordan narrowed his eyes, and it didn't take long for him to catch my meaning. From the waist up, the young women were covered by casual winter coats, but from the waist down, they wore white leggings that fed into athletic shoes.

"They look like gymnasts. Or maybe ballerinas. So what?"

"So that sort of thing makes them stand out," I said. "Were anyone hunting for them, they wouldn't be difficult to spot. Also, watch their movements. See the way they're peering around? They're looking for someone."

"Probably just a friend."

"Most likely," I said. "But you want to avoid anything that might set you apart from the crowd. That's why it's better to take your time, and keep your movements smooth. Just fly casual."

Agent Gordan nodded, then blinked. "Did you just quote—"

"I'll never admit it if I did," I said. "Oh, and while you're at it, avoid looking into any cameras."

"Cameras?"

I nodded. "It's not only good guys who use them. If your target clues in to the fact that you're tailing them, they'll try to establish their own counter surveillance. This is why it's helpful to have a partner to pass the target back and forth. And if all else fails, start picking your nose."

Agent Gordan stopped short. "My nose?"

I grimaced, then reached out and took his arm, gently nudging him forward into step alongside me, as if we were a couple just out enjoying the mall. "Most people are disinclined to sit there and watch someone fishing up their nostrils. They instinctively look away."

"You're just making fun of me now."

I shook my head and held up two fingers. "Scout's honor. Next time you're in a stakeout car, take a hard look at the floor and lower end of the dashboard. I guarantee you'll find leftovers."

"That's disgusting."

"Granted," I said. "But its effective."

"I'll take your word for it," he said. "In the meantime, what do we do when we spot Sullage?"

I debated a moment before answering. We'd used our dispatch computer on the way over to pull Corwin Sullage's identification card. He didn't have a valid driver's license, but anyone who's been found guilty of a crime in the state of Massachusetts is required to have a government ID. His picture showed a young man with a pinched nose and dark hair buzzed short. He was sneering in his photo, and there was a hollow sheen to his eyes that didn't match the baby fat clinging to his face. The glimmer staring back spoke of a youth who'd already traveled too far down the path of lost adolescence to ever come back. He'd turned eighteen the previous summer, and while I wasn't able to access the specifics of his juvenile record, the number of court dates on record suggested he was intimately familiar with the arraignment process.

"Nothing," I said. "At least not right away."

"Nothing?"

I shook my head. "Sullage knows it's only a matter of time before Ricky's body is found, and even if he thinks he's in the clear, the lizard part of his brain will be on alert for anyone looking for him. That means he'll be hyper aware. The last thing we want to do is spook him."

"So, what do we do?"

"Standard operating procedure is to call in backup and surround him."

"We don't have any backup."

"Which means we'll need to hang back and wait for him to move into a secluded area. Fewer people mean less chance of collateral damage, or God forbid, a hostage situation."

Agent Gordan nodded. "Mitigate the risk. Smart. So we wait for our moment and then we arrest him?"

"That's the plan. Just know that if he sees us coming, he's likely to run."

"Then what?"

"He goes to jail tired."

"What if he decides to fight?"

"Fight back."

"And if he starts shooting?"

"Shoot back," I said. "But aim for the leg."

Agent Gordan frowned. "That's easier said than done."

"No argument," I said. "But keep in mind that, right now, that gold is the only lead we have to discovering the identity of our leprechauns, and the only other person besides Sullage who knows for certain where it came from is lying dead in an upstairs bedroom in Charlestown."

"You think Sullage knows?"

I nodded. "Even a complete idiot wouldn't execute Ricky Brannon without finding out where the gold came from. The only way we're going to find out is to take him in alive so we can question him."

"I guess I should probably aim for the leg then."

"Good idea."

"Do you really think he'll tell us?"

"Won't know unless we try," I said.

"Seems like we're overlooking something."

"What's that?"

"Before we can affect any sort of arrest, we still have to find him. How are we going to do that?"

"The old-fashioned way," I said. "We look."

"That's it?"

I nodded. "We know he's got money to burn, so we start with the obvious places. Music stores and jewelry shops. If we come up empty then we'll move on to sunglass stores and vaping shops."

"Or we could just hone in on the loud-mouthed idiot throwing free money around the Eataly food court."

"Yeah," I said. "If only it were that easy."

Agent Gordan cleared his throat. "Might want to look to your left, Sergeant."

I blinked, then glanced over and felt my stomach drop.

Standing in the middle of the Eataly food court, surrounded by maybe three dozen teens, was Corwin Sullage. Dressed in baggy jeans with a black windbreaker, he was standing with one foot up on the back of his chair, a wad of cash in his hands, flicking singles out toward the crowd while shouting profanities. His alleged accomplice was beside him, a young man of approximately the same age, dressed in a red hooded sweatshirt. The half-smile on his mouth said he was enjoying the spectacle as much as the others, but there was a wariness to him that made me think he knew Sullage was making a mistake. Watching the contrasting murderers might have been comical in other circumstances, but there was nothing funny about the memory of Ricky's body, or the remnant sounds of his sister's crying echoing in my ear.

Unfortunately, I let my gaze linger too long, and Sullage chose that exact moment to glance up. All the things I'd said about lying low and not letting the target spot you went right out the window as soon as our eyes met. He caught my gaze, and then his eyes dropped, not to my chest, which would have been par for the course when dealing with young men, but lower, toward the gun holstered on my hip. I saw recognition flash across his face, followed by panic. He shouted something to the other young man, then leaped off the chair and took off, racing down the nearest aisle. The wary young man peered back at us, then cursed and bolted in the opposite direction.

"Get the accomplice!" I snapped

"But—"

I never got to hear what else Agent Gordan had to say because I was already in motion. My legs carried me forward through the food court and past the adolescent crowd who were busily scraping dollar bills from the floor. Ahead of me, Sullage glanced back, and I had the satisfaction of seeing his eyes widen an instant before he jerked back around.

A fierce grin lit my face, and I took off after him.

Catch a Killer if You Can. March 15th 1346hrs

CHARGING RECKLESSLY THROUGH A crowded mall after an armed and dangerous murderer is generally not the smartest idea. The chance of collateral damage is just too high, and that goes doubly so for female officers.

Bostonians might have been more accustomed to violence than other places, but people are people, and we all tend to react the same when confronted by unexpected conflict. The last thing I wanted to do was start a panic. Not only because it would hinder my pursuit, but because any would-be-white-knights who saw a female officer chasing a suspect might get it into their heads that it was their duty to intervene. That would be bad. Not because their hearts weren't in the right place, but because most people lacked the physical know-how, not to mention the athletic prowess, to effectively subdue a fleeing criminal.

Sullage had already killed one person today. I wasn't in a hurry to add any more victims to that list. For that reason, I kept my pistol in its holster, and pointedly didn't announce myself as I raced down the walkway.

Sullage ran ahead of me, his movements uneven and jerky, lacking the easy grace and finesse of a more seasoned runner. He was trusting more to youth than skill, allowing his fear and adrenaline to carry him forward.

As he ran, I kept watch of his arms, noting when his left hand dipped down and grabbed something from his waistband. Fear shot through me, but I didn't allow it to slow my steps as we reached the end of the walkway.

Sullage jerked right, nearly plowing over a trio of elderly ladies before he raced through a service door with the words "Parking Garage. Employees Only" written on it. I followed on his heels, dodging around the flabbergasted ladies and some other shoppers who'd stopped to help them, and pushed through the door into the service hall. I glimpsed Sullage as he turned the corner up ahead, and a dozen strides carried me forward into an L-shaped intersection. I turned the corner and drew up fast, skidding the last couple of feet before not-quite-crashing into the side of the doorway leading into the parking garage.

Which leads me to the other problem with foot chases.

I had no way of knowing what was on the other side of that door, and any bad guy worth their salt would recognize it as an ideal place to set a trap. Not only would the light in the hallway create an ideal silhouette

83

of me in the doorway, but it would take my eyes a second to adjust. If Sullage was so desperate to stay out of jail that he was willing to blow my head off, all he had to do was set up on the other side and wait for me to come barging through the door.

As traps go, it was simple, but effective.

Unfortunately, I didn't have time to double back. If I was wrong, then Sullage was getting further away every second, and if I let him go now, I had next to no chance of finding him again. Now that he knew for certain we were looking for him, he'd go to ground within Charlestown, and trying to dig him out of there would take time I didn't have.

I drew in a deep breath and reminded myself that while there are lots of facets of police work, one of them meant going through doors you don't want to go through, knowing full well that danger may be lurking on the other side. I exhaled, drew back my leg, and kicked the door open a split second before I hurled myself through the doorway.

There was a flash of light, and the concrete above my head exploded, bursting apart and showering broken bits down as the gun's report caught up with it. I screamed, and dove forward, turning into a roll and coming up to one knee behind a fancy-looking Rolls-Royce the color of pale milk. My pistol came free of its holster, and I focused in on where I'd seen the muzzle flash and fired three times.

The gun's reports echoed through the garage, and glass shattered an instant before Sullage appeared. He'd been crouched behind a red sedan, and he took off running, casting frequent looks back as he raised his arm and fired. He held his gun sideways, shooting blindly, which while visually stimulating for movies, was not ideal for actually hitting your target. That said, he could always get lucky. I came out from behind the Rolls in a low crouch, keeping close to the parked vehicles and using them for cover as I pursued him.

Once upon a time, back when I'd been a brand-new traffic cop, my field training officer, Sergeant Barron, told me that a criminal is never more dangerous than the moments before they're placed under arrest. Most of them will say they can feel the net tightening, the last moments of their freedom slipping away like sands in a glass timer. There's a fear associated with it. A sense of impending doom that causes them to act out, desperate to delay the inevitable.

As I slipped between the cars, I started wracking my brain, trying to come up with a plan. Going from car to car exchanging gunfire was dangerous, and every step I took only carried me deeper into the garage and away from possible help. I didn't know for sure if anyone had called the police, but even if they had, it would take the respondin g officers time to ascertain what was happening, and then even longer to set up a perimeter, which would only add to the danger. If Sullage felt like he couldn't escape, then he would start looking for another avenue of egress, and that most likely meant taking hostages.

I quickened my step, bolstered by adrenaline and no small amount of determination. Sullage was dangerous, but I reminded myself that I still needed him to help unravel the mystery behind the leprechaun's gold. Otherwise, more people might suffer the same fate as Ricky Brannon. Which meant my best chance of ending this quickly was to disable him and hope he didn't bleed out. It wasn't great, as far as plans go, but it was all I had.

Unfortunately, chance got involved, and I was a second too slow, as headlights came around the descending ramp, illuminating Sullage. The car screeched to a jerky halt, and the driver blared their horn. Sullage shouted something in response, then turned and fired his pistol into the vehicle's hood. The bullet punched through the exterior and ricocheted throughout the engine block. It must not have hit anything too vital, because the car shot forward a second later, tires squealing as the driver fled down the aisle in my direction. Sudden realization dawned, and I threw myself between two cars an instant before it blew past. Had I been a moment slower, the driver likely would have splattered me. As it was, he sped by without so much as a backward glance, crashing through the gate arm and sending wooden bits into the street as he fled the garage.

Sullage reached the edge of the parking lot and took off in the direction the car had come, racing up the descending ramp. I started to follow, then slowed, halting my steps as something occurred to me. Chasing Sullage like this wasn't going to end well. I needed to approach it from a different direction, and that meant asking myself what he wanted.

Freedom.

Sullage was on the run, and dim as he was, even he had to recognize that there were only two ways out of this garage. The first would take him back through the mall, where he ran a high risk of coming into contact with more officers. The second was right out the front exit, which would allow him access to the street. Changing floors wasn't going to help him, not unless he was able to lead me up after him and then double back down through the other side. I debated a moment, weighing my odds before deciding that it was worth the risk. I turned and raced away toward the opposite side of the garage, drawing up behind one of the pillars nearby the ascending ramp. Then I dropped into a crouch and waited.

The ascending ramp, when traversed on foot, led back down to the street level and was only a short sprint from the exit. It was a stroke of luck that there were no windows on any of the other floors, else Sullage might have tried his luck with the cold, ice-slick sidewalk. As the seconds passed, seeds of doubt began to grow, gnawing at my chest and whispering that maybe I wasn't as clever as I thought I was. That I might have just let a murderer go free.

I started counting in my head as the tension continued to build, and sixty seconds passed before I finally caught wind of Sullage's footsteps. His shoes slapped against the concrete as he sucked in air through his mouth, and a fierce grin split my face as I rose half an inch, holding myself tight until the second I saw him come off the ramp.

He had his head turned, peering backwards up the ramp, likely trying to ascertain if I was behind him. I waited for him to draw close, then shot out from behind the pillar and hurled myself toward him. He heard me coming, but I was faster, and I slammed into him, driving my shoulder into his back and riding him down to the pavement. We hit hard, but I kept my balance, and managed to stay on top, rotating as he twisted and digging my knee into his back. His arm, still holding the pistol, rose, but I seized his wrist and slammed it onto the pavement.

He screamed as his knuckles cracked, and the gun slipped from his numb fingers, clattering down onto the concrete. I shifted my hips and kicked it out of his reach. Then I turned and twisted his arm, using my leverage to bend it behind his back. A low, animalistic whine came from Sullage as I holstered my pistol and drew my handcuffs. I heard the familiar *click* of the first bracelet as it secured itself around his wrist, and I started to reach toward his opposite arm, but something caught my eye. I raised my head and glanced back toward the garage, catching sight of a lithe figure as she moved into view.

I recognized her as one half of the duo I'd seen back inside the mall. She'd discarded her coat and was dressed in a long-sleeved white unitard with black dots arranged in a spiraling star pattern that ran up her midriff and around her shoulder. She was a few hairs below average height, with dark hair drawn back into a tight ponytail and a white swan mask adorned with long-tipped feathers covering her face. She was gripping a sword, a double-edged straight blade that reminded me of the ones you see people using to practice Tai Chi in the park. She wielded it in one hand and twirled her wrist as she walked, each rotation eliciting a whistling note as the blade cut through the air, the echo of its passing reverberating off the cars.

"Who the heck is that?" Sullage asked.

It's possible that's not exactly what he said, but just because he uttered something doesn't mean I'm obligated to repeat it. Instead, I shook my head and said, "Honestly? I have no idea."

The Swan-Sisters. March 15th 1352hrs

THERE'S A REASON WHY police officers prefer to go in pairs when responding to fights or domestic violence calls. It's a safety issue, not only because you have someone to watch your back, but because it allows you that extra second for threat assessment. No matter how diligent or situationally aware you might be, no single person can watch two directions at once, and when dealing with multiple reporting parties, being able to figure out ahead of time which one is more likely to try to kill you can be paramount to surviving high-risk situations.

I ran the numbers.

On one side, I had an approaching young woman armed with a sword and, presumably, the skills to employ it. On the other side, a known murderer with a hatred of law enforcement and all the survival instincts of a rabid weasel. I couldn't handle both of them at the same time, which meant my only chance was to get Sullage secured and then deal with the young woman, preferably before she drew close enough to bring her weapon to bear.

I turned my attention back to Sullage, but the split second's hesitation had cost me. As I moved to secure his other arm, he rolled onto his side, brought his knees up to his chest, and kicked out hard. I tried to dodge, but I was a hair too slow, and his feet slammed into my chest. My Kevlar vest helped to soften the blow, but only a little, and the shock of impact still tore a breathless gasp from my throat as I crashed over onto my back. The back of my skull struck the concrete, and black stars flashed across my vision, dancing across my sightline like macabre holiday lights.

I blinked rapidly and shook my head, but that only made them worse. At the same time, warning sirens began sounding in my head, and a voice, not unlike the old drill instructor from my police academy days, began barking orders, urging me to get up, get moving, and most importantly, to fight. I struggled for several seconds, my limbs jerking spasmodically before control finally reasserted itself. I scrambled up to a sitting position, blinking my vision clear just as Sullage threw himself forward and seized his pistol from the ground.

He closed his hands around the gun and howled, a sound filled with equal parts bloodlust and madness. He spun back around, and then, much as I had done only moments before, he hesitated, his eyes darting from the white-clad young woman to me. It only lasted a second, then he turned and jabbed his gun out toward me, finger caressing the trigger.

The drill instructor in my head shouted a warning, and I threw myself backward, rolling behind a maroon pickup truck and taking cover behind its heavy engine block. My head cleared the bumper just as Sullage fired, blasting two holes through the vehicle's hood before he cursed and spun back toward the white-clad woman.

What happened next is hard to describe.

Sullage started firing, and the young woman... She didn't dodge the bullets. This wasn't the Matrix, after all. It was more like she flowed around them, bending and twisting her body so that each movement carried her free of Sullage's line of fire. She moved like a gymnast, spinning, leaping, even cartwheeling with no hands, and each movement prevented Sullage from catching her in his sights. I was crouched behind the truck and used the opportunity to circle around to the opposite side of the vehicle, keeping so low to the ground that I was practically moving on all fours.

Sullage rapidly depressed the trigger, emptying the magazine in the space of a few panicked breaths. Bullets shattered glass windshields at the opposite end of the garage, and car alarms blared, each whirling note causing those around it to begin emitting similar cries, until the entire garage was joined in a symphony of anti-theft deterrents.

And still the young woman came forward.

She swept past me in a blur, leaving the faint scent of jasmine and lily in her wake as she leaped through the air and drove her foot into Sullage's face. His head snapped back, and the spent pistol tumbled from his grip as he crashed to the floor. It was a solid blow, but Sullage recovered fast, spitting and cursing as he rolled onto his stomach and began to rise. He made it as far as his knees before the white-clad woman came down beside him. She swung her left leg around, rotating her hip and kicking Sullage's hand out from beneath him. He crashed back to the floor, blood dripping from his nose down onto the concrete pavement, and made to rise again, but the swan-masked woman swept her sword around and struck his side with the flat of the blade, spinning him up and over onto his back. Her next strike came down almost too swiftly for my eye to follow, and her blade halted a hair's breadth from his throat.

"Stay where you are," she snarled at him. "Attempt to run, and I will slice you from—"

She never got to finish her threat, because I chose that moment to emerge from behind the vehicle and launched myself toward her. I didn't know who this woman was, or what she wanted with Sullage, but I couldn't just stand back and let her harm him. I needed him to bring justice to Ricky Brannon's family, as well as to discover where the gold had come from.

The swan-masked woman sensed me coming at the last moment, but it was too late. I struck her hard, driving my shoulder into the small of her back. Her feet left the ground, and I ended up carrying her a handful of steps before hurling her into the side of the nearest vehicle.

She struck hard enough to leave a giant dent in the door and crashed to the ground in a senseless heap. To my right, Sullage started to rise, and I jerked around, drawing my pistol in one smooth motion and aligning it onto him just as he regained his feet.

"Don't even think about it, you mangy piece of—"

I never got to finish my sentence, because a second swan-masked woman came bounding over the adjacent car. She was dressed similarly to her sister, save that her black star pattern ran the opposite direction of her body, and her swan-mask, rather than being purely white, held tiny touches of orange along the tips of the feathering. She somersaulted over the vehicle's roof and landed beside me, spinning on her heel and swinging her sword around in a crisp upward arc. The blade struck the underside of my pistol barrel and slid back, shaving the skin from my fingers even as it tore the weapon from my grip. I screamed, and jerked my hand back, but wasn't fast enough to avoid her second strike. She kicked out hard and slammed her foot into my stomach, driving the air from my lungs and sending me stumbling backward. I hit the maroon pickup truck and gripped its side, using it to keep myself standing even as every inch of me wanted to double over until the pain subsided.

From behind the woman, Sullage took a hesitant step back. I saw him glance toward his fallen pistol, but he evidently thought better of it and took off, pumping his arms as he ran for his life. The second Swan-Sister snapped her head to the side and said something harsh in a language I didn't recognize. Whatever it was had an immediate effect, and the first sister hauled herself up, shaking her head free of cobwebs before she retrieved her sword from the floor and took off after Sullage.

I forced myself straight and made to join the pursuit, but the second Swan-Sister took a half step to the right, blocking my path, and raised her sword.

"You sure about this?" I breathed, my voice shaky. "He's getting away."

The corner of her lip curled up into a half smile. "My sister will see to him. And I will see to you."

"Don't suppose you'd be willing to tell me who you are, or what it is you want?"

"What would be the point, since you will not be here much longer?"

I nodded and set my feet into a striker's stance. "Might want to rethink that. I'm a police officer. Killing me will bring all sorts of heat."

"Perhaps your death will serve as a warning to the other officer, that we are not to be trifled with."

"Afraid it doesn't work like that," I said. "In this city, we look after our own."

"And yet, here you stand. Utterly alone."

She had a point, but it wasn't one I wanted to dwell on. And neither did she, apparently, since she chose that moment to attack.

People think looking down the barrel of a gun is scary. They're not wrong, but they are uninformed. The blessing of a gun is that, in most cases, you're already shot before you realize it. That's not the case when dealing with melee weaponry. Trust me when I tell you that there is a whole new level of fear when you find yourself facing off against someone wielding something sharp and pointed with the intent and skill to use it. I peered around and spotted my pistol nestled beside the tire of the pickup truck. In order to retrieve it, I'd have to get past the swan-masked woman, which was easier said than done.

She came on fast, her sword flickering with lightning quickness and darn near perfect precision. I say darn near perfect because, angled as we were between two cars, her options of attack were limited. She could jab, but every circular strike or cutting blow she tried was hindered by the close proximity of the nearby cars. Had that not been the case, I likely would have died within seconds. As it was, I couldn't do much other than retreat, each flick and jab sending me backward. I couldn't get to my pistol, not before she stabbed me, and I didn't have a flashlight or retractable baton to try to parry her strikes. In fact, I was running pretty short of conventional options, so I decided to try something new. Namely, fighting dirty.

She was fast, graceful, but there was a predictability to her movements, and I waited for the moment her blade began to retreat backward. I didn't try to cross the entire distance, I was nowhere near fast enough, and the chances of me getting past her blade unscathed were next to none. So I settled for crossing half the distance, blitzing in close and slamming my foot, my nice big booted foot, down on the front of her shoe. I felt the heel dig down, felt it push through the relatively soft athletic exterior and smash down onto the toes beneath.

The Swan-Sister's eyes snapped open and her body snapped up straight, almost as if she'd been given an electric shock. A low, breathless hiss tore past her throat, rising in volume as I drew back my arm and threw a straight cross punch toward her mouth. My knuckles struck clean, and her head snapped back, sending her stumbling half a dozen steps. She caught her balance and glared, eyes smoldering hatred even as one hand rose to touch her lip. A trickle of blood leaked from the edge of her mouth, staining the base of the feathers along her mask.

"And there's plenty more where that came from," I said.

I shot forward, intent on retrieving my pistol from beside the tire, but the swan-masked woman saw me coming and swept her sword down. I jerked my hand back a split second before she would have severed my fingers, and the blade sailed past, struck the concrete and sent up a stream of sparks. Positioned as I was, I couldn't halt my momentum in time, and didn't even try, Instead, I threw myself forward, crashing into her and taking advantage of my height and weight to force her off balance. She grunted and stumbled, and tried to bring her sword around, but I'd already anticipated the movement, and I seized her sword-wielding arm with both of my own.

My fingers closed around her wrist, and I pushed her forward into the nearest vehicle, bending her backward over the hood. I forced her hand up and slammed it down onto the vehicle hard enough to dent the hood. Once, twice, on the third slam, her hand sprung open, sending her sword crashing to the pavement. A frustrated scream ripped from her mouth and she snapped her opposite fist toward my face. Striking my cheekbone. Her fist struck flush, but angled as she was, she couldn't bring her full power to bear. I lowered my chin and used my shoulder for cover as she struck again. The third time she drew back her arm, I beat her to the punch, literally, and backhanded her across the face, snapping her head around. Unfortunately, I shifted my torso in the process, surrendering leverage, and the motion allowed her to slide her hips up and over the edge of the car. There was a brief flash, as her leg swung over my head, and somehow, my arm ended up trapped between her knees as she turned and rolled off the hood. I had two choices in that moment. I could either roll with her, or I could hold firm and watch my arm break. I went with option A, and dropped my head, allowing myself to be carried along by her rotation. She jerked her hips and tossed me head over tail. I hit the pavement and skidded five feet, grinding to a graceless halt even as she popped back to her feet. In the distance, a vehicle's engine roared, but I hardly had time to register it, much less dwell on the significance.

The second Swan-Sister retreated over to where her sword had fallen and used her foot to scoop the blade, kicking it up and then snatching it out of midair before she turned. Cold fury radiated from her eyes as she stared toward me, the blade dangling down by her knees. A little tremor passed through me as I realized that playtime was at an end, and whatever brief enjoyment she'd had during the course of our melee had run its course.

I forced myself up to my feet, trying hard to ignore the twinging in my shoulder as I brought my hands up in a defensive boxing stance. I couldn't reach my gun, and a brief glance around revealed that there was nothing I could use as a makeshift weapon. I was also fairly certain I couldn't outrun her. My only shot then, was to either knock her silly, or hold her long enough for help to arrive, assuming it ever did.

I set my feet, still not sure which option I was going to go for, but in the end, it didn't matter, because a third option presented itself, one that I hadn't even known about or considered until right that very moment. All I actually needed to do, as it turned out, was take a step back.

The revving engine I'd heard moments ago grew louder, revealing its source as a large, midnight black, Trans Am muscle car. It barreled in from the street, turned down the wrong-way lane, and growled thunderously as it sped forward. I suspect my backhand had left the second Swan-Sister's head ringing, because she didn't notice it right away. When she did, she acted swiftly, leaping up into the air, but the Trans Am adjusted its course and angled hard, twisting around and skidding sideways to slap her out of the air. The vehicle struck with a heavy thump, and the force of the blow sent her flying over half a dozen cars before she crashed down in an explosion of broken glass and dented metal. I saw her bounce and disappear between two vehicles before I peered back toward the car and caught a brief glimpse of the occupants inside.

There were three of them, all dressed in heavy black attire with long flowing leather coats. The driver had long blonde hair spilling down past his shoulders, and a hunch to his shoulders that suggested he had to work to fit inside the vehicle. I didn't have time to notice much more than that, because they blew by in a flash, tires squealing and filling the air with the scent of burned rubber as they righted themselves and took off in the direction Sullage and the first Swan-Sister had gone. I watched as they disappeared around the corner, the revving engine echoing across the stonework, and then broke into a heavy jog, retrieving my pistol from beneath the tire of the maroon pickup and jamming it down into my holster. I picked up Sullage's pistol as well, careful to avoid touching the grip as I shoved it down into my pocket. Then I took off after them.

Sword Fights Make Everything Better. March 15th 1358hrs

THE RUMBLING ENGINE OF the Trans Am served as a homing beacon, ensuring I didn't lose my way as I followed it up to the next floor. Coming around the corner, I spied Sullage. The Charlestown native hadn't made it far before the first Swan-Sister caught up with him, and she had his back against the wall, forcing him up onto his tippy-toes to avoid the blade beneath his throat.

The two were speaking, though it appeared that Sullage was doing more cursing than actual talking. Their words, however, were drowned out by the sounds of the Trans Am as it came to a rumbling halt, its engine left idling as three men got out.

The driver was tall, and God help me, dressed like something out of a pirate movie, wearing a white shirt lined with ruffles and lace around the collar and a sleeveless leather doublet beneath a cape that clasped at the neck. Thigh-high boots that would have been more at home on a drag-queen performer than a grown man clicked against the concrete pavement and sheathed across his back was a short sword with a cross-pommel. Something in me pegged him as the leader of the group, a suspicion that was confirmed as the two other men moved out to flank him.

The henchman to his left was shorter, thicker, with black spiked hair and heavy sunglasses despite the florescent lighting. Opposite him, the second henchman was heavyset, with a piercing gaze. Both were dressed in black tactical gear similar to what our Special Response Teams wore, along with flowing black leather coats that belonged on a set of Buffy. Each man wielded a retractable baton, and at a word from their leader, they started forward, spreading out to either side of the first Swan-Sister.

I was too far away to shoot accurately, not that I would have necessarily known who to aim for at that point anyway. I started forward, moving at a swift jog as the men encircled the Swan-Sister. I could see the leader speaking, but his words were lost in the rumblings of the Trans Am. Regardless, I could tell that his message was poorly received. The Swan-Sister lowered her sword and kicked out Sullage's legs, dropping him onto his butt before she stepped out to confront the two hench-men. Sudden fear rose up in my throat, as my mind began calculating her odds of survival.

The henchmen had every advantage they could hope for. They had height, weight, even the numbers. And one hit from one of those batons would shatter the petite woman's skull like an egg. A warning cry erupted from my throat, but I don't know if anyone even heard it, because a split second later the men attacked.

The taller of the two, the one with the piercing stare, came at her first. He shot forward and swung his baton in a sideways arc. It wasn't the most graceful attack I'd ever seen, but it was efficient, powerful, and had it struck, it likely would have knocked the girl senseless. But it didn't. Instead, the Swan-Sister ducked, dropping below the swing and kicking her leg up. It came around her back like a scorpion's tail, snapping her heel into the tip of the henchman's nose. His head snapped back, and he stumbled, one hand rising to cup his wounded f-ace.

His partner, on seeing this, screamed and launched himself forward. He moved carelessly, even recklessly, trusting on his bulk and size to carry him overtop the Swan-Sister. But she was faster than she looked, and she side-stepped around him, spinning as he passed and swiping out with her sword. The blade cut into the back of the henchman's thigh, and he screamed an instant before he hit his knees. That much weight coming down couldn't have been good for the henchman's knee joints, but he had bigger problems. The minute his blood hit the ground, it served as a sort of unofficial signal that caused all three of the combatants to get a lot more serious.

The henchman with the piercing stare recovered his wits and came forward, swiping his baton through the air, allowing his companion to rise back to his feet. The two men spread apart, circling around the Swan-Sister before launching themselves forward. Had they worked together in unison, it's likely they would have been able to subdue her. But they didn't. Instead, they relied on their size, their strength, and pure ferocity to bring her down. I suspected they'd used that same trick in the past, probably with positive results, but this time was different. The Swan-Sister, whoever she was, clearly had training, and she flowed through the men's attack, dodging, parrying, and avoiding their strikes while launching back with plenty of her own. Even from a distance, watching them was like being front row in one of those old kung-fu movies. The Swan-Sister didn't try to throw everything she had into one single blow, instead, she launched out with rapid fire strikes, often to the body, which struck me as a mistake at first, until I saw how it impacted the men's breathing. People who've never been involved in combat sports don't understand the physical toll it takes, or the way adrenaline and stress can deplete your cardiovascular system. Every strike the Swan-Sister landed robbed the men of a single breath, and bit by bit, their movements slowed, until she gained enough of an advantage that she was able to move through them at will.

She ducked beneath a lazy strike, and leaped into the air, driving her knee into the black-haired henchman's nose. His head snapped back, and he crashed to the ground and lay still. Standing five feet away, the henchman with the piercing gaze seemed to suddenly realize that the tide and momentum of the conflict had turned against them, and he decided to risk it all on one last barrage. He yelled and came forward, swinging his baton with reckless abandon. The Swan-Sister saw him coming, and she took a quick step, bringing her feet together and twisting her body to allow his strike to pass before raising her knee and snap-kicking her foot into his temple. His head jerked, and he took an unsteady step to the side, swaying drunkenly as the Swan-Sister spun and brought her heel around, snapping her foot across the henchman's face. He let out a low grunt, and his eyes rolled back into his head a split second before he collapsed.

For a long second, nobody moved, then the blonde-haired leader came forward. As he walked, he kept his hand down, drawing the tip of his blade along the concrete, sending up a steady stream of sparks as he came to stand before the Swan-Sister. He reached up with his opposite hand, unclasped his cape and let it fall to the floor with a dramatic flourish.

"You have skill, little one," he said. "But those are warriors of God you've just attacked."

The first Swan-Sister snorted. "If those are the best warriors your god can muster, then he is more worthy of pity than reverence."

"Blasphemy," the blonde man said. "We are ordained by God himself, and I have slain legions of demons who sought to hide in the shadows. To stand against us is to pit yourself against the will of the Almighty himself."

The first Swan-Sister cocked her head to the side. "And does your god demand that you only speak of violence? Or do you ever act?"

"Ah, I see what you are now," the blonde man said. "You come in sheep's clothing, but there is darkness beneath the flesh." He took a quick side-step and snapped his sword up in a flourish. "Very well then, demon. Come forth, and have at thee!"

The first Swan-Sister snarled and came at him, her blade leaping out with lightning quick strikes, each of which the blonde man managed to turn. The two circled each other, launching themselves forward and exchanging flurries of quick cuts and violent thrusts before stepping back. They clashed, and parted, and clashed again, neither giving an inch of quarter or respite. The Swan-Sister was faster, that much was evident, but the blonde man had the reach, and unlike his henchmen, he was patient, and careful not to overextend himself. His strikes didn't flow together with the same technical precision, but there was an unorthodox approach to his attacks, an almost cartoonish aura to him, as if he'd formed his style from practical tips and choreographed movies. The unconventional flow of his footwork kept the Swan-Sister perpetually off balance, forcing her to constantly readjust her stance and prevented her from landing any clean strikes. Their back-and-forth took on a musical rhythm, albeit an unsteady one, and it lasted until the first Swan-Sister slipped. It wasn't a big mistake. She thrust in, and the toe of her foot slid on the concrete, forcing her to extend just a hair too far. The blonde-haired man recognized the error, and took full advantage, pressing forward with his attack and driving the Swan-Sister back to the edge of the garage. Her back hit the wall, and she ducked, jerking below a strike that would have taken her head off. The blonde-haired man's sword cut a nasty furrow in the concrete, sending bits of broken debris and particle dust into the air as the Swan-Sister regained her balance. The two resumed their melee, striking back and forth with savage tenacity, and all the while, Sullage was forgotten.

By everyone but me.

I slowed to a halt and jerked my pistol from its holster, my aim wavering between the two combatants, unsure who to align on. I didn't doubt that any shot would bring the melee to a swift and violent conclusion, but I suddenly realized that I didn't know which side I wanted to win. The brief hesitation allowed me to notice Sullage as he slithered to his feet. For a brief instant, I thought he was going to run, but he thought better of it in the last moment, and dropped his head, sprinting in my direction. I realized what he intended, and I took off, crossing the distance and reaching the still idling Trans Am a split second after he did. He threw himself into the driver's seat, and I repeated the motion on the opposite side, coming down into the passenger's seat and snapping my gun up so that it aligned with his te mple.

"Freeze!" I said.

Sullage's mouth tightened, and he slowly lifted his hands from the wheel. "You taking me in?"

I glanced out through the front windshield, noting the henchmen beginning to stir, and beyond them, the blonde-haired man and the first Swan-Sister, still locked in mortal combat.

"Actually, you're taking yourself in," I said.

Sullage blinked. "Eh?"

"You heard me. Get us out of here, and if you even think of trying to run, just remember I can shoot you in the balls just as easily as the head."

Sullage hesitated, then he shifted the car into reverse and took off, spinning us around and carrying us down the ramp toward the exit. As we came around the corner, I caught sight of the second Swan-Sister. She'd roused herself, and her eyes widened a split second before she set herself directly in our path.

"Uh, you seeing this?" Sullage asked.

"Punch it," I snapped.

He blinked. "Seriously?"

"You heard me," I snapped. "Just do it!"

I reached out and slammed my hand down on his knee, pushing his foot down onto the accelerator to emphasize the point. The Trans Am roared and sped forward, the front wheels nearly lifting from the ground as it sped across the lot. I saw the Swan-Sister hesitate, watched her run the figures in her mind. She didn't like her chances, and her mouth tightened a moment before she sprung free of our path, bounding over the nearest car and landing on the hood as we roared past.

Sullage threw back his head and screamed, equal parts excitement and reckless abandon as he maneuvered us through the exit, past the already broken gate and out onto the street. He gripped the wheel and turned hard, twisting the car to avoid crashing into the adjacent building as we sped off down the street.

"Ah yeah," Sullage said, and cast me a half-smile. "That was some darn fine driving, if I do say so myself. Looks like I'm your cabby. Where we headed?"

"The police station," I said.

Sullage's grin slipped. "Wait, for real? After I saved you and everything?"

"Yeah," I said.

"But—"

I raised my pistol. "No buts, Sullage. You and I've got some unfinished business. Now head for the station, and keep it under the speed limit."

"Darn," Sullage said and shook his head. "You're one cold witch."

"Best not to forget it."

A Most Unusual Interrogation. March 15th 1430hrs

Sullage drove us to the police station, and I directed him into the "Law Enforcement Only" lot. We drew more than a few raised eyebrows from other officers as we parked, but I didn't have time to explain, and pointedly avoided making eye contact as Sullage killed the engine. I plucked the keys from his hand and kept my gun trained on him as I made my way around the car to the driver's side door. It swung open with a metallic groan, and I motioned him out of the vehicle. He exited reluctantly, muttering under his breath as I turned him around and secured his hands behind his back.

On the drive over, I'd debated heading for Blue Moon headquarters, but space inside our little hobbit-hole was limited, and the closest thing we had to an interrogation room was a dinky conference room with water stains along the walls. Not exactly the most secure of environments. Plus, I realized I wasn't sure exactly how far our exile went. Blue Moon division might have been booted from the police station, but I was still a sergeant within the department, and as such, should have full access to the facilities within.

Of course, should doesn't always mean would, and I held my breath as I scanned my keycard into the door at the rear of the station. A subjective eternity passed, then the light flashed green, and the metallic lock opened. I hauled open the door and motioned Sullage inside, leading him down a hallway and around the corner to where the holding cells, as well as the interrogation rooms, were housed. We made our way past a final security gate before I motioned him into a yellow box with accompanying hand prints painted on the wall. Department policy dictated that no personal belongings were allowed inside the interrogation rooms, and I turned him so that his face was against the wall before I donned my own gloves and set about emptying his pockets.

He had no wallet, no credit cards, and no ID. What he did have were loose 9mm shells, a couple of soggy business cards from massage parlors, each with various hand-written prices in the corner, a bent-up flyer for an online sport's betting site, and a wad of cash that was easily two inches thick when folded. I deposited it all into a plastic evidence bag, then sealed the top, securing the red tape and penning the date and time, along with my name. I repeated the procedure again with Sullage's pistol, which I'd recovered back in the garage. It would need to be finger-printed by our forensic technicians, and I filled in all the pertinent information, as well as a disclosure that they should expect to find my prints on the weapon as well. Once that was done, I helped myself to a couple of arrest forms and led Sullage into the interrogation room.

The room was small and cramped by design, the furniture arranged in such a way that any stray movement could cause an officer to invade a suspect's personal space. A small recording camera was perched in the ceiling corner, and the walls were painted the most boring shade of beige known to man. I seated Sullage down in the first chair and handcuffed his wrist to the table before lowering myself down opposite him. Then I spread my forms out onto the table in front of me, clicked my pen and began filling in the boxes, all the while humming softly to myself.

People think being a detective is all about mind games, tricking people into confessions and admissions of guilt using complex clues and misdirection. And sure, there's a bit of that, but mostly, being a good detective is about leveraging the little things. Most criminals have seen enough television to have at least a rough idea of what to expect, and to make matters more difficult, they're often the only ones who know for certain what actually happened and what they want to keep hidden.

So they lie.

And that's where the art of interrogation comes into play.

Being a detective is a lot like being a carpenter. You start with a shapeless, formless block of wood, and you shave it, peeling away one lie at a time, guiding your cuts by what you know of the crime scene and the forensic evidence until the truth begins to take form. The criminal's job, or inclination in most cases, is to divert the officers' hands from the truth, to steer them away from the correct cuts and attempt to craft another picture. It's a complex game that involves a lot of backtracking, but if you play it long enough, you begin to develop an ear for the truth, a sort of sixth-sense for the falsities. And all the while, you keep leveraging the little things.

Starting with personal space.

Most men are inherently uncomfortable with another man between their legs, so when an officer scoots his chair so that his knees are between their own, most criminals will give up something small, a tidbit of truth, if only to get the officers to roll their chair back. I've seen similar tricks where officers will chew raw garlic cloves before stepping into the interrogation room, or douse themselves in expired body spray and pungent cologne. Anything to put subtle pressure on the criminals. To make them so uncomfortable that their resistance is overcome by their desire to create space within the room. The tricks are countless, limited only by the officer's creativity, but they're just that. Tricks. And they don't always work.

Sometimes you run across someone who's been hardened by the system. Someone who's grown up knowing nothing but hate and discomfort, who's convinced themselves that any attention at all is better than the alternative. Often times, the best way to combat those types is to do nothing at all. Boredom and lack of stimuli have a power all on their own, and I've seen the passing hours break more than a few hardened criminals in my time.

Sullage struck me as one of those.

I leaned back in the chair, my full attention seemingly on the arrest report form in front of me, absently clicking the pen's tip as I filled in the little boxes. I kept humming, keeping my tone intentionally off-tune, punctuating it with the steady *clicking* rhythm that couldn't be easily ignored. Evidently my musical prowess didn't sit too well with Sullage, and no more than five minutes passed before he started fidgeting in his chair.

"Yo, cop-lady," he said. "Are we going to be here all day?"

I glanced up, blinking as if I'd forgotten he was there. "Most of it. Why? You got somewhere else to be?"

"Darn right. I'm starving. Aren't you supposed to offer me a soda or a cheeseburger or something?"

"Afraid we're all out of soda and cheeseburgers. I'd like to tell you that they'll feed you dinner at the jail but the way things are going, it looks like we're going to miss that too. Tough break. But don't let it get you down. Breakfast comes quick this time of year."

He snorted. "You think you're going to get me talking by starving me? That ain't happening."

"Who said I need you to talk?"

"I know how this game is played," he said. "You cops always got little tricks up your sleeve, but I'm not stupid."

"I can tell," I said. "I'm just surprised you're in such a hurry to get back to prison, given the scope of what you're facing."

"I've done time before."

"Not like this you haven't," I said. "This isn't some simple assault and battery case, or a low-level felony drug bust. You're going down for murder."

He sneered. "Fat chance. You got nothing on me."

I honestly couldn't tell if he was trying to be funny or not, but I turned in my chair and leaned forward a fraction of an inch. "I've got everything on you, Corwin. I've got an eyewitness who can place you at the scene. I've got motive. I've got forensic evidence that is going to match your gun to our murder victim. And even if, by some unthinkable twist of fate, you manage to avoid all of that, I've still got you for what happened back at the mall. You're looking at aggravated assault, illegal possession of a firearm, reckless discharge of a firearm, attempted murder, and at least half a dozen more charges that I can think of off the top of my head, each of which could put you away for fifteen to twenty years. I've got all that I need and more."

The corner of his lip split into a humorless smile. "You don't got the gold."

I tilted my head to the side and tried to keep my face smooth. "What gold would that be, exactly?"

114

"I told you I don't like games," he said. "You know what gold. It was all over the news a few months back. Those Irish-looking micks knocked over that big bank, looks like Fort Knox."

Leave it to a Charlestown native to see someone in a leprechaun outfit and label them as a "Irish-looking mick." "What makes you think I'm interested in that?"

He snorted. "Like I said, I'm not stupid. You might be a cop, but you're no different from those other clowns. Else it would have been the uniforms that brought me in. You want that gold just like everyone else."

"What do you know about those other clowns?" I asked.

He shook his head. "Nothing worth repeating. All you need to know is that everyone thinks all that gold up and disappeared. But it didn't, see, cause I know where to find it."

"And you're willing to tell me?"

"Depends," he said. "First you gotta get me a lawyer, then have him work out one of those deals like you see on television."

"What kind of deal?"

"The sweetheart kind," he said. "The ones that let me walk outta here a free man. Get me one of those, and then maybe I'll show you. Otherwise, you can kiss that gold goodbye. Swear on my mother, even if I live to be a hundred years old, I'll never tell a living soul."

"Let me get this straight. You expect the district attorney to just hand you full immunity based on your word?"

"My word is the only one that matters, since I'm the only one who knows where the gold's stashed."

"Says you, but I'd be willing to bet—"

A knock sounded on the doorway, cutting me off. I dropped my pen on the desk and rose, crossing the room and opening the door. Special Agent Alexander Gordan stood in the hallway. His soft brown hair was wind blown, and his suit was wrinkled beneath pink cheeks. If I didn't know better, I might think he ran all the way here from the Prudential Center.

"Where have you been?" I asked, keeping my voice low as I slipped into the hall and closed the door behind me.

"I ran all the way here from the Prudential Center," he said.

"Seriously?" I asked. "Damn. Did you get him?"

By "him" I meant Sullage's accomplice. Even though I was reasonably certain Sullage was my shooter, there were two people responsible for Ricky Brannon's death, and I meant to see them both answer for it.

Agent Gordan shook his head. "No. Sorry."

"What happened?"

"When Sullage fled, it started a panic. I tried to give chase but ended up slipping on a five-dollar bill. By the time I regained my feet, he was long gone."

"Damn," I said.

"How about you? Any word yet about the gold?"

"Nothing definitive," I said. "He claims to know where the rest of it is."

"You don't believe him?"

"Honestly, I don't know," I said. "A part of me thinks he's just stalling."

"What are you going to do?"

"Stall back I suppose," I said. "A couple more hours should soften him up. If not, I'll try to figure something else out."

"It's a good plan," Agent Gordan said. "But you'd better do it quickly."

"You're not overly familiar with the definition of stalling, are you?"

"It's not me. There are people looking for you."

"What kind of people?"

"Police officers. Deputy Superintendent Bulwark is leading them."

My eyes snapped open. "Bulwark is looking for me? Why?"

"I don't know, but he certainly seems determined," Agent Gordan said.

I frowned, feeling the wheels in my head begin turning. Deputy Superintendent Bulwark was a third generation Boston police officer. A bureaucratic elitist who hadn't hesitated to try to tank my career in order to appease the political powers that be. Even though I reported to Lieutenant Kermit now, Blue Moon division was technically still under the umbrella of the department's Bureau of Community Engagement, which meant Bulwark was still my boss, an unfortunate fact that I suspected neither of us cared to openly acknowledge.

In the three months since he'd ordered me transferred, I hadn't heard a peep from him. If he was looking for me now, then it meant something serious had happened, and my gut told me that it couldn't be anything good. I'm not a coward, but I'm also not stupid. It would be all too easy for Bulwark to reassign me to the Crime-Tip hotline, or God forbid, the counter at the Licensing and Public Service Division, where I'd be responsible for managing permits and sorting mail for the various sightseeing tours throughout the city.

I might have still been learning the ropes of Blue Moon, but I was getting better every day, and had no desire to give it up, especially now, with the leprechaun heist and Ricky Brannon's murder still unresolved. I needed to get out of here and back to our little hobbit-hole inside the government parking garage. Before I could do that, though, I needed to find out everything Sullage knew about the gold. And the only way I was going to do that was to break him down, fast and hard.

"Give me three minutes," I hissed, and made my way back into the room.

"Bad news, Corwin," I said. "There's not going to be any sweetheart deals."

Sullage's eyes narrowed. "Why not?"

"Turns out, we've got your partner in the other room. He already started talking on the way over. Bad news for you."

"He's lying," Sullage said. "He's never even caught a sniff of that gold."

"Funny, he told us you'd say that. Unfortunately, it looks like his word is going to win out. The other detectives have already put in a call to the district attorney and are waiting on an answer back."

"He's playing you," Sullage said again. "You mark my words, this time tomorrow you'll be begging me to take your deal."

"Not likely," I said. "Your partner may be lying, but so are you, and right now, he's doing it better."

"How do you know I'm lying?"

"Basic mathematics," I said. "See, unlike you, I have a pretty good idea how much those coins are worth. And that stack of cash you had in your pocket? Even if you sold those coins for twice that, you still got ripped off big time."

"Ain't nobody got ripped off."

"Oh no? How much did he give you?" I waved my hand in front of my face. "Off the record."

"Off the record? Six large."

I groaned and rubbed my eyes. "It's worse than I thought." I turned back toward the door. "Hey, Agent Gordan."

There was a second's pause before the door opened and Agent Gordan stuck his head in. "You rang?"

"How much were those coins worth again?"

"$19,000."

I allowed Sullage a moment to absorb the information. "So you expect me to believe that you accepted less than one third their value, knowing full well that you would have hundreds of more pounds to unload? Nope, sorry. Not buying it. Now stand up."

Sullage blinked. "Eh?"

"You heard me. Stand up."

Sullage hesitated, and then slowly stood, his features drawing into a frown of confusion as I uncuffed his wrists.

"You high or something?"

I shook my head. "I already told you, I have everything I need. Your gun coupled with our forensics team is going to tell the story of Ricky Brannon's death better than I ever could."

"So, why are you letting me go?"

I shrugged. "Jails are overcrowded. Plus, it means less paperwork for me. You'll get a court summons here in about a week. Probably want to find a lawyer between now and then. Now hurry up and get out of here so I can get ready for the deputy superintendent's press conference."

Sullage frowned. "Press conference?"

"Regarding Ricky Brannon's death. He'll expect me to be at his side, and I'll need to announce that we've arrested our murderer, that would be you, and that you've been released on your own recognizance." I hesitated a moment. "I'll also need to mention the gold too. I mean, there are still plenty of people looking for it."

Sullage's frown deepened. "You joking, right?"

"Do you see me laughing?"

"You put out word that I know where the gold is and every townie in a twelve-mile radius is going to be looking for me."

"That's probably true. Of course, you've got bigger problems than that."

"Eh?"

"Have you forgotten about the Swan-Sisters? Or those jackasses in the long leather coats? They certainly seemed to want a piece of you, and the fact that they found you as quick as they did makes me think they can probably do it again. Plus, this time, you won't have a gun."

"I got plenty of people on the outside can help me."

"I'm sure you do," I said. "But you have to wonder, how loyal are they really? Once that press conference airs, everyone who believes you've got more gold stashed away is going to be lining up to take a swing at you. Might be you can find a friend to lend a hand, but I think you'll have a harder time than you think. Anyone with half a brain will be able to see that you're up a creek without a paddle. Helping you will only make them a target in return." I lowered my voice. "They're going to tear you apart, Corwin, like vultures fighting over a rotting carcass."

"You can't do that."

"Watch me," I said. "You're living on borrowed time. The safest place in the world for you right now is prison. Worst thing that will happen there is some other inmate shakes you down for deodorant and toothpaste. But outside these walls?" I shook my head. "I fully expect to find your body on the side of the road or in a ditch sometime in the next week or so. Tough break for you, but at least it'll save the taxpayers the expense of a trial."

"It don't bother you? The thought of them killing me?"

I schooled my face to stillness and prayed he didn't notice I was holding my breath. "I've seen a lot of guys just like you come through these walls, Corwin. And I can count on one hand the number of them that turned their life around and became upstanding citizens. Way I figure, you're going to get what you deserve either way."

"Cold witch."

"Time to go."

"Hold on now," he said. "Let's just talk about this. You want something. What is it?"

"I want to solve this case," I said. "But since you're not willing to cooperate..."

He considered it, then sat back down in the chair. "I didn't say I wasn't willing to cooperate. But things are complicated."

"Complicated how?"

"What if there was no more gold? What if I was just saying that?"

I feigned a shocked expression. "You mean you were lying?"

"Just suppose. What then?"

"Well, in that case, I'd still need to know how Ricky came to be in possession of the gold. Specifically, where he found it."

"I tell you that, you let me stay?"

"No. First you tell me where Ricky found the gold. Then you tell me who you sold it to. Do that, and I *may* consider letting you stay." I leaned forward, pressing my fists down into the table's top. "But you lie to me again, Corwin, and I'll broadcast your release on every major news station in the city. I'll walk you out of the station myself, uncuff you right on Concord Street, and then I'll sit back and watch the feeding frenzy. Now start talking."

My Kind of Coffee. March 15th 1451hrs

"NORTH POINT PARK," I said, as the door closed behind me.

Agent Gordan was already waiting for me inside the adjacent interrogation room. He held a Styrofoam cup in either hand, and my stomach rumbled as the scent of coffee reached my nose. It suddenly occurred to me that it had been a while since I'd last had anything to eat or drink, and I accepted the offered cup with a low groan, tossing back my head and letting the first sip linger in my mouth for several seconds before swallowing.

It wasn't great coffee. Police station brew usually isn't, but there was a kind of twisted pride in it. As if the beans themselves had taken on the personality of the department. You could almost hear them murmuring that, even though it wasn't pretty or graceful, somehow, someway, we'd get the job done and make it through another day.

It was, in short, my kind of coffee.

Of course, I could be deluding myself. It was entirely possible that I was romanticizing the sub-par sludge the department served in an attempt to trick myself into believing it was more palatable than it really was. It was a theory further supported by the face Agent Gordan made after his first sip. He swallowed with effort, and then gently set his cup down pn the table. I thought I heard him murmur something about hamster droppings before he cleared his throat and shook his head clear.

"What do we know about it?"

I held up a finger, then took another swallow before answering. "First things first. Were you seen?"

He nodded reluctantly. "I couldn't exactly go sneaking around without raising even more suspicion. Luckily, I don't think anyone's made the connection between us yet."

That was good. If Bulwark had his posse roaming the halls, then it was only a matter of time before they spotted me. I'd left Sullage handcuffed in his chair, a lukewarm soda and a plastic wrapped hoagie roll for company, and called for a transport vehicle to take him to the county jail. I felt drained, emotionally and physically, by his confession, but also strangely hopeful.

"So, the park?"

I shrugged. "It's just north of the Charles River, leading into Cambridge. Eight acres, give or take. According to Sullage, Ricky and his sister were walking along the banks when Ricky spotted the bag nailed to a tree. The sister was so busy watching the ducks that she didn't even notice. Ricky figured it was just a gag, but decided to take it with him just in case."

Agent Gordan made an acknowledging sound. "Cause you never know."

"Exactly."

"I don't suppose either of them had any idea who might have put it there?"

"No, and Sullage doesn't remember seeing any markings or writing on the bag itself, although he wasn't entirely sure."

"Mysteries within mysteries."

"For now," I said. "But it might be that we can clear some of this up if we find the bag and the rest of the coins."

"Did he cough up the name of who he sold them too?"

I nodded. "Guy named Red Sammy."

Agent Gordan let out a low grunt.

"You know him?"

"Not personally," he said. "But his name has popped up on the Bureau's radar once or twice."

"Mind filling me in?"

"Jamaican immigrant, runs Red Diamond Pawn, over in the South End. Right next to the BU Medical Campus."

"Is he legit?"

"Not even close," he said. "Rumor is Sammy immigrated over when he was in his late teens and got a job working for the pawnshop. Two years later, he shows up at city hall with a business purchase agreement and signed bill of sale granting him full control of the business. The pawn shop's previous owner sold it to Sammy for pennies on the dollar, then promptly fled the city, leaving behind his home and most of his possessions. The owner's daughter reached out to local law enforcement a few months after he left claiming he'd been coerced, and they referred her to the Bureau. Our agents made contact with the previous owner, but whatever Sammy said scared him good. He refused to speak about the sale and requested not to be contacted again. That was ten years ago."

"And now?"

"From what we can tell, Sammy hasn't cleaned up his act much. He's been implicated in multiple cases for accepting stolen goods, mostly jewelry, but he's smart enough to keep a good lawyer on retainer. Nothing's stuck so far. He's also not shy about fleecing the nearby colleges, spreading the word that any students struggling with their tuition can receive quick cash for their valuables."

"I'm guessing there's a hefty discount in his favor."

Agent Gordan nodded. "He's scum, a bottom feeder, but just smart enough not to get caught."

"Not yet at least," I said. "But he hasn't run up against us before. I say we get over there and press him. Shake him out and see what comes loose."

Agent Gordan's mouth split apart into a boyish smile. "I think that sounds like a fine idea."

"Good," I said. "Then all we have to do is get out of here without—"

The interrogation room door swung open, and a familiar figure stepped into the room. She stood a foot shorter than me, with a petite frame and shoulder-length hair dyed blonde and styled into messy, chaotic curls. She was dressed in a police cadet uniform, or at least what a cadet's uniform would look like if it were designed by an adolescent teenage boy. The sides had been taken in, drawn tight to accentuate the bust, and the pants had been hemmed and trimmed, giving it a more form-fitting appearance that clung to her rear and thighs. The unencumbered duty belt sat snug along her waist, the nylon fabric accentuating the curves that would have otherwise been nullified by the standardized sizing. She looked, quite simply, like a stripper-cop, more akin to attending bachelor parties than solving actual crimes.

"Stick em up, partner," she said, and raised her hands, aiming her finger at me as if it were a gun. "Boom. Boom. Boom."

The Newest Member of the Force. March 15th 1454hrs

ON THE VERY FIRST day of the academy, officers are taught that, when confronted by a criminal wielding a gun, they have three options. You can go for your own weapon, try to fight back. You can flee, seek cover, and call for backup. Or you can do nothing, and, most likely, die.

There was nowhere for me to flee within the tiny interrogation room. And I couldn't in good conscious reach for my weapon. So I did nothing and tried to ignore the way my stomach dropped as each of the imaginary bullets struck home.

"Those are solid hits, sister," stripper-cop said. "Looks like it's game over for you."

"Cambrie," I said. "What the *hell* are you doing here?"

It had been a few months since I'd seen my sister. Last time we'd spoken, she'd been in the hospital, recovering from her ordeal at the hands of the bay-spurned cultists, as well as trying to attract a rich doctor who might be interested in giving her more than just a checkup.

Cambrie let her arms drop, and her mouth turned into a pouty frown. "Now what kind of greeting is that? Almost makes me think you're not happy to see me."

"Have you lost your mind?"

"Me? You're the one who's got half the force out looking for her."

I blinked and felt my chest give a little tremor. If that were true, then things were a lot more serious than I thought. I knew there'd be fallout from what happened at the Prudential Center, but I hadn't allowed myself to dwell on just how bad it might be until now.

"You're just lucky I found you first," Cambrie said. "You and..." she turned her head and her eyes widened, her lips transforming from a sullen pout into a wide grin. "And your friend here. Hubba, hubba, sailor. Who might you be?"

Agent Gordan cleared his throat. "Uh, Sergeant Mayfield. Who's your friend?"

I gritted my teeth. "Agent Gordan, this is Cambrie Mayfield. My sister."

"Her much younger sister," Cambrie said. "And, yet, far more adventurous." Her eyes shined with wicked delight. "Although, maybe that's not the case anymore. What exactly were you two getting up to in here, I wonder?"

"Working," I said. "You might try it sometime."

Cambrie's disbelief was plain on her face. "I'm sure you were."

I bit back my response and shook my head. "Agent Gordan, would you mind waiting outside? I'll be along in a minute."

"Of course." He nodded politely, and exited the room, the tips of his ears reddening as he disappeared down the hall, though whether in embarrassment or amusement I couldn't say. I watched him go, then turned to Cambrie and bit back a sigh.

Sibling relationships are often complicated, and mine was no exception. Cambrie and I might have grown up in the same neighborhood, but we'd taken very different paths. While I'd graduated college and gone right into the police academy, she'd spent eight years lingering around campus, subjecting other students to her off-key renditions of the school's song and trying to land a wealthy husband who would support her for the rest of her days. That hadn't happened and in the midst of a crisis last year, she'd decided to follow in my footsteps and join the police academy. I'd had my doubts initially, and the sight of her uniform was all the convincing I needed to know that they were well founded, but good luck convincing her of that. Watching my sister's life was kind of like watching a train when the conductor called in sick. It was only a matter of time before it ran itself off the rails.

"Alright," I said. "Spill it. What are you really doing here?"

"Saving your career, sister," she said. "I wasn't lying. Deputy Jimmy is searching high and low for you. Much longer and he's going to start thinking that you're purposefully ignoring him."

Deputy Jimmy? "You mean Deputy Superintendent James Bulwark?"

"Oh, you know him?"

"Course I know him," I said. "He's my boss. How do you know him?"

"He comes by the academy two to three times a week to speak with the new recruits," she said. "I think he likes the attention."

"Sounds like him," I said. "Speaking of attention. What the hell have you done to your uniform?"

Cambrie's smiled brightened, and she did something with her back that made her rear stand out as she turned in a slow circle. "Oh, you mean this old thing? Do you like it? I had my tailor make some improvements. All it needed was a little nip-tuck and *baboom*, it's fabulous."

"It's something all right," I said. "How are you ever going to fit a vest under there?"

Cambrie blinked. "You mean for next winter? I'll just wear a wind-breaker."

"No, that's not what I—"

"In the meantime, just look at that ass. You can smack it if you want."

"I'm not going to smack your ass."

"Don't be shy," she said. "Lord knows everyone else does it." She drew back her hand and, God help me, slapped her own ass, the sound of impact echoing through the room. "Tight as a freshman coed."

I drew in a long breath and held it, slowly counting backward from three before exhaling. "Okay, well as much fun as this has been, I have real work to do, so if you'll excuse me."

Cambrie's smile fell. "Afraid not, girlie. Jimmy says I'm supposed to bring you straight to him. He gave me these, in case you try to resist arrest." She drew a pair of handcuffs from her pocket, letting them dangle loosely from one hand. "Now are you going to come along quietly, or am I going to have to—"

I snatched the cuffs out of her hand, earning me a startled surprise, followed by a hurt look as she brought her fingertip to her mouth. "Ow, what the heck, Chloe? What's the big idea?"

I opened my mouth, then closed it again. Much as I hated to admit it, Cambrie had a point. Whether I liked it or not, Deputy Bulwark was my boss, and avoiding his attention wasn't the same as outright ignoring it. The first one I could plead ignorance. The second was insubordination, which would get me fired right quick once he inevitably found me. I may not have respected my sister, but she was only doing her job, limited in scope as it was. I didn't doubt I could get past her, but it wouldn't be very sisterly of me to make her look bad so early in her career. Besides which, she wasn't actually responsible for the day's events. That was my mess, and it was up to me to clean it up. No reason I needed to drag her through the mud alongside me.

"Okay," I said. "You win. Let's go see *Jimmy*."

"Well, that's more like it," Cambrie said and held out her hand. "Ahem."

I lowered her handcuffs into her waiting palm and tried not to roll my eyes as she moved to walk beside me.

"That a girl," she said. "Try not to look so worried. I'll put in a good word for you."

"Yeah, that's all I need."

"What's that supposed to mean?"

"Nothing."

"No, seriously. What's your problem exactly?" she asked. "You've got a serious burr up your butt."

"You really want to know?"

"I asked, didn't I?"

"Fine. In that case, I have many problems, but the one annoying me the most in this second just happens to be you."

"Me?"

I nodded. "You told me last year that you wanted a fresh start. That you wanted things to change. But they're not. You're still treating this as if it's some kind of game, and you're playing the same way you always have."

"Meaning what?"

"Meaning you found yourself a tight dress and you're schmoozing the upperclassmen. Explain to me how this is any different from your first week of college?"

"What's wrong with being personable?" she asked.

"Nothing," I said. "But this is a real job and the people who call us need actual help. You won't always be able to get by with just a wink and a wiggle. You've got to be able to make quick decisions, and then you've got to be able to live with the consequences. Keep treating it like playtime, and you're going to get someone hurt."

"Or maybe I'll do things my way and have like, you know, an *actual* career. Unlike some people I could mention."

I blinked. "Excuse me?"

"Nothing."

"Nope, too late for that. Spill it."

Cambrie drew in a breath, and let it out in a huff. "Look, Chloe, I don't want to rub salt in the wound, but your reputation around the department isn't exactly stellar, girlfriend. You and your lieutenant are basically laughing stocks. I mean, ghosts, and goblins, and now leprechauns? How exactly does that relate to real police work?"

"You wouldn't understand," I said.

"Sure, keep telling yourself that," she said. "But be careful. Rumor is the brass is just looking for an excuse to get rid of you both. And since I'm clearly not *serious* enough for your liking, you can forget about me putting in a good word for you. In fact, I don't think you should bother asking me for anything anymore, since that's how you feel. Watch your own back, because no one else is going to."

I didn't have anything to say to that, and a heavy feeling came over me, nesting in my chest and making it hard to draw in a full breath. I tried to tell myself that her words didn't matter, but couldn't quite bring myself to believe it. Like it or not, this was my career, and the opinion of my co-workers, no matter their own personal shortcomings, still held weight. I knew that the work we were doing was important, but it bothered me that the other people within the department couldn't see it. It made me sad, and that feeling lasted until we came around the corner, and my heart skipped a beat at the sight in front of me.

Deputy Superintendent James Bulwark stood in the hallway with his hands raised. He was balanced up on his tippy toes, a heavy stack of reports gripped in one fist, and his mouth was open in a silent scream.

Standing beside him was the blonde swordsman I'd seen back in the parking garage. He had his sword drawn, and the blade was pressed underneath Bulwarks throat, a hairsbreadth away from severing his windpipe. I wasn't the only one watching. Half a dozen other officers looked on helplessly as the caped swordsman drew back his arm, seemingly savoring the moment before he would thrust home.

"Chloe," Cambrie started to say, but I didn't let her finish. I snapped my arm out, shoved her roughly into the wall, and jerked my pistol from its holster, bringing the barrel up just as the swordsman's blade began to slide forward.

Vermont Wensdale. March 15th 1505hrs

TIME SLOWED AS THE surge of adrenaline hit my system, and I watched in slow-motion as my pistol rose, my sights aligning on the blonde swordsman. His mouth was drawn back into an almost comical expression, and the surrounding officers' expressions alternated between fear and horror. In the wake of the time distortion, I caught sight of the swordsman's two henchmen. Both were still wearing their tactical vests, half-hidden behind thick leather coats, their expressions unreadable behind their thick sunglasses. Briefly, I wondered how they'd gotten inside the building dressed like that without tripping any alarms, but it didn't matter now. They were here, and apparently, intent on dismantling the police department from the top down.

Well, I wasn't about to sit back and allow that. Deputy Bulwark might be a self-serving asshat, but he was still a cop, and no way in hell was I going to be caught flat-footed while he was sliced open like a lamb for slaughter.

Someone screamed from behind me as my finger caressed the trigger, but I ignored it, exhaling and aligning my shot on the swordsman as time returned to its normal speed. I drew a bead on his forehead just as he finally noticed me out of the corner of his eye. His sadistic smile slipped, and there was a moment's shock on his face as I depressed the trigger.

Something hit me from behind, striking me hard and sending me crashing into the wall. My sight picture shifted a split second before I pulled the trigger, the barrel jerking upward as the bullet departed, escaping from the tunnel and blasting apart the fluorescent light fixture halfway down the hallway.

The gun's report echoed through the hallway, and in the wake of its shot, people sprang into action. The blonde swordsman stumbled back, his earlier mask dissolving into a mixture of shock and disbelief even as his black-coated henchmen moved up to surround him. Bulwark stumbled, and grabbed the far wall, his head snapping back in our direction even as the surrounding officers drew their pistols and took aim... at me.

The sight of them with their guns pointed at me hit me like a brick to the face, and confusion washed over me even as Bulwark stepped back into the middle of the hall, his hands spread out to either side.

"Cease fire!" he screamed. "Everyone, holster your weapons this instant. I repeat, for God's sakes, put your weapons down!"

A second or two passed before the officers at the other end of the hall holstered their weapons, their faces ranging from concerned, to confused, to anger. Bulwark watched to make sure they did as ordered, then turned back to me.

I gulped.

I thought I'd seen Bulwark mad before, but what I'd mistook for anger had been merely self-preservation. This was new, and the light gleaming from his eyes, not to mention the tightness of his jaw, suggested that he wanted nothing more than to hurl me in a dark cell filled with fire ants and throw away the key.

"Sergeant?" he said, his voice a tight wire.

I blinked, then hurriedly holstered my own weapon, the scent of the expelled gunpowder causing my nose to itch. Bulwark's eyes narrowed, and for a brief moment, I gained a sudden insight into how his mind worked.

At his core, Bulwark was a behind-the-scenes guy. He enjoyed the quiet peace that comes from a well-run department. In his mind, screw-ups were to be handled quietly, with the offending party either quickly corrected or dismissed and never spoken of again. In his perfect world, he managed his division from a position of comfort, secure in his role and the respect of his peers, unvexed and unchallenged.

Which, let's be honest, I had a habit of doing.

As Bulwark glared at me, I could see him weighing his options.

Option one. He could eviscerate me. I still wasn't exactly sure what was happening, but things were clearly not what I'd assumed them to be. Depending on how badly I'd miscalculated, he could end me, here and now, strip me of my badge and gun and show me the door. But it would be messy, and there would be questions, both from the upper-brass and from our union reps. There was no way to know how it would all shake out until the end, and I could always argue what I'd s een.

Option two, was a bit more underhanded, but with less risk, and I watched Bulwark settle on his choice before he lowered his arms and drew himself up, straightening his collar.

"And that, gentlemen, is why we drill weapon safety as often as we do." He glared at me for a moment, then turned back to the surrounding officers. "No one, no matter how experienced, can afford to let their guard down even for a single minute. What you've just witnessed here today is a classic weapon's misfire. Let it sink in." He motioned up, to where the shattered fluorescent light stood, one broken bit dangling by a loose cord. "Let yourself feel the gravity of knowing just how easily it could happen, and how easily someone could have been hurt. Feel it, down in your guts, gentlemen, and make sure you never, ever, find yourself in a similar situation as our Blue Moon sergeant here."

Translation: don't be an asshat. Like me.

Bulwark allowed a moment for the other officers to absorb his words, then he turned and snapped his heels together. "Alright then, fun time is over. Return to your work, officers, and remember what you've just witnessed."

The officers slowly dispersed, some mumbling quietly among themselves as they departed. Several of them glanced back at me over their shoulders as they departed down the opposite hallway, their looks similar to the ones they might have given an unwelcome turd found hidden beneath the covers of their bed. I tried hard to ignore them, and a few moments later the hallway was empty except for Cambrie, Bulwark, the blonde swordsman and his two flunkies.

Bulwark cast me a hard look, then turned to Cambrie. "That will be all, Officer Mayfield. Good work."

"Thank you, sir," she said. She started to turn, then hesitated, looking as if she wanted to say more before deciding against it. She slipped past and departed down the hall in the same direction the other officers had gone, and I couldn't help but notice the way Bulwark's eyes followed her. He tried to be discreet, but his gaze lingered a touch too long on her as she left. The blonde swordsman, and his flunkies, didn't even bother with discretion, and openly admired my little sister as she passed. The fact that Cambrie was aware of their gazes was undeniable, but it didn't seem to bother her. She didn't revel in it, or flaunt herself in a way to make the moment last longer. More like she merely took it as a matter of course, merely the natural order of things that men should seek to watch and appreciate her.

"Sir," I said, forcing Bulwark back to the present. "There's something you should know about that man. Earlier today, he—"

"I am well aware of what he did," Bulwark said, roughly cutting me off. "And I suggest, Sergeant, that you thank him profusely, and avoid giving him any other reason to think badly of our department, if such a thing is possible." His mouth split apart into a grin void of mirth or warmth, and I could see him grimacing behind the facade. "Now come with me."

He turned and led me over to the swordsman and his flunkies, drawing to a halt beside them and offering a disarming smile.

"My apologies for the delay, gentlemen. As well as the ruckus."

"Of course, Deputy," the blonde swordsman said. "Think nothing of it."

"You're very gracious," Bulwark said. "I felt it was important that Sergeant Mayfield here have the opportunity to personally thank you for your assistance." He turned and gave me a hard look. "As well as returning their car."

I stared at him. "Return their *car*, sir?"

"Indeed," he said. "I believe it's still parked in our lot out back. I assumed you have the keys?"

I nodded, and wordlessly pulled them from my pocket, handing them over without a word. The blonde swordsman accepted them from my grip, and handed them off to his flunky, who bounced them in his palm, before slipping them into his coat.

"Much obliged," the blonde swordsman said.

"Of course," Bulwark said. "Now, Sergeant Mayfield, isn't there anything you wish to say?"

"Oh, there are many things I wish to say, sir," I said. "But maybe it would help me organize my thoughts if someone could explain what's happening." *And why, for example, the three men in front of me weren't currently in handcuffs.*

Bulwark's mouth curled down into a small frown, but he clearly didn't want to show dissention among our ranks beyond what they'd already seen. "I suppose that's fair. Sergeant Mayfield, allow me to introduce Vermont Wensdale, along with his associates, Stefan and Arthur. I'm surprised you've not heard of them, given the similarities within your professions."

"Begging your pardon, sir, but what similarities might those be?"

"Mr. Wensdale here is a renowned monster hunter, famous for his battles against the supernatural. He's received multiple commendations for his heroic efforts and is fully endorsed by the Archdiocese of Boston. Your entire division, in fact, is largely based on his exploits."

I snorted, and muttered, "Bet Tempest would love to hear that."

Evidently, I didn't speak low enough, because Vermont's face flickered, his facade momentarily cracking before it reappeared back into place. "You're far too kind, Deputy Bulwark," he said and held out his hand. "If you would allow me the honor?"

Bulwark nodded, and lifted his arm, revealing that what I'd first taken for a stack of report forms clenched in his fist was actually a hardback book. Vermont accepted the book and turned it over, revealing the black and white portrait, his portrait, on the back. He opened the cover to the title page and wrote a brief dedication before signing his name, penning the final letter up with a flourish before snapping the book closed and handing it back. "And, of course, Stefan?"

The shorter of the two flunkies stepped forward and handed Deputy Bulwark a cell phone. His cellphone, I realized a moment later, when Bulwark unlocked the screen and swiped to the picture section. My stomach dropped at the sight of him together with Vermont Wensdale, and I had a sudden flashback to moments before, the new information allowing me to recognize their posturing for just that. The sword, the fearful expression, all done for the sake of the camera. And I'd almost shot them for it. I felt suddenly sick, but also angry, my earlier determination burning strong in my chest.

"With all due respect, sir, accolades and endorsements are all well and good, but they don't excuse obstruction of justice or interfering in an official police investigation. I have some questions for Mr. Wensdale and his associates, and they'll need to be answered to my satisfaction to ensure that no charges are brought before them."

"Charges?" Vermont said, his mouth curling up into an amused smile. "Imagine that."

Bulwark evidently didn't share his view, and his voice dropped half an octave. "Mr. Wensdale came here of his own accord. In fact, I was just about to congratulate him for his bravery and thank him for his civic service."

"Thank him? Are you kidding me?"

Bulwark cocked his head to the side and raised an eyebrow.

I coughed and cleared my throat. "Apologies, are you kidding me, sir?"

If Bulwark was mollified by my show of deference, he didn't show it. "No, as a matter of fact I'm not. Mr. Wensdale showed a remarkable amount of courage when, according to his own statement, he spotted one of our officers under attack by masked assailants."

"I wasn't under attack," I said.

Bulwark raised his eyebrow again.

"Okay, well, I guess I kind of was," I said. "But it's more complicated than that. And that's sure as heck not what he was doing."

"Oh, really?" Bulwark asked. "Very well then. Enlighten me, Sergeant."

"He was..." I said, before my voice trailed off. I couldn't exactly explain that Vermont and his cronies had come hunting leprechauns, and suggesting that he'd been pursuing Sullage in hopes of recovering the gold reeked too much of speculation and not enough of fact.

"Clearly, you've given this matter a lot of careful thought," Bulwark said, his voice dripping with sarcasm before he turned back to Vermont and his cronies. "Forgive me, Mr. Wensdale. Sergeant Mayfield has been suffering with several health-related problems as of late. Her judgement is clearly more impaired than initially believed. Please believe that I will be taking whatever steps necessary to remedy the situation. In the meantime, on behalf of the entire Boston Police Department, allow me to thank you for your heroic actions and selfless courage in coming to the aid of one of our officers. I'm sure the chief will want to reach out personally but, in the meantime, this is my personal cell phone." He extended his hand, one of his business cards clenched in between his fingers. "Please don't hesitate to reach out to me directly if you encounter any more difficulties during your stay here in Boston."

Vermont accepted the card and flipped it once before slipping it in his coat pocket, flashing me a smirk as he did. "That's very generous of you. I just thank God I was there when Sergeant Mayfield came under attack. Otherwise, who knows what would have happened. She could have gotten seriously injured."

"Oh, you lying son of a—"

"That will be quite enough, Sergeant," Bulwark said. "Your demeanor during this meeting is bordering on insubordination, and make no mistake, we will discuss your conduct shortly. In the meantime, I believe you have a prisoner in custody?"

"Yes, sir."

"Good. Then attend to that, and count your lucky stars that Mr. Wensdale is not seeking to press charges for your commandeering of his vehicle during your apprehension. Otherwise, you might very well find yourself sharing a cell alongside your charge. Dismissed."

Evidently, if Bulwark couldn't project an aura of cooperation, then he was going to settle on authoritative control. Unfortunately, there wasn't much that I could do in that moment except to nod my head, turn on my heels, and make my way back down the hall. I could feel Vermont's eyes on me as I departed, and it took a conscious effort of will not to shiver under his gaze.

Anger, frustration, embarrassment, and half a dozen other emotions reared up, each vying for control, and I was so distracted by the battle raging inside that I didn't notice the man lying in wait until I rounded the corner and he seized me by the throat.

Everett Mackleroy. March 15th 1512hrs

Spend enough time among seasoned cops and you're bound to hear the phrase "rookie bravado" uttered at least once.

It's a phenomenon that runs rampant through first year officers, especially those who regularly play video games. The symptoms are a combination of enthusiasm, naivety, and recklessness that convinces them they're invincible. That they're somehow special, unstoppable little ninjas in blue uniforms who can wade into any situation, head-shotting enemies with reckless abandon, and defend themselves at the drop of a hat.

Older, seasoned officers, however, know the truth.

No matter how much you practice, how many hours you train, or even how many certifications you complete, sometimes, you just don't see it coming. Anyone can get caught flat-footed, and I was no exception.

As I came around the corner, the man sprang, launching himself forward. Strong hands seized me beneath the throat, and my feet left the floor as he swung me around, slamming me into the wall. The back of my skull smacked against the hard plaster, and black stars flashed across my vision, my muted scream ricocheting in my throat.

"You think this is some sort of game? That you can turn around and screw with my investigation and I won't do anything about it?" the man snarled.

A faint hint of recognition flickered somewhere inside, and I blinked my gaze clear, forcing my eyes to focus until I saw Detective Everett Mackleroy. He was still moving with his cane, but evidently didn't need it to steady himself as he choked me. His face was scrunched, his ears burning red, and there was something dark and scary in his gaze as he held me pinned to the wall.

It occurred to me suddenly, that there is a stark difference between someone threatening to kill you and someone actually trying to kill you. Mack had threatened me earlier, and I wasn't too proud to admit it had scared me, but this scared me a whole lot more. Of course, the police station offered me some level of protection. Mack couldn't exactly choke me lifeless and then drag my corpse out through the halls. Not with Bulwark and all the other officers, not to mention the recording cameras, so close. Not even he had that sort of influence, right?

My eyes must have shifted, because Mack craned his head around the corner, catching sight of the figures at the other end. He snorted and leaned in close. "What are you looking for? Bulwark? You think that spineless twerp is going to save you? I've had his balls in a vice ever since my first week on the job. I could bend you backward over his desk and snap your neck and he wouldn't make a peep. Face it, Chloe, you're all alone."

A part of me feared that was right. I had no friends, no partner, to watch my back. And if the entire department was willing to look the other way, well, that's the way it goes. At that moment, I felt the first tendrils of despair creeping up, wrapping their blackened vines around my heart, even as my lungs burned.

But I'd forgotten something.

Unorthodox as my methods might be, they were effective, and that little voice in my gut that whispered warnings to me wasn't something that could be outsourced or taught. Maybe I wouldn't be winning any popularity contests among the department, but there were still people who saw the value in me. Who were depending on me to solve this crime, and bring justice to the victims.

"On the contrary, she's far from alone," a male voice said from behind us.

Mack stiffened, and his grip released a fraction of an inch, allowing me to draw in a shaky breath. He never turned to look back, but I watched his face as realization dawned.

"Beat it, you penny-pinching prick," he said. "This doesn't concern you."

"As a matter of fact, it does," Agent Gordan said. "That's my partner, and I don't much care for the way you're treating her. I suggest you either release her, right now, or prepare to kiss your career goodbye."

"I'd like to see you try it," Mack said. "I eat pencil-pushing nerds like you for breakfast."

"So I've heard. Except it doesn't always work out that way, does it?"

"Meaning what?"

"Way I heard it, it was a pencil-pushing, penny-pinching prick like me who put three rounds in your chest last year." There was a sound of metal being drawn back, and a pistol slide coming forward. "Of course, one thing we know for certain is that history never, ever, repeats itself, don't we?"

This time Mack did glance back, and his eyes narrowed at the sight of Agent Gordan with his duty-weapon drawn, the barrel pointed at his back.

Mack stared at him for a long moment, then let out a disdainful snort. "You think you're tough because you got a gun? You're lucky I don't shove it up your prissy little ass."

"Wouldn't that be something for the cameras?" Agent Gordan said. "Of course, it would be a short-lived victory."

"How do you figure that?"

"Isn't it obvious? The world is changing, detective. Nerds are in charge of things now, and we don't take kindly to bullies. Strange things have a way of happening. For example, I've some friends at the IRS who are just bored stiff now that tax season is over. They'd love nothing more than to sink their teeth into a wayward detective's personal return. Of course, I'm sure all your affairs are in good order, not a blemish to be seen. Otherwise, they might be forced to freeze your accounts, and that sort of thing makes life very inconvenient, as I'm sure you can imagine."

Mack's face darkened, and several seconds passed before he released his grip. He straightened, and stared at me for a long moment, before the corner of his lip curled up into a snarl. "You want to play hardball, Chloe? Fine by me. I don't need to skirt the rules to end you. All I need to do is tell Bulwark how you and your number-cruncher boyfriend purposefully withheld information in my murder case all so you could try to apprehend him yourself, thereby placing countless pedestrians at risk. Way I hear it, he's just looking for an excuse to give you the boot."

"I wasn't withholding anything," I said. "Remnants of gold related to the Federal Reserve heist were found at the scene of your murder. I was merely following up my own investigation."

"It's a good story. He might have even believed it, except we all know your credibility is shot in this department. Fact is, you and your little boy wonder here almost let a murderer get off scot-free."

"Agent Gordan and I single-handedly caught your suspect for you and recovered the murder weapon. You're welcome, by the way."

"You went too far on this one, Chloe. Mark my words you're going to regret this."

"Yeah, that's what you keep saying, Mack. But, so far, the only thing I regret is not realizing what a pathetic scumbag you were when I first met you."

Mack's sneer never wavered. "You dug your own grave. I'm going to make damn sure you sit in it."

"That's enough, detective," Agent Gordan said, his voice firm. "If I hear you threaten my partner again, I promise you'll regret it. In fact, I would strongly advise you to leave. Now."

Mack turned slowly and spent several seconds eyeing up Agent Gordan. "That's a nice jacket," he said. "Shirt's a little thin though. Light hit's it just right, you can practically see right through it."

"I'll be sure to take it up with my tailor," he said. "Now, are you finished, or are we going to escalate this further?"

Mack nodded, mostly to himself, then turned and made his way down the hall without a backward glance, leaning heavily on his cane and whistling softly to himself. Agent Gordan and I watched him go, each letting out a soft sigh when the notes of his song finally faded.

"Are you alright?" Agent Gordan asked.

I started to answer in the affirmative, mostly out of habit, but something made me hesitate. I allowed myself to dwell on the feeling and eventually concluded that there was more to it than a simple yes or no could convey. On one hand, I was tired, drained, hungry despite the coffee I'd recently ingested, and more than a little sick of dealing with department politics. On the other hand, I was more determined than ever to catch these leprechauns and find justice for Ricky Brannon and his family. True, I may have caught the shooter, but the way I saw it, the leprechauns were just as responsible for his death as Sullage. And they needed to be made to answer for it.

"Sergeant?"

"Fine," I said. "Just fine." I gave myself a shake, then let out the breath I hadn't realized I was holding. "Come on. Time's wasting."

"Where are we going?"

"Nowhere yet," I said. "First, we're going to swing by the armory."

Agent Gordan frowned. "Did you need a bigger gun?"

I shook my head. "We need to get you a vest."

Agent Gordan blinked, then instinctively touched his chest, fingers tracing over the fabric of his dress-shirt and tie, the indentation revealing the absence of Kevlar beneath it. It suddenly occurred to him what Mack had been alluding to, and his face tightened.

"Don't worry," I said, before he could speak. "We'll handle him."

Agent Gordan snorted. "Who's worried?"

"That's the spirit," I said, and pretended not to hear the uncertainty in his voice. "Come on. Let's get you suited up and then go find some gold."

The Power of Belief. March 15th 1532hrs

THE ARMORY INSIDE THE police department headquarters was a favorite hangout of those officers lingering on the edge of retirement, many of whom had prior military service. The smell of oil, metal, and gunpowder were old friends for them, and they congregated there on a regular basis, taking solace in the comfortable familiarity of the tools around them.

Running the division was our chief armorer, who was aptly named Robert Warman. He was an old school blacksmith who had joined the department as a reserve officer a few years prior, dividing his time between law enforcement and a successful chiropractor practice before making the jump to full time. In addition to maintaining all of the department's weapons and armor, he was an accomplished knife maker and had twice been featured on the cover of *Knives Illustrated*.

"Hey, Warman." I made my way up to the counter and extended my fist out. "What's shaking?"

Warman glanced up at my entrance, and a friendly smile split his face before he rapped his knuckles against my own. Standing a hair under six feet tall, he was built solid, with a full dark beard and black-rimmed glasses. His fist easily dwarfed my own, and his forearms were lined with layers of thick corded muscles earned through endless hours working the anvil.

"Hey there, Chloe. Haven't seen you for a minute. What can I do for you?"

"We need some Kevlar. Something to keep the bad guys from putting holes in us." I hesitated, and then added. "Make sure its front and back."

"For you?"

I shook my head and motioned toward Agent Gordan. "For him."

Warman looked him up and down, frankly assessing. "Not much to him."

"Maybe not, but I'd like to keep what there is intact. Think you can help?"

"Course I can. Bring him over and let's get started."

Warman went to work, assisted by the other officers who drifted in and out, and in no time at all they had Agent Gordan stripped to his undershirt with a vest across his torso. I turned my back as he worked through the kinks, adjusting the fit until everyone was satisfied.

"One last thing. It's a personal touch." Warman drew a slender knife from his pocket. It was a thin blade, but it fit neatly into the sheath he'd sewn into the Kevlar vest. "Just don't forget about it."

"I won't," Agent Gordan said.

"Good. Oh, and Chloe?" Warman slipped behind his counter and came back out a minute later holding an open knife case. A quick glance inside made my breath catch.

Art is subjective, most people would agree, and can take many forms, so believe me when I tell you the object inside was no mere knife. It was a piece of art, handcrafted and adorned with beautiful inlays.

I let out a low whistle. "Wow."

"Stainless steel with contoured rosewood handles and an anodized aluminum pivot ring." He extended his arm out. "For you."

"You sure?"

He nodded. "I've a feeling you might need it."

I accepted the knife, drawing it from the box and sliding it into its sheath before attaching it to my belt, where it fit seamlessly. "Thanks, Warman."

"You be careful out there," he said and gave us a meaningful look. "Both of you."

We said we would, and I thanked the other officers and Warman again before the two of us made our way back through the station to the large garage that served as headquarters for our Fleet Management division.

The FMD was comprised of civilian mechanics, rather than officers, and were responsible for keeping the department's vehicles in tip-top shape. Whether it was pounding out dents, patching over bullet holes, or just rotating the snow-tires, they worked hard to ensure the officers were able to do their jobs and, unfortunately, didn't always get the credit they deserved.

A couple of years ago, there'd been talk about outsourcing the care of the fleet to a third-party company and reducing our on-site staff to a handful of part-timers. Word got around, and the entire division went on strike the following day, effectively grinding the entire department to a halt. Turns out, arresting someone isn't worth much if you can't actually deliver them to the jail. Within seventy-two hours, the upper brass had reconsidered. Rumor was that the division only agreed to come back to work once they had a signed contract from the city ensuring that the department would continue to employ their division for a period of no less than ten years. Granted, it was probably more expensive for the department, but a part of me cheered that the folks at FMD had successfully stuck it to the man, and I was reasonably certain that none of the mechanics had needed to buy their own drinks since.

I walked into the garage, breathing deep the smell of oil, gasoline and exhaust, and made my way over to the front desk, where I was greeted by a copper-haired man whose nametag read: *Wrench*, of all things. I told him what I needed, and he drew out a single sheet form, attached it to a clipboard and slid it over. I filled out the necessary information, and he took it back and tossed a pair of keys across the counter.

In addition to maintaining its normal fleet, the department kept a dozen or so loaner cars on standby, useful for visiting officials or in circumstances like now, when my car was still parked at the Prudential Center and I didn't have time to go retrieve it. The loaner cars weren't flashy, but they'd get us from point A to B, and right now that was all I needed.

I took the keys, and we made our way back out the rear exit, stepping through the doorway and into the late afternoon sun. The row of loaners stood parked at the far end of the lot, and we were halfway across when I noted a figure lingering nearby, presumably waiting for us.

Vermont Wensdale stood at ease, idly leaning against one of our loaner cars. He had his sword sheathed across his back, and his ruffled shirt sleeves rolled up to the forearm. I angled right and drew up across from him.

"Can I help you with something?" I asked.

"On the contrary, Sergeant, I would very much like to help you."

"Is that so? You've got a funny way of showing it."

He tilted his head, conceding the point. "That performance with Deputy Bulwark was regrettable, but necessary, to ensure we understand one another."

"Strange, cause from where I'm sitting, it seems to have had the opposite effect."

"Meaning?"

"Meaning, how about you tell me what it is you actually want?"

Vermont's face took on a puzzled expression. "Isn't it obvious? I'm here for the leprechauns."

"Uh-huh," I said. "By which you mean the gold."

He shook his head. "I've no interest in Boston gold. It is the leprechauns themselves that have brought me here."

"Wait a minute. You're talking about actual leprechauns?"

"Is there any other kind?"

"You honestly believe leprechauns robbed the Federal Reserve?"

He blinked and looked at me. "You honestly believe they didn't?"

I'll admit, up until now I'd just assumed that it was all an act, but there was something in Vermont's face, a lack of guile, that left me convinced that he was telling the truth. Or at least the truth as he believed it to be. He wasn't playing a character. He was living out his delusions, and the consequences were frightening.

Plenty of people believe in the supernatural. But those who do often try to keep it at arm's length, or embrace it under the guise of magic spells and positive rituals. It's rare that a true believer will try to tap

into unseen forces in order to do harm, and even rarer still that someone who wholeheartedly believes would then turn around and declare
war on its denizens. No, not just war, Vermont had built his entire
career, hell, his entire reputation, off fighting the supernatural. To
suggest that none of it was real was to rob him, not only of his enemy,
but of his entire life's work. It hit me suddenly, just how deep his belief
in the supernatural went, and the depth frightened me a heck of a lot
more than any ghost or spook could have.

"Sergeant?"

I gave myself a shake. "No, I don't believe they did."

"Why not?"

I blinked, momentarily unsure how to answer. "Well, for starters, they
don't exist."

"Says who?"

"Pretty much every scientific journal or organization in the world. If
fairies or leprechauns existed, then we would have found irrefutable
evidence of them by now."

"Who's to say we haven't?" he asked. "You think you're the only
government division dedicated to policing the supernatural? Far from
it."

His words sent a tiny shiver sweeping through me. I'd heard plenty
of stories about government agents, men in black as they are often
called, over the past few months, but had dismissed them as merely

more flights of fancy. Vermont however, was speaking as if it were common knowledge. Such a revelation would be... well, it would be something.

Vermont read my face. "Alas, I fear I must disappoint you. For the time being, the governing authorities believe it safer if the population believes the world around us to be harmless, and must therefore remain hidden from the public. Their existence, were it common knowledge, would cause public outcry such as could not be controlled."

"How convenient."

"You should not allow their fear of discovery to dissuade you from the truth."

I gave myself a shake. "Even if there is some shadowy government agency dedicated to the supernatural, it still doesn't prove any of it is real. The facts still don't support it, especially in this case."

"What facts are those?"

"The thieves uploaded a computer virus into the Federal Reserve's surveillance system to hide their crime. You going to tell me you think leprechauns started taking computer classes at night when no one's watching?"

"Entirely unnecessary," he said. "Even the simplest of practitioners knows that magic can befuddle technology."

"And how about the fact that they fled the scene in a Ford cargo van?"

"A simple glamour."

"And that the only recorded picture shows them wearing body armor and wielding machine guns?"

"Glamours upon glamours," he said. "Leprechauns are crafty beings, prone to trickery. They allow you to see that which you wish to see, thereby causing you to dismiss, not only their actions, but their entire being. If you are to truly catch them, then you must begin to think like them, and before you can do that, you must believe."

"Uh-huh. Sure."

"Look here." He shifted his shoulders, unsheathing his sword and holding it out lengthwise in his hands. The blade caught the late afternoon sun, casting its glare across the nearby vehicles. "This sword was given to me by Benedictine monks. The blade itself was quenched in holy water, and its hilt contains one of the nails used to pin Jesus Christ to the Holy Cross."

"Sounds like quite the collector's item."

Vermont's face softened, and he slid one finger along the flat of the blade. "I have born witness to its power, a mere vessel of the Almighty, as it slew demons, witches, and other denizens of the lower realms. There is power here, sergeant. Only your stubbornness keeps you from seeing it."

"Keep waving it around and you're going to catch a charge for openly carrying a weapon."

He snorted and muttered something. It sounded like he was complaining about all Blue Moons being the same, but I couldn't say for certain, and he shrugged his shoulders and let out a long exhale before I could question it. "As you wish, Sergeant. I don't blame you for being a non-believer. But if you'd seen the things I'd seen, you'd feel differently."

"I've seen more than my fair share," I said. "And none of it has served to change my mind."

"Perhaps that will change once I find my prey." He smiled. "Leprechaun gold is the purest known to man. It's said to sing when the sun hits it, yet not even that will protect them from the wrath of the Almighty. Their mischievousness and wickedness must come to an end. But in order to do that, I must ask you to allow me and my people space to work."

I blinked. "You want me to back off?"

"Only temporarily," he said. "Allow me three days, and I will catch these beings, and purge them from this city."

"You've lost your mind."

"Think carefully, Sergeant," he said. "If you continue to pursue this case as you have been, then there is a good chance our paths will cross again. If this proves detrimental to my cause, I will have no choice but to reach out to your commanding officer and report that you are harassing me again. That wouldn't go well for anyone, would it?"

I drew in a breath and let it out slow. "What is it with everyone threatening my career today? Since when did I become public enemy number one?"

"It would be better for everyone were you to simply acquiesce to my request."

"See, that's what everyone keeps saying. That things would only go smoother if I did what was asked of me. But the more I keep hearing it, the more I've come to realize that they really mean it would go smoother for them if I looked the other way, and not one time has anyone been able to explain how it's better for the city of Boston." I shook my head. "You want to use your influence to get me canned? Go right ahead. But until they take away my badge and gun, I'm going to keep on doing my job, and that means not letting puffed up morons like you run roughshod over my city. You want to stay in Boston? Fine, I can't stop you. But if I find out that you're going around threatening my citizens, then you and I are going to have one heck of an unpleasant conversation. And if I get wind of you wielding your little poker stick, then, by God, I'm going to stick it someplace not even the Holy light can reach, all the way to the nail-cross pommel." I lowered my voice. "Now do you believe that?"

Methadone Mile.
March 15th
1559hrs

There's nothing quite like the threat of forced sodomy to bring a conversation to a quick and uncomfortable close. Vermont strode away without another word, his boots clicking against the pavement as he rounded the building and disappeared from view. I watched him go, then shook my head and made my way over to the loaner vehicle, unlocked the doors and dropped down into the driver's seat with a heavy exhalation.

"You alright?" Agent Gordan asked as he lowered himself down into the passenger's seat beside me.

"Long day," I said. "And it's not over yet."

"Who was that guy?"

"His name is Vermont Wensdale," I said. "He's a—"

"The vampire hunter? That was *him*?"

I blinked. "You know him?"

Agent Gordan shook his head. "No, but I've seen his books at the airport. I always just assumed it was a fictional pen name. You know, like Richard Castle."

I shook my head and inserted the key into the ignition before bringing the engine to life. "He's real enough. He's looking for the leprechauns, apparently so he can smite them."

"And the gold?"

"Claims he's not interested."

"You believe him?"

I considered it as I pulled out of the lot and into the street. I headed east, intending to pass through downtown and the Old State House before crossing over the Congress Street Bridge and turning south near the Convention Center.

"Chloe?"

"I'm not sure. He seemed pretty dismissive of it."

"And the rest of it?"

"Obviously not," I said.

"Not even a little bit?"

I glanced at him. "Are we really having this conversation?"

"Why not?" he said and shrugged. "I'm curious."

"About what?"

"You, mostly," he said. "You spend all your time hunting ghosts, vampires, goblins—"

"Leprechauns."

"Leprechauns," he said. "And yet, you seem entirely disenchanted with all of it."

"It's because I'm not really hunting any of those things," I said. "I'm hunting people, criminals, who use their visage and myth to exploit others for gain. We keep saying leprechauns, but really, we're just hunting thieves in Halloween costumes."

"Unless we're wrong."

"Unless we're wrong," I admitted. "In which case, we've got even bigger problems than I thought."

"Isn't there even a little part of you that wants to believe?"

"Maybe a bit," I said. "But I'm of the mind that if there really are fairies, gnomes, or magic beings in this world, then they've probably learned by now to stay as far away from people as possible. It's better that way."

"Better for who?"

"Them, certainly. And probably us too."

"You really think that?"

"You don't?" I asked. "I mean, come on, you must have noticed how we tend to treat one another. How many old grandmotherly types have you had show up at your office, spouting the same sob story about how Junior, who they've raised since he was a baby, stole their life savings and went on a bender down at the local games store?"

"I don't see the connection."

"Think long and hard about how people treat each other. Then imagine what we'd do to something that wasn't technically human but had all the same feelings and features."

"Ah," he said.

"If there are any supernatural creatures lurking out there beyond our view, I'd caution them to stay there. For their own safety."

"I guess that's fair," he said. "What about the rest of it?"

"The rest of what?"

"Our investigation," he said. "Where do we stand?"

"Depends on which part you mean."

"Ricky Brannon?"

"Well, we've got Sullage pinned for the murder, but we still need the accomplice," I said. "Charlestown kids need to know that if you go that route then there are consequences. Nobody gets any free rides when it comes to murder. Not in my city."

Agent Gordan raised an eyebrow. "Your city?"

"Sure," I said and shrugged. "I mean, someone's got to take responsibility for her. Why not me?"

"Spoken like a true native."

"I'm a homer, no doubt about it. The city may be cold, and the people discourteous, but when push comes to shove, there's no place else I'd rather be."

"If that's the case, then you're going to need to make some changes."

"Oh?"

"Come on, Chloe," he said. "We both heard what Detective Mackleroy said. He and those loyal to him are gunning for you now. You let your guard down, even for an instant, and they'll jump all over you."

"Guess I can't let my guard down then."

He shook his head. "It's not that simple. I've seen situations like this play out before."

"You have?"

"Well, okay, maybe not to this extreme, but that only makes my point. Detective Mackleroy seems pretty determined to have his way. Either you'll need to go, or he will."

There wasn't much I could say to that. He was right, I knew that. I could feel it, deep down in my guts. Mack was the human equivalent of a junkyard dog. Once he had his teeth in you, he wasn't going to let go unless you made him. Which meant I either had to hit him so hard that he learned to steer clear of me, which, let's be honest, didn't seem like something I could reasonably expect to pull off, or I needed to make peace, which, for the moment, seemed equally unlikely. Unfortunately, that put me in a tough spot, with no clear way out.

"Mack's a problem for another day," I said. "I'll deal with him if push comes to shove, but I'll do it my way."

"You'll let me know if you need anything?"

I blinked and glanced at him, feeling a burst of surprise that quickly faded to gratitude. "Yeah. Sure."

He nodded. "Alright then. What else?"

"We still need to figure out where the gold came from," I said. "We know Sullage sold the coins to Red Sammy and his pawn store. We need to go there, and get Red Sammy to hand them over."

"Suppose he's not feeling cooperative?"

"Then we apply pressure until he changes his mind," I said. "Blue Moon might not have a lot of sway with the upper brass, but this is a federal investigation. I'm not above ripping Sammy's entire world apart if it means preventing more deaths."

Agent Gordan grinned. "I knew there was a reason I enjoyed riding with you." A thought struck him, and his smiled slipped. "We're not the only ones searching for the gold though. What do we do if those sisters show up? The ones with the swords."

"The Swan-Sisters," I said.

"Is that what we're calling them?"

"Seems appropriate."

"Okay, what about the Swan-Sisters?"

"No idea."

"Nothing at all?"

I shook my head. "We don't know who they work for or what they want, beyond the obvious."

"Hmm," he said. "Might be we should find out?"

"Any ideas?"

"There are cameras in the mall. We could track them back, find out what door they came in from, then try to track them back to their point of origin using street cameras and nearby business surveillance systems."

"How long would something like that take?"

"Depends how many officers we can assign to the task."

"It's just you and me for the moment."

He frowned. "Days. Maybe weeks."

"We don't have that kind of time," I said. "For now, let's just keep our eyes peeled and hope they don't pop up again."

"Seems like kind of a slim hope."

"Granted," I said, as the road elevated, carrying us over the highway. "But slim hopes are what we seem to rely on these days. Now look alive. We're almost there."

Red Diamond Pawn was located on the intersection of Melnea Cass Boulevard and Massachusetts Avenue, a crossing more commonly referred to as the Methadone Mile. Generally regarded as ground zero of the opioid and drug crisis within the city, mismatched tents lined the streets, stretching two blocks in every direction, and there were barrels placed strategically along the curbs, some with makeshift grills overtop their lids, the remains of last night's burned offerings clinging to their bodies.

A few years back some high-ranking city official's daughter had overdosed there, and in the wake of her passing, he and his wife had declared it their mission to clean up the area. They'd held fundraisers, thrown fancy memorial dinners, and schmoozed everyone who needed schmoozing until at last, the combined power of the city stood behind them. The cops had gone in like an invading army, tearing apart the tent streets, sweeping the gutters clear of discarded needles, and arresting the dealers and the other bad weeds. For a few weeks, it seemed as if the area really had turned around. Then the media coverage died down, and the cops left as overtime funding waned, and slowly, bit by bit, the weeds grew back, until the street returned to its original state.

The tents had since been replaced, and even expanded in some places, their roofs sewn together to form giant tarps that covered makeshift stalls like the kind you might find at an outdoor flea market. People milled around along the sidewalks and within the small lots, talking softly among themselves or, in the cases of those who'd already gotten high, swaying unsteadily on their feet, their eyes half-closed. I spotted more than a few slumped down with their foreheads aimed toward the floor, engaged in what the narcotics officers referred to as the fentanyl crawl, characterized by off-kilter, jerky movements and heavy leaning as they edged their way toward the buildings. To the west, I could just glimpse the top of the BU Medical Campus, the surrounding streets serving as a stark reality check to those incoming medical students as to what can happen when drugs are misused or treatments gone awry. I took the next right turn, traveling west for two blocks before pulling into Red Diamond Pawnbroker's parking lot.

A two-story red brick building with green and white awnings, pictures of gold and jewelry lined barred windows. The lights were on inside, but there was a heavy gate strewn across the front door, blocking the entrance.

"Doesn't look like they're open," Agent Gordan remarked.

"Lights are on," I said and narrowed my eyes at the open padlock. "And the gate's unlocked."

"Maybe they're having a private party?"

"Maybe they are," I said. "Let's take a peek around first."

We pulled out of the lot and took the next right turn, making our way down a narrow alley flanked by red-brick buildings on either side. Coming around the back of the building, we caught sight of a black van with heavily tinted windows idling near the rear entrance.

"Hello," I said. "And who might you be?"

"Chloe?"

"Let's just take a look," I said.

I turned into the next lot, which belonged to a laundromat, and angled back, parking at the edge of the lot in a way that would allow us a clear view of the black van. All the while, my Spider-Girl sense was whispering that something wasn't right, and the hairs along the back of my neck voiced their agreement.

I slid down in my seat and drew my phone from my pocket, setting it up along the dashboard. I wasn't quite hidden, but from a distance, I would just look like someone playing on their phone and waiting for their laundry to finish washing. It wasn't perfect, as far as covers go, but it served to allow me to blend in enough that no one took notice.

Peering over the top of my cellphone, I had a clear view when the back door of the van opened and two men stepped out. They were both dressed in black tactical gear, like the kind our SWAT officers wear, glow sticks and zip ties attached to their flak vests. One was noticeably heavier than the other, but otherwise there was nothing differentiating them. There were no badges or patches along their arms or chest, and they both wore hockey masks, the kind that wrap around the entire head, the yellow and black designs depicting the Boston Bruins logo. The first one had a pistol in one hand, with a red-dot scope attached to the top and a flashlight along the under barrel. The other one...

I swallowed.

The other one had a Mossberg 12-gauge shotgun with an extended drum magazine attached to the underside. The sight of it in his hands sent a tremor running through me, and it was one of those times where familiarity with guns worked against me, because I knew that anyone who was on the receiving end of that barrel wouldn't have time to feel it, much less utter any final words before they were, quite literally, shredded.

Agent Gordan evidently knew it too.

"You need to call this in," he said as the two men began briskly walking toward the Pawn Store's rear entrance. "Any idea what the response time down here is?"

"Depends which shift is on," I said, which was, unfortunately, the truth.

Most of the locals were smart enough to steer clear of this area, which meant that the majority of the crime that occurred here was addict-on-addict. I couldn't really blame the officers for their lack of enthusiasm. It can be frustrating, going to all the effort of investigating and reporting a crime, all the while knowing full well that your addict-victim probably isn't going to bother to show up for court, much less meet with the district attorney's office ahead of time. It begins to feel a lot like babysitting, and it was common knowledge that most officers weren't willing to hurry down here unless it was something really serious. Suspicious men lurking about the pawnshop wasn't going to qualify in most cases. Besides, there was another factor to consider.

"You call it in," I said.

Agent Gordan blinked. "Me?"

I nodded as the two men drew up alongside the doorway. They tested the knob, and when it proved to be locked, the taller of the two reached inside his vest and drew out a small, handheld device. It looked like some sort of miniature drill, and he lined it up to the metal bit and bit into the deadbolt lock. No more than ten or twelve seconds passed before the lock gave way, and the exterior plating dropped to the cement. The two men kicked it aside, then slipped the door open and disappeared inside.

I watched them go, then pushed open my door. "I'm going in."

Agent Gordan's eyes widened. "You're what?"

"You heard me."

"Hold on. Let me put in the call and then we can go together."

I shook my head. "Can't do that."

"Why not?"

I motioned toward the still idling van, and it only took Agent Gordan a moment to spot the slender trails of smoke rising from the front window, revealing the third man sitting in the driver's seat.

"If we both go in, we could end up surrounded. You have to stay here and keep eyes on the driver."

"If only one of us is going, then it should be me."

I shook my head. "You said it yourself. Mack and those loyal to him are going to be gunning for me. We don't know who's on shift right now, but if they see my name, they might shelve the call."

"Dammit," Agent Gordan said. He looked like he wanted to argue further, but my reasoning was sound, and after a moment he let out a defeated sigh and fished his cell phone from his pocket. "Be careful in there. Don't go getting into a gunfight you know you can't win."

"Wouldn't dream of it," I said.

I closed the door, suddenly aware of the rising cold coming off the tiny patches of leftover snow still clinging to the street. They called to me, worming their way into my feet, trying desperately to keep my heels glued and preventing me from taking another step. I allowed them a moment, then gave myself a shake, and conjured the memory of Ricky Brannon to the forefront of my mind. The recollection of his body brought warmth fueled by anger that burned away the cold's touch. I savored the heat, then I unzipped my coat, loosened my gun in its holster, and started toward the pawnshop.

Red Diamond Pawn. March 15th 1617hrs

I COULDN'T GO IN the back without the driver noticing, so I eased my way back toward the front of the building, waiting until I passed the corner before breaking into a swift jog and crossing the street. I made my way over to the front entrance. Along the way, I couldn't help but to note the broken surveillance camera in the corner, wires erupting from its body like an octopus giving birth. Assuming the one around back was not in any better shape, it meant that Red Sammy was more dependent on his reputation to keep his business safe, which was a real possibility based on what I'd already heard or someone had been here ahead of time and taken measures to keep their activities secret. Either way, it didn't bode well.

I came up beside the front door and seized the gate, the one with the open padlock, and pushed it aside. It gave way reluctantly, the metal hinges groaned as they were forced closed. I'll say one thing for Sammy.

He was cautious. The bars of the gate were intentionally bent a little further down, allowing the gate to only open so far, ensuring that anyone who came inside had to do so in a single-file line.

Once past the gate, the front door could have been a problem. Obviously, I didn't have a key, and while I could have broken a window, the noise would have carried to anyone inside, alerting them of my presence. Thankfully, luck was on my side, and whoever had forgotten to lock the padlock had also been negligent with the front door. It turned with ease, and the door swung away, allowing me entry.

At first glance, Red Diamond Pawn was a junkyard masquerading as a pawnshop. There were shelving units along the walls, loaded down with all manner of items such as tools, electronics, musical instruments, and sporting equipment. It was all stacked haphazardly, with a thin layer of dust coating most of the surfaces and more than a little rust visible along the tools. One glance would have been enough to send most seasoned treasure hunters on their way, but a more seasoned eye, or a more skeptical one depending on how you wanted to look at it, would have taken a closer look and realized that the store's haphazard appearance was no mere accident. It was a front, designed to weed out those looky-loos who had no real business there, while simultaneously funneling those in the know towards the heavy glass counter by the register. A lone swivel chair sat alongside a handmade table containing a digital scale, a weighted counterpart, a black testing stone, and a small collection of magnifying glasses. Everything someone might need in order to work as a gold broker.

I loosened my pistol in my holster, and slipped through the empty storefront, pushing around the counter and back behind the register. As near as I could tell, the armed men had entered into the storage room, and were likely searching the hallways. I knew I didn't have long, so I walked as silently as I could, and stayed low, keeping my head down and my ears open. As a result, I caught wind of men's voices, coming up from the floor. It took me a second to realize that whoever was speaking was doing so from the basement. I pushed deeper into the hall, and the first door I came to led to nothing more than a storage closet. The second door, however, opened to reveal a metal staircase descending into an expansive subbasement that ran the entire length of the building. More voices rose, and this time they seemed to be arguing, the frustration heavy in the cadence even if the words were indecipherable. The tone sent warning bells ringing in my head, and I drew my pistol, holding it close to my chest as I descended the stairway, keeping my footsteps light until I reached the base and stepped out onto a bare cement floor. It was noticeably cooler down here, but the chill that went through me as I skulked along had little to do with the cold. If the upstairs had been messy, the basement was worse. A large workbench stretched the length of the west wall, loaded down with everything someone might need to work with gold. There was a large testing stone surrounded by little bottles of acid, a smelter that resembled a crock-pot, and various graphite cups surrounded by tongs and shaping tools. There were several different sized brick molds, and heavy gloves hung from a tack on the wall, along with thick leather aprons and several pairs of protective glasses.

"Come on now, boys," a man's voice said from deeper inside. "Let's say we stop playing these games, eh? Red Sammy knows what you're up to, and I'm telling you right now, I want in."

The "boys" response was murmured, and I couldn't make out the words, but whatever they said clearly didn't sit well, because I heard the sound of metal smashing against wood, followed by a curse.

"What's the problem, eh? My money not good enough for you. Or maybe you just think you're better than me? You're thinking you're going to keep all the money for yourselves and leave old Sammy out in the cold. Is that it?"

I followed the sounds of the voices, slipping through the dimly lit basement until I eventually came to a small room walled off by a four-foot fence and windows made of chain-link fencing. I dropped into a crouch and peered over the edge at the figures inside.

The first person I saw was in his early twenties and dressed in baggy flannel clothing with a bandana over his head and a short-barreled rifle slung across his chest. He was leaning against the wall, watching the scene unfold with a bored expression across his face.

The second person was Red Sammy.

He was shorter than I expected, but he was lean, with wiry muscle that made me suspect that whatever he lacked in size, he made up for in speed. Dressed in loose olive green BDU pants and a black sleeveless shirt with a gun barrel sticking out the back, he kept his hair cut short, and his dark eyes shone with anger as he peered at the pair of figures seated in the middle of the room.

The first was in his mid-thirties and thin to the point of being gawky. He was dressed in a gray suit that was at least two sizes too big, with a receding hairline and the kind of soft features that some women might find comforting but would never be rated as traditionally attractive. He was also, to put it in a single word: terrified, sitting ramrod straight in his chair, clearly not comfortable but too afraid to stand.

The man beside him seemed to be suffering no such compunctions. He slouched at ease, his wide back and heavy thighs spilling over the edges of the chair. He had a blue collar look about him that reminded me of the bricklayers who worked in north Boston. Black shaggy hair hung low past his ears, and his heavy features and sloping brow heralded back to a simpler time, when men bludgeoned one another with sticks and axes made of stone.

Sammy stepped between them and held up his hand. In his fist, he clenched an antique leather coin purse. There was something engraved on the side of the bag, but I couldn't make it out, beyond a mere glimpse. My heart skipped a beat when I heard the sound of the coins clink inside, though.

"This is the way it's going to be, boys," Sammy said. "You're going to take this here bag, and consider it a down payment. A gesture of goodwill, if you like. And three months from now, you're going to come back and bring me double its worth."

"Three months?" the suited man sputtered. "That's not, I mean, we can't—"

"Three months," Sammy repeated.

"But we're talking about elements that won't be discovered for *years*."

"Then you'll have plenty of time to think how to pay me back for my investment," he said. "Double in three months. And the same again three months after that. And so forth."

The suited man's eyes bulged. "For how long?"

"Until I say it's enough."

"Oh, now hold on just a moment."

"No holding on," Sammy said. "This is the way it is. And I know what you're thinking. What if you don't pay? Well, that would be a very bad choice. I can always hop a flight over to London and find you. And if it comes to that, I'm going to have my man here twist your head off. You feel me?"

The suited man's mouth curled into a rounded "o", and a soft squeak slipped past his mouth. Beside him, the heartier one only nodded his head, not bored exactly, more like he hadn't fully registered what was happening.

Sammy turned and flipped the bag of coins to the suited man, who raised his arms more by reflex than any conscious thought. He fumbled the bag before eventually catching hold and pulling them to his chest.

"W-what are we supposed to do with these?" the suited man said.

"You're the metal man, aren't you? You figure it out, and remember what I said. Double, or else I'll come looking for you and the coins."

"You won't have to look very far," I said as I came around the door. Four pairs of eyes snapped in my direction, and the man leaning against the wall started to raise his barrel, but I was faster. I aligned my pistol on him, and a quick warning sound halted his hands. He slowly lowered his rifle back to his chest and removed his hand from the grip.

Red Sammy stared at me for a long moment, then turned his glare on his associate. "For heaven's sake, man. Didn't I tell you to lock the damn door? How many times I gotta say it? We can't have little bippies walking in off the street at a time like this."

"I'm sorry, Sammy," the man said.

"Yeah, damn right you're sorry. Sorry in all kinds of ways. And as for you." He turned back to me. "Who are you?"

"Boston PD," I said. "I'm here for those coins."

Sammy snorted. "Damn cops. Either show me a warrant or get yourself gone. Otherwise, I'll be siccing my lawyers on you."

I shook my head. "You've got bigger problems than me. Two heavily armed men just broke in through your back door and are prowling around upstairs. I don't think they're here to browse."

Sammy's face twisted in confusion, and he debated a moment before he turned to the other man and motioned with his jaw. "Go take a look and see what all the fuss is about."

The man pushed himself off the wall and made his way past, angling wide around me. I kept my pistol pointed at him, and he passed without incident and headed back toward the stairs I'd come down. I watched him disappear from view, then turned back to Sammy, who still hadn't bothered reaching for his gun.

"What's your interest in my coins?" he asked.

"They're not yours, for starters," I said. "They're leprechaun gold."

"Oh, they're mine. Bought and paid for."

"Yeah, and I know exactly what currency was used," I said. "Meanwhile, you've got—"

I never got to finish my sentence, because at that exact moment Sammy's associate came sprinting back through the darkness. He still had his rifle, and I hadn't heard any gunshots, but something must have spooked him good, because he stumbled back into the room and crashed against the wall, gripping the chain-link fence to keep himself up. He tried to speak, failed, and tried again, managing little more than a bubbling gurgle.

"What was that?" Sammy demanded. "Come on now, out with it, man."

Spurred by his words, his associate straightened, his face going slack an instant before he opened his mouth and blood came pouring out. Wet spittle spewed, then dissolved into a thick flow that spilled down his chin to the floor. Confusion reigned, all of us too stunned to move, as the man swayed. That was when I noticed the steadily expanding wetness on the front of his shirt. I followed it back, angling my body and peering behind him to note the sword hilt sticking out his back. It was a delicate blade, with a carefully wrapped hilt and a soft white tassel hanging from the bottom of the pommel. I stared at the hilt for a long moment, and then realization dawned, and I spun around as one of the Swan-Sisters came hurtling out of the darkness.

The Blade versus the Bullet. March 15th 1623hrs

DRESSED IN A FULL white unitard with an aptly named visage mask, the Swan-Sister leaped into the room, moving with blinding speed. She targeted me first, snapping her foot out and kicking my arm at the wrist. Pain flashed through my forearm, followed by a tingling numbness as my gun flew from my hands, striking the far wall and dropping to the concrete.

Sammy saw it happen and started to move, but the Swan-Sister had angled her attack, and she came down in a crouch in front of him, spinning around with all the grace of a professional figure skater and sweeping his legs out from him before he could take his first step. Sammy's body went sideways, and he crashed to the hard cement, his head rebounding off the floor just in time for her to rise up and deliver a vicious soccer kick to his face. The force of her torque spun her around in a full circle as Sammy's head rolled back.

My gun hand was throbbing, the nerve tips along the edges of my fingers burning, but I ignored it and threw myself forward, drawing back my opposite arm and launching a heavy punch. It wasn't my best shot, not by a long shot, and it showed. The Swan-Sister parried my punch aside with contemptuous ease and then snapped the same hand around, back fisting me in the face and sending me crashing into the wall.

At the same time, the two figures standing in the center of the room finally stirred. The suited man was gripping the coins to his chest, and he raised his feet off the floor, bringing them up to his chest as if he'd seen a mouse. The heavier of the two finally seemed to take note of what was happening and decided to intervene. He rose from the chair and took a slow, lumbering step forward, reaching out and seizing the Swan-Sister's shoulder.

"Hey now," he said. "That's enough—"

The Swan-Sister jerked around and did something with his wrist. I couldn't see what it was, but the effectiveness was clear. The heavy man let out a surprised exhalation a split second before he spun head over heels and crashed down with a heavy *thud* that echoed through the basement.

I tried to push myself off the wall, but my head was still ringing, and I stumbled half a step before falling to one knee. The Swan-Sister noted my movements, and her lip rose in a snarl behind her feathered mask. She took a quick step up beside Sammy's henchmen, seized her sword, and, with a single motion, jerked it free of his back, sending a

191

scarlet ribbon of blood onto the cement as she spun and brought it up underneath the suited man's throat.

"Coins," the Swan-Sister said.

The suited man's lip trembled, and his hands were shaking so hard that the bag slipped from between his fingers, landing on the chair in between his legs. The Swan-Sister glanced down, her mouth compressing into a thin line as her fingers tightened along the sword's grip. Suddenly realization hit me like a physical slap, and I forced myself up with a heavy grunt, stumbling two steps before lowering my shoulder and charging forward.

The Swan-Sister didn't block, and she didn't parry. She didn't need to. Instead, she spun her body, twisting away as if she were a matador and I was merely a charging bull, too stupid to realize the cape wouldn't be there when I passed.

I stumbled past her spinning form without making contact and crashed into the suited man, the unbalanced force knocking his chair over and sending the two of us crashing down to the ground. A subjective eternity passed before we managed to untangle ourselves, and when I turned, I found the Swan-Sister standing over us, her arm drawn back to strike. She started to bring her sword forward, but then she hesitated, just for a moment, eyes flickering as she debated which of us she should skewer first. The momentary hesitation cost her, as the heavyset man rose from behind her. He'd grabbed the henchmen's rifle, and wielded it like a club, swinging it around and bringing it down across her back. The Swan-Sister's body jerked, and her eyes rolled back in her head a split second before she crashed to the ground in a heap, her sword clattering from her suddenly unconscious fingers.

I stared at her still form for a long moment, then I scrambled up to my feet, kicking her sword across the room before peering around for my pistol. I spotted it over against the far wall, and I could feel the big man's eyes on me as I retrieved it, double-checking the magazine and barrel before I turned back.

The suited man and his associate were halfway to the door before I ordered them to stop. They came to a halt slowly, trading a long glance before turning back to face me. I noted the big man was still holding the short-barrel rifle.

"Yes?" the suited man asked.

"Coins," I said, still fighting against the dizziness. "I need them."

The suited man blinked, then glanced down to his hand, seemingly surprised to find that he was still gripping the bag. He must have seized it as a reflexive action, and he tossed it underhand toward me. I caught it with my numbed hand, or tried to. I didn't think anything was broken, but my nerves were still firing sporadically, and I fumbled the bag before kneeling down and scooping it up. I kept one eye on them as I tore open the leather cord with my teeth, peeling back the edges to peer inside.

The sight of gold greeted me.

The golden coins reflected the fluorescent lighting with a familiarity that both surprised and scared me. They were identical to the ones I'd seen before, stamped with violence on one end and a broken crown and maimed eye on the other. I stared for a long second, then seized one end of the cord with my teeth and closed it back up before slipping it into my pocket.

"I-is that all?" the suited man asked. "Can we go now?"

I considered it for a moment, then nodded. "You can go, but not out the front."

"Eh?" the big man asked.

"I wasn't bluffing, there are armed men upstairs. If we go that way, I don't know what will happen, but I don't think it will be good."

"Is there another exit?" the suited man asked.

I glanced toward the opposite way, noting the heavy shadows that fell across the walls as the hallway turned. "Only one way to find out," I said. "Let's go."

"Wait," the big one said and motioned to where Red Sammy and the Swan-Sister had fallen. "What about them?"

It was a good question, and if I weren't so scatterbrained, I would have thought of it already. A bag full of coins wasn't going to give me any answers or earn me any goodwill on its own. I still needed Sammy, scummy as he may be. And there were still plenty of questions surrounding the Swan-Sisters and what their connection to all of this was. The only one who could give me any definitive answers was currently unconscious, and it occurred to me that it might not be such a bad thing to have her in custody if her sister showed up. Much better than leaving her here where she could presumably be abused and possibly killed.

"Okay," I said. "Here's the plan. First, what are your names?"

"I'm Basic," the heavy one lumbered.

"Pleasure," I said and turned to the suited one. "And you?"

"Hilary," he said.

"Say again?"

"Er, Brian," he said. "Brian Clinton. But everyone calls me Hilary. And this here is James, but everyone calls him—"

"Basic," I said. "I got it. I'm Chloe. Everyone calls me Chloe, or Sergeant Mayfield if you're feeling formal. Listen closely now. We're getting out of here, all of us, but we need to do it carefully. Basic, can you carry Sammy and the girl?"

"Don't see why not," Basic said.

"And Hilary," I said. "I need you to hold the rifle and take point."

"Uh, me?" Hilary asked. "I'm not really a big fan of guns. The police don't use them back home."

"Well, we use them here," I said. "If the men from upstairs find us, then they'll most likely come down the same way we did. That's why I'll cover our rear. If we can get outside, I have a car waiting." I didn't bother mentioning that the armed men had a car as well. Hilary seemed scared enough as it was. There was no reason to terrify him further. And Basic, for his part, seemed strangely fine with the events unfolding all around him.

I started to take a step, but a loud bang suddenly came from the opposite side of the basement. It took me a moment to recognize that it was coming from the doorway I'd descended through, and then another to realize that Sammy's associate, or possibly the Swan-Sister, had evidently barred it from the opposite side.

Unfortunately, whoever was responsible hadn't done a very good job. Two more loud bangs sounded, followed by the sound of the wood snapping as the door gave way. A single flashlight beam appeared, illuminating the stairway and forming a circular shape on the basement floor.

Whoever Hilary and Basic were, they clearly weren't stupid. As soon as the first sound rang out, Basic handed Hilary his rifle and stepped over to scoop the Swan-Sister from the floor. Hilary held the rifle gingerly, as if afraid he might get oil on his hands, but I didn't bother to reprimand him. We knew what direction the gunmen were coming from now, and it would be up to me to hold them off while we made our escape. Speaking of which...

"Come on," I hissed, fearful that my voice would carry.

Basic threw the Swan-Sister over his shoulder, then stepped back and reached down for Sammy. Unfortunately, that's where things took a turn for the worse.

Red Sammy, as it turned out, wasn't as unconscious as we had believed. In fact, he'd been playing possum. As soon as Basic went to grab him, he spun around and came up to his feet, yanking the pistol from behind his back and pointing it at us.

"Ain't nobody going anywhere," he snarled. "Not until I get some answers."

"Shh," I snapped. "Keep your voice down?"

Sammy's eyes snapped to me. "Who are you to tell Sammy to stay quiet in his own house?" He glanced back over his shoulder, noting the flashlight for the first time. "Who that there? What's your name, boys? You come here for Red Sammy? Well, here I am. Take your best shot, because if you don't, then I'm going to—"

We never got to find out what Red Sammy was going to do.

As soon as the first gunman descended low enough to see into the basement, he turned and began firing. I caught a brief glimpse of a muzzle flash, followed by a deafening report, and then Sammy's chest blew apart like... well, there aren't too many good ways of describing what happens when someone takes a shotgun blast to the chest. Picture a watermelon being blasted apart, and it was basically the same thing.

We were all in the splash zone, including the Swan-Sister, whose white unitard suddenly resembled something out of a polka dotted Dr. Seuss book. Sammy's remains crashed down to the cement, the sight of his lifeless body sending tremors running through me. Unfortunately, we didn't have long to mourn him, because the gunman was even now lining up his next shot. I snapped around and raised my pistol, firing rapidly at the midway point of the stairway. Sparks flew where the bullets struck the concrete, and the gunman cursed and jerked back, pressing himself up above the sightline.

"Run!" I screamed.

Neither Basic nor Hilary needed any additional encouragement, and the three of us took off, racing away from the stairway and down the far hall as the gunman dropped his shotgun down and began blind firing.

People think you have to aim in order for guns to be effective, and for the most part that's true, but there are exceptions. Namely, when you have an overabundance of ammo, or in this case shotgun shells, to fill the air.

Each shot delivered nine to ten pellets, and the air suddenly became awash in horizontal lead rain. I positioned myself at the rear as we funneled into the hallway, and it was a good thing I did, because five steps from the corner I felt one of the shells strike my back. It hit hard, shredding my jacket and crashing into my Kevlar vest like a baseball bat to the back. My feet went out beneath me, and I crashed face first into the cement, skidding to a graceless halt just as Hilary and Basic disappeared around the corner.

It was only by sheer luck and divine mercy that I held onto my pistol, but as I went to bring it to bear, I suddenly realized that my body wasn't responding right. Might be it was the fall, more likely the shotgun blast, but as I struggled to turn, I couldn't manage more than a graceless, flopping motion, like a fish plucked from the ocean.

Behind me, the barrage ceased, and I distinctly heard the sound of a magazine being removed and a fresh one slapped in its place. Footsteps sounded, heavy boots touching down upon the stairs as the gunman descended. No, make that *gunmen*. There were two of them, based on the cadence of the footfalls, speaking softly to one another as they descended.

A little voice whispered that once they reached the bottom stair and caught sight of me, I was done for. Unfortunately, there wasn't much I could do about it. My pistol, even if I could wield it properly, was of limited use from this range, whereas the one wielding the shotgun could afford to be a little more liberal with his aim. That, coupled with the fact that the two gunmen wore Kevlar vests not unlike my own, meant I would need to score not one, but two headshots. And while I was considered a fair shot, I was not a miracle worker.

Luckily, I didn't have to be.

As the gunman's foot touched the concrete floor, a hand snapped out of the hall to my left, seized me by the shirt, and hauled me into the air. My feet cleared the ground just as the gunman took aim and blasted apart the section of concrete I'd been leaning against. I could feel the ricochets striking against my leg as my rescuer hauled me down the hallway and overtop his shoulder. Several seconds passed before my brain caught up with my body, and I realized that Basic had me over his shoulder, bouncing alongside the still unconscious Swan-Sister.

I drew in a long breath, then another, as Basic and Hilary fled down the hall. Once I was sure my feet wouldn't immediately collapse beneath me, I slid from Basic's shoulder, holding his arm until I caught my balance and resumed running alongside them.

We fled down a pair of winding hallways, the gunmen hot on our tails, before coming upon a gradual ramp that led to a swinging iron doorway meant for easy deliveries. Basic and Hilary reached it first, the latter seizing hold of the door and throwing back the lock before swinging it open.

As the first rays of daylight appeared, something flashed across our view. A reflection of metal was all the warning we had before the second Swan-Sister came through the door. She had her sword out, and would have taken Hilary's head off, but Basic seized him by the back of his shirt and ripped him back hard enough to give him whiplash.

The Swan-Sister's sword struck the wall, sending up a long row of sparks before she came around for another strike. I started to raise my pistol, but Basic had other ideas.

He didn't try to grab or strike at her. Instead, he gave her exactly what she wanted most, shrugging his shoulder and tossing her sister into the air. The second Swan-Sister only had a moment to respond, and she dropped her sword a split second before her sister came down on top of her.

I knew firsthand just how strong each sister was, especially for their size, but there are limits, and having the entirety of your own body-weight, or close enough in this case, dropping down on your head is a lot for anyone to handle. The second Swan-Sister went down under the weight of her sister, the pair of them crashing to the floor in a tangled heap.

We stepped over their prone forms, and I kicked her sword out of view as I went past, noting something as I did. A business card, one that hadn't been there for long judging by the lack of grime. One that might have been knocked loose when the Swan-Sisters went down. I snatched it up off the floor, jamming it down into my pocket without looking and then followed after Hilary and Basic, the three of us escaping the building and racing out onto the street.

It took me a second to get my bearings, then I realized where we were. We'd come out the north side of the building, and I turned left, motioning for Hilary and Basic to follow. We turned the corner and raced past the front of the pawnshop, crossing the road and angling back to where I'd left Agent Gordan. He was sitting in the driver's seat with his window down, and he saw us coming, shifting the vehicle into reverse and backing out of the spot. Unfortunately, he wasn't the only o ne.

As we crossed the street, we came into view of the black van, and the driver, who'd evidently heard the gunshots and had exited the vehicle. I turned my head just as he caught sight of us, and there was a brief moment as our eyes met, fear, anger and surprise flashing between us in an instant.

Then we went for our guns.

I was faster, partially because I already had my weapon out, and partially because he was slowed by his heavy gloves. Either way, I brought my weapon to bear a full half-second before he did and started firing, emptying half the magazine and sending him scurrying for cover even as the windows of his van shattered, spraying glass everywhere.

Agent Gordan hit the accelerator, sending the vehicle up and over the sidewalk before pulling out in the street beside us. I kept firing as Hilary and Basic piled into the car, then threw myself in after them, crashing down into the passenger's seat and slamming the door shut before screaming for Agent Gordan to drive.

He didn't need any additional encouragement, and we sped down the street, passing the pawn shop just as the two gunmen appeared. For a brief second, I thought they were going to open fire, but they just watched us go, their gazes following us as we turned the corner and drove like mad.

Back to Blue Moon. March 15th 1705hrs

We headed back to Blue Moon headquarters, passing through downtown without incident and pulling into the police station adjacent to our garage. I kept my head down as we made our way through the law enforcement parking area, not wanting to risk another encounter with Mack or Bulwark.

Inside the Government Center Parking Garage, Agent Gordan parked at the end of a long line of government vehicles, and we exited the car to find that it was probably five degrees cooler inside the garage than out, a phenomenon made possible by the lack of heating combined with the wind blowing in from the Charles River. The smell of steel and gasoline was prevalent, and only half the lights overhead were in working order. We piled out of the car and walked to the end of the garage and took the stairs, descending two floors to the subbasement, where our hobbit-hole headquarters lay. Hilary hesitated at the base of the stairs, and his eyes widened at the Blue Moon division sign taped to the doorway, but I motioned him inside before he could comment on it. He stepped through the door, and he and Basic took a long look around, their faces clearly conveying their dismay before they caught sight of the refrigerator and headed that way. If they expected to find anything in there, they would be sorely disappointed.

As it stood, the entire Blue Moon division contained only two people, and I was one of them. As such, while I expected to find Lieutenant Kermit inside, it came as a bit of a surprise when I walked inside and found a young man sitting at Topher's old desk, busily typing away at his computer.

He was in his mid-teens, thin, with curly red hair and two black studs in either ear. There was a splattering of facial scruff along his face and neck, but not enough to really qualify as a beard. He had dark eyes, and was dressed in a plain gray t-shirt with khaki pants and a brown coat. He had the side of Topher's computer opened up, and wires stretched from the base over to where an old television sat on the third desk. It was an older model with bunny ear antennas. I'd seen it before, stacked in the far corner, and just assumed it didn't work.

"Uh, hi," I said. "Who are you?"

The kid glanced up and flashed a half smile that lacked any emotion behind it. I'd seen the same, on high school kids when they were going through the motions of trying to be accepted into the adult world. "Robbie," he said.

"Got a last name, Robbie?"

"Rutledge."

"Pleasure," I said. "I'm Sergeant Mayfield. Mind if I ask what it is you're doing?"

"Trying to drag you people out of the dark ages." He nodded toward the television. "I got your basic cable tv working. Give me another half-hour and I'll have the Wi-Fi up and running."

"We have Wi-Fi already."

He shook his head. "Actually, you don't. You've been getting runoffs from the main headquarters building, but it's so weak you couldn't download a jpeg if your life depended on it. Never mind being able to stream or go live."

"Are you supposed to be doing this?"

"No one told me I was supposed to *not* be doing it."

"That's not really the same thing."

"I couldn't agree more," Lieutenant Kermit said as he appeared from his office. "Point of fact, we've already discussed how a lack of specific prohibition does not give one the inherent right to act. Haven't we, Robbie?"

"Did we?" Robbie asked. "Funny, because it didn't seem like much of a discussion to me."

"Child," Lieutenant Kermit said, his voice firm. "I will allow you certain allowances due to your lack of a father figure, but if you continue on this route, I will bend you over my knee and give you the length of my belt."

"Kinky," Robbie said, but he kept his head down when he said it.

I shook my head and made a note to steer clear of whatever this was. Instead, I glanced toward my desk and found something sitting atop it. It was some sort of electronic device, one that resembled a motherboard, with a little red light on it. "What's that?"

"The source of today's friction, I'm afraid," Lieutenant Kermit said. "It seems my enterprising nephew here devised a means of blocking all cellular communication within his school."

"I'm not really your nephew you know."

"I am married to your aunt, young man, and have been for longer than you have been alive. Hence, we are related."

"A DNA test wouldn't support it."

"Regardless," Kermit said. "Our blood relationship is not the issue at hand. Your actions are."

"The teachers are always complaining about the students being on their phones. I was doing them a favor."

"So you said," Kermit said and turned to me. "Unfortunately, there came a large outcry once the teachers realized that their cell phones no longer worked either."

"Technically, they shouldn't be on them during work hours," Robbie said. "If anything, I'm saving the school district money."

"Your actions also would have prevented anyone from contacting emergency services in the case of a real emergency. What you did put hundreds of lives at risk."

"They were already at risk," he said. "It's high school."

"One more word, young man, and it's the belt for you."

"Word," Robbie mouthed, but thankfully the sound didn't reach Lieutenant Kermit.

Kermit stared at him for a long moment, then snorted and motioned me back into his office. Once the door closed, he let out a loud sigh and dropped into his chair. "What am I going to do with that young man?"

"Families can be hard," I said, thinking back to my last conversation involving my own sister.

"I spent all day in the principal's office arguing on his behalf. They wanted to expel him, you know. There was even talk of filing charges. I convinced them to let me intervene and allow him to serve out his detentions here. If he fails to live up to his end of the bargain, he'll most likely be expelled, and with college right around the corner..."

"You just looking for a friendly ear, sir, or do you want some advice?"

Lieutenant Kermit spread his hands. "By all means, Sergeant."

"Tell him."

"Beg your pardon?"

"You're sticking your neck out for him, right? Tell him that. He's old enough to understand that actions have consequences. Tell him what you're doing, and make it clear that this is his last chance."

"You think that's wise?"

"I think he's fast approaching the age where he doesn't actually have to listen to anyone anymore. Give him the chance to turn things around, and if he throws it away, then you can step back knowing you did all you could." I shrugged. "Who knows? He might even surprise you."

"You may be right." He considered it for a long moment, then gave himself a shake. "Enough about my family affairs though. We have more important things to discuss. Let's hear your report."

I drew in a breath and started at the beginning. "I arrived at the scene of Ricky Brannon's murder shortly after I was dispatched. I'd expected you to meet me there, sir."

"My apologies."

"Understood," I said. "But you could have at least warned me."

He blinked. "Warn you of what?"

"About the gold," I said. "And Ricky Brannon's killer."

Lieutenant Kermit's expression was carefully neutral, but something in his eyes told me he wasn't sure what I was talking about.

"Wait a minute, if you weren't sure what I was going to find, why did you send me there?"

"A friend who works in the jewelry business called me this morning. He was approached by a young man looking to sell some gold coins. The man refused to say where he'd gotten them from and left in a hurry when he suspected my friend might report him. It struck me that there was a good chance that the coins could be related to our heist, and since my friend pegged the man's accent as Charlestown born, it seemed as good a place as any to start."

"Well, in this case you and your friend were right on the money," I said. As briefly as possible, I filled him in on all that had happened, starting with Ricky Brannon's murder, my apprehension of Corwin Sullage, and the appearance of both Vermont Wensdale and the Swan-Sisters.

"Vermont Wensdale, here in our city," Lieutenant Kermit said. "That's not ideal."

"You can say that again."

"And these sisters, you've no idea who they work for or what their motivation might be?"

"None," I said, then stopped. I suddenly recalled the scrap of paper I'd taken off the floor, and I fished it from my pocket, turning it over and straightening it out to reveal a business card with indented text.

"Huh," I said.

"Something to report?"

"Not yet," I said. "It could be nothing, but let me look into it first."

"As you wish," he said. "Anything else?"

I continued my debriefing report, although I intentionally downplayed the confrontation with Mack at the police station. Lieutenant Kermit was a good supervisor, and likely wouldn't stand for his officers being overtly threatened, but I didn't want him involved any more than necessary. It wasn't that I didn't trust him, but if I was going to make it in this division, then I needed to fight my own battles. Something in his expression told me he recognized what I was doing, but he didn't push, and I continued on to our meeting with Red Sammy and the gunmen.

Lieutenant Kermit's eyes widened when I got to the part about Hilary and Basic.

"You're sure those are their names?"

"Positive," I said. "You can ask them yourself if you like. They're in the kitchen."

Lieutenant Kermit rose from his chair, and we made our way back out to the office area, arriving to find Basic looming over Robbie, who looked about as uncomfortable as a human can possibly look.

"Pizza," Basic said, delivering the word slowly.

"I heard you," Robbie said. "Now can you, like, back off?"

"Is there a problem?" I asked.

Hilary cast me an apologetic look. "Sorry about all this. The fridge is empty, you see, and the young man here says we can't order pizza until the internet is up and working."

"And I can't get that going with this mouth-breather leaning over my shoulder," Robbie complained.

"Pizza," Basic said again, sounding out the vowels.

"Boys," Lieutenant Kermit said. "What on Earth are you doing here?"

Hilary's eyes widened, and Basic's mouth curled into a pleased smile at the sight of Lieutenant Kermit. The three came together, and the next thirty seconds were filled with handshakes and several claps along the arm and shoulders.

"You all know each other?" I asked.

"Of course we do," Lieutenant Kermit said. "We met some time back, shortly after our division was formed. I traveled back home to hammer out the details with Tempest Michaels, and he was kind enough to introduce me to the group, such as it were. As I recall, there may even have been a few pints involved."

"Maybe more than a few," Hilary said.

"It's wonderful to see you boys, but what are you doing here?"

"We're on tour," Basic said.

"Tour?"

"More of a recruiting drive, really," Hilary said.

"Recruiting for what?"

"Investors."

"For your stealth plane business?" Lieutenant Kermit asked.

"No, no," Hilary said. "That's all squared away. We're making money hand over fist. This is something new."

"We're selling precious metals," Basic said.

"Of a sort," Hilary agreed. "We recently began a new enterprise, focusing down on a specific niche."

"Which is what?" I asked.

"Unique and rare metals. The first of which is called Tremenderium."

I frowned, something about the name sounding off. "I don't think I've ever heard of that."

"That's probably because it doesn't exist yet," Basic said.

I blinked. "Come again?"

Hilary's face slipped, but was back in an instant. "Yeah, I probably should have clarified. We're currently recruiting investors interested in purchasing undiscovered precious metals."

"By undiscovered you mean... not real?"

"Undiscovered," Hilary clarified. "Allow me to explain. Think back to high school chemistry. Do you remember the periodic table of elements?"

"Vaguely," I said.

"It's chock full of metals," he said. "Almost 75% in fact. And when we were younger, there were all these gaps, where scientists knew the atomic number but not the corresponding element."

"So you're selling the elements that fill in the gaps?" I asked.

"Uh, I hate to break it to you, but I'm pretty sure they filled in the table back in 2015," Robbie said.

"They did," Hilary said. "Which is why we couldn't sell those. Even back then, those were the *known-unknown* elements."

"So what are you selling?"

"We're selling the *unknown-unknown* elements."

"I don't think I get it."

"Think of it like this," Hilary said. "Right now, the Periodic Table only goes up to #118, but scientists think the maximum atomic number could fall somewhere between #170-210. No one knows what #119 will be. Or #125, or #155 for that matter. It's a total blank slate."

"We're getting in on the ground floor," Basic said.

"Exactly," Hilary said. "No one knows what these elements might be capable of or when they will be discovered. That's why we're selling them ahead of time, so that our investors will have a legitimate claim on them should they ever be discovered."

"That doesn't sound entirely legal," I said.

"Well," Hilary said. "It's not illegal, exactly. I mean, you can't patent something that doesn't exist."

"Uh-huh," Robbie said. "You hear that, Uncle Kermit? Lot of not-quite-illegal things happening around here lately."

"Quiet you," Kermit said. "Focus on that internet you keep going on about."

Robbie muttered his reply and resumed typing. A moment later, the television came on, and white noise filled the screen, flipping occasionally to reveal a local newscast before the signal slipped away.

Lieutenant Kermit turned to Hilary and Basic, his face serious. "Boys, I can certainly appreciate the ingenuity, but are you sure about this? Discovering elements is, well, it's tricky business."

"Oh, no," Hilary said. "Our company will take no part in the actual discovery process. Just the distribution afterwards if and when the elements become commercially available."

"And how do you intend to do that exactly?"

"Through the Post Office," Basic said with a smile.

"Well, yes," Hilary said. "That is, each investor is awarded a certificate, based on their initial investment, to be compared to the element's value at a later time. Once the elements become commercially available for individual purchase, then our company will set about distributing th em."

"Isn't that risky?"

"All new business ventures require some level of risk, but ours is minimal," Hilary said. "Even comparing it to Rhodium, which is the most expensive element in the world, valued at approximately $260 dollars per gram, and taking into account stock market fluctuation and inflation, we still stand to net ourselves a hefty profit."

"You're some sort of chemist, or metallurgist?" I asked.

"Er, not exactly," Hilary said. "Once the idea for the business came about, I spent several months reading up on the subject, learning everything I could about precious metals in order to better market the idea."

"And this business, does it have a corporate headquarters?"

"Not at the moment."

"Any employees?"

Basic frowned. "What for?"

"Uh, there's really no need for any additional employees until the element is discovered." Hilary said. "And since there's no telling when that might be..."

"So, just so I have this straight. You two started a company that doesn't actually exist in any tangible form outside of a single document recorded at city hall, and are selling undiscovered elements which may one day be discovered?"

"It's not as crazy as it sounds," Hilary said. "In fact, you could make all the same argument about cryptocurrency. Take that latest news story, Fidelitycoin I think it's called."

"And people are paying you for this?"

"Big time," Hilary said. "In fact, that's how we ended up at the pawnshop. Word got around the city and Sammy decided he wanted in. Wouldn't take no for an answer. Not that we were going to take his money of course. He seems, er seemed, like a bad guy to do business with."

"Bad business," Basic said.

"Exactly," Hilary said. "We just hadn't figured out how to handle him yet."

"Well, he's been handled now," I said. "Unfortunately, it leaves us in a bit of a lurch. Without him, we have no way of finding out any more information about these coins." I reached inside my pocket and withdrew the bag, tossing it down onto the desk. As it landed, I suddenly saw something. A symbol, of some kind, engraved into the bag. I'd noticed it before, back at the pawnshop, but in all the fear and excitement it had slipped my mind.

I took a step to my left and smoothed out the bag, turning the engraving up for easier viewing. It was a square shape, roughly about the size of my palm, with three smaller squares inside.

"Anybody recognize this?" I asked.

A round of blank looks greeted me, even Agent Gordan, who was our go-to financial analyst, seemed at a loss. Several seconds passed, then Robbie let out a bark that wasn't quite a laugh, and whispered something to himself.

"You say something?"

"I said it's a good thing you're cute, because even a two-button mouse is too complicated for the likes of you."

I stared at him, too confused to be insulted. "That some sort of computer joke?"

"Oh, for Pete's sake," he said and threw up his hands. They shook the table as they came down, and the television snapped into focus, displaying a local newscaster speaking into the camera. "This is too sad to even be funny. The symbol on your bag? It's a QR code."

"A what?"

Robbie rolled his eyes. "You know that black and white symbol that the cashier scans on every product you've ever bought?"

"I guess."

"Well, this is the same thing, except it's on the bag. Look, just scan it with the camera app on your phone."

I stared at him for a moment, then fished my phone out of my pocket and opened the camera app. I held it over the bag, noting the yellow square as it came into focus and then... nothing.

"Uh, Robbie?"

"Yeah, hold on," he said. "It doesn't work without internet. Give me just another minute, and then..." His voice trailed off, and when he spoke again, his tone sounded different. "Uh, Sergeant? Uncle Kermit. You probably want to look at this."

We turned away from the table, noting the way his gaze lay glued to the television. He pressed a button, and the sound rose, the local newscaster laughing at something her co-anchor had said before she began.

"Thanks so much, Sally. Spring is definitely in the air here in Boston, and for some lucky residents, St. Patrick's Day has come a little early. For those just joining in, city goers have, as of last count, reported thirty-seven leather purse bags such as this one found in different locations around the city." She raised her hand, holding up a bag that was identical to the one on the desk in front of me. *"What's inside? Well, that's where it gets interesting. Each of these bags is said to contain sixteen gold coins which, if real, would hold an estimated value of approximately $20,000. City authorities have yet to release any official statement, but*

local crime-fighting sleuths have already suggested that this gold could be related to the recent Federal Reserve heist that took place at the end of last year. As if that wasn't mysterious enough, each bag comes engraved with a QR code that when scanned, leads residents to a website." She raised her phone and scanned the QR code, flipping the screen around to reveal the corresponding website. I stared at it and felt my stomach drop.

The website itself was blacked out, save for a lone timer in the middle, with green digital numbers counting down.

"Who these mysterious benefactors are, and what connection they may have to the Federal Reserve heist is, as of now, unknown, but the real question on everyone's mind is what are they going to do next?"

The Countdown Begins. March 15th 2O49hrs

SHORTLY AFTER THE NEWS station went off the air, Robbie got our internet going, and we scanned the QR code engraved on the bag and were treated to the same black screen with green timer. The countdown was set to end at 3:00 PM the following day, but there were no other clues that any of us could see.

We'd tried researching the website itself, thinking that if we could find the host, then maybe we could discover who it belonged to, but there was nothing to go by, and whoever set it up had taken steps to keep it from appearing in any search engines. Even Robbie, who was the only one of us with any real technical proficiency, was eventually forced to conclude that it was hopeless.

With our only possible avenue of discovery taken, we ordered pizza and spent the next several hours trying to piece what we knew with what we suspected and come to any sort of conclusion. To say it wasn't going well was a massive understatement.

"Okay," I said. "Let's take it from the top."

A round of groans greeted my statement as I turned back to face the room. The air inside our little hobbit-hole was stale, runoff vehicle fumes coming through the air vent from the parking garage above our heads, mixing with the too-spicey pizza sauce we'd devoured and basic body odors. My eyes felt like someone had slipped sandpaper beneath my lids, and my breath smelled of garlic and buttered crust.

Basic and Hilary were seated with their backs against the wall, and Agent Gordan had his feet up on my desk. Lieutenant Kermit had removed his jacket and rolled up his sleeves, and Robbie was doing slow circles in his chair, his head lolling backwards and wordless groans slipping past his mouth. Evidently, our attempts to discover the identity of the leprechauns had ceased to amuse him, and since the game package we had on the computer consisted only of Solitaire and Minesweeper, he was convinced that he was circling the drain in his own personal bubble of hell.

"Let's try this a different way," I said, biting my fist to stifle a yawn. "Instead of focusing on what we do know, let's focus on what we don't."

"You tried that an hour ago," Robbie said, momentarily halting his groaning.

"Well, let's try it again," I said. "We know that whoever's distributing these coins is likely the same people who stole them in the first place."

"The Leprechauns," Hilary said.

We'd taken some time to bring him and Basic up to speed. They'd handled the news of the leprechauns pretty well, all things considered. Based on our, albeit brief, conversation, it clearly wasn't the weirdest thing they'd ever had to deal with.

"Right, the leprechauns," I said. "We know they went to a lot of trouble to steal this money. Twenty-five million dollars is nothing to sneeze at. So what would be their motivation to turn around and just give it away?"

"Perhaps they fancy themselves as modern day Robin Hoods?" Lieutenant Kermit said.

"Possibly," I said. "Except that doesn't track. I can get behind the steal from the rich and give to the poor angle, but if that was their real aim then they would have selected their beneficiaries better. They hid bags all over the city. There's no way they could have reliably predicted who was going to find them, or even if they would turn them in once they did."

"What do you think the ratio of people who've come forward versus those who just took the coins home is?" Agent Gordan asked.

"There's no way to know for certain," I said.

"Spitball it."

"Maybe five to one?"

Hilary raised an eyebrow. "That bad?"

"Unfortunately," I said. "It could be higher."

"Let's assume five for the moment," Agent Gordan said. "Each bag contains sixteen coins, which equals one pound. Assuming your ratio is correct, then forty people have come forward, and two hundred people have not."

"What's your point?"

"We know the thieves stole approximately 1,365 lbs. worth of gold. If our numbers are correct, then they've given away seventeen percent of their entire haul."

"Safer to round up to twenty percent," I said.

"Right. Twenty Percent," Agent Gordan said. "That seems like a lot."

"That's because it is, especially considering how hard they worked to get it," I said.

Silence fell, and I sighed and rubbed at my eyes. I felt, in a word, bad. The pizza sauce was burning my stomach, and the cheese had left my forehead feeling greasy. I was tired, sore, and longing for my bed. For all that though, I couldn't shut my mind off. It kept trailing down the same paths, searching for something we may have missed, but coming up empty.

"Okay, let's try coming at this from a new angle," I said. "What purpose does giving away their wealth serve?"

"Attention," Agent Gordan said immediately. "Which shouldn't be something they want."

"Granted," I said. "What else?"

"Notoriety," Lieutenant Kermit offered. "News of the coins is certain to renew public interest in the Federal Reserve heist."

"Okay."

"Anonymity," Hilary offered. "Introducing that many coins will dilute the market, making it impossible for the authorities to track which coins came from where. That could be useful, in case they want to sell them."

"They'd be paying a hefty tax just to offload their haul," I said.

I took three steps and let my head roll back, staring up at our aged ceiling panels. Attention. Notoriety. Anonymity. They were all good options, but we were missing something. I could feel it, like a sour taste on the tip of my tongue, just waiting to be spit out. I closed my eyes and focused on the sensation, allowing my body to sway for several long seconds before it finally occurred to me.

"Credibility," I said.

A soft hush fell over the room.

"What now?" Agent Gordan asked.

"That's the answer," I said. "This whole thing is just a stunt designed to buy them credibility."

"Why would they need that?" Lieutenant Kermit asked.

"Because giving away these coins isn't their endgame," I said. "It's just another step in their plan. Distributing the gold this way builds public trust. People know they're serious, and that the money is real." I nodded and rubbed my hands together. "One of the side effects of credibility is attention. There are a lot of people out there who could happily use an extra twenty grand. You can bet every one of them will be watching this timer, and waiting for what happens when it runs out."

"What *does* happen when it runs out?" Robbie asked.

"No idea," I said. "But we know they've had a long time to plan it. Safe to say it will be worth the price."

"Actually," Hilary said. "They might not have had as long as you think."

I blinked. "What?"

"Something's been bothering me ever since I heard your story," Hilary said. "I couldn't put my finger on what it was until now. It's the smelting. Or, more specifically, the timeline surrounding it."

"What about it?"

He raised his hand, stalling my question. "First answer me something. In your opinion, would the leprechauns be concerned about the purity of their gold? That is, would they care if the product they put out was less valuable than the one they initially stole?"

I hadn't considered the question before, and it took me several seconds before I could answer. "They're leprechauns, or at least they want us to think they are. They'd want it to be better."

"You're sure?" he asked.

I nodded. "If nothing else, it goes back to their credibility. If they're putting out subpar coins, if one bag is worth more than the other, then they could be accused of playing favorites. In order to maintain the public's trust, each bag would need to be a uniform weight and purity."

"Uh-huh," Hilary said. "That's what I thought too. And that's good news for us."

"Why is that good news?"

"Because it means they would have needed to smelt the bars down, as opposed to just melting them."

"Is there a difference?"

Hilary nodded. "A big one. Melting is relatively straightforward. You throw it in a hot stove and turn it from a solid to a liquid and then pour it into a mold and let it cool. It's what pawnshops do to old jewelry, scrap coins, and cufflinks. It's effective, but crude. Smelting, on the other hand, involves removing impurities caused by metal oxides and oxide waste. It requires heat, pressure, and chemicals like potassium cyanide and mercury. It's also a much slower process." He glanced at Agent Gordan. "How much gold did you say they stole?"

"1,365 lbs." Agent Gordan said.

"And the heist happened back in December?"

"December 16th," he said. "So what?"

"Eighty-nine days," Hilary said. His eyes were distant, and I got the feeling he was running calculations in his head. "How much of the gold do you think they would want to turn into coins?"

"I would imagine most of it," Agent Gordan said. "Easier to move, not to mention giving it a more uniform appearance."

"Okay then," Hilary said. "1365 lbs. of gold in eighty-nine days equals roughly fifteen pounds of gold per day. Let's assume they didn't want to leave the final batches to the last minute and round that up to twenty pounds. That's a heck of a lot of gold to smelt. Way more than the average person could handle."

"How much more?" I asked.

"Too much," he said. "You have to understand, melting the gold isn't the problem. A good industrial strength induction furnace can liquify that amount in less than an hour. It's the purifying that takes time. You'd need between two and three hours for every few pounds. At twenty pounds, with the right equipment, you'd be looking at fifteen-hour days."

"You say the right equipment. You mean like the stuff Red Sammy had back in his basement?"

Hilary shook his head. "No. That was a pieced together kit. Useful for melting down scrap jewelry and Grandma's silver forks. He'd be lucky to do a pound or two a day. To accomplish what you're talking about would require a dedicated facility. You'd need industrial strength equipment."

"You mean like the kind you'd find at an ironworks facility?" I asked.

"Exactly."

"That's good to know," I said. "But it doesn't really help us. There's no shortage of forges or ironworks facilities here in the city. Especially near the waterfront. And that's assuming they didn't take the gold out beyond city limits."

"I think we can rule that option out," Agent Gordan said. "Traveling with that much weight carries a high level of risk. The last thing they'd want to do is break down on the side of the road. It's more likely they made their getaway and retreated to a nearby safe house."

"Even so, they could be in any one of a dozen facilities and we would never have noticed."

Another hushed silence fell over the room broken a minute later when Basic spoke.

"Someone would have."

Until now, he'd been silent, his genteel, good-natured presence serving as a calming but otherwise quiet addition. His sudden contribution took me by surprise.

"What do you mean?" I asked.

Basic pointed up toward the ceiling. "Snow."

I frowned and wrinkled my brows, trying unsuccessfully to absorb what he was saying.

"Don't hurt yourself trying to decode the mouth-breather, Sergeant," Robbie said. "I can do that too. Watch. Fire. Ice. Earth."

"Snow," I repeated.

Half a minute passed, then it hit me, and I straightened. A quick glance over revealed Agent Gordan had gotten it as well, and it was a fair toss-up whose face was more incredulous.

"He's right," Agent Gordan said.

"Wait, what?" Robbie said. "Seriously?"

"Does it hold up?" I asked Agent Gordan.

He nodded. "It's certainly worth a try."

"Well done, boy," Lieutenant Kermit said, having evidently figured it out as well.

"What's worth a try?" Robbie asked. "Would someone mind filling the rest of us in?"

"Snow," I said again.

"Yeah, I heard that part."

"We've been bombarded with it for weeks. More snow than we've had in the past ten years."

"Yeah, so what?" Robbie asked.

"So, the leprechauns couldn't have planned for that," I said. "Remember the news reports? They all agreed that the storm had come out of nowhere. There was no advance warning."

"I repeat, so what?" Robbie asked. "I thought we already established that they were holed up in a facility somewhere."

"They were," I said. "But no one else was."

"Come again?"

"The leprechauns couldn't afford to sacrifice the weeks until the snow melted. Not if they wanted to get the gold processed in time."

"Smelted," said Hilary.

"Smelted," I agreed. "They were working around the clock practically as it was. Meanwhile, all the other warehouses and ironworks facilities were closed down due to the snow."

"I'm still not clear how this helps us," Hilary said.

"Those industrial ovens give off smoke," I said. "You'd need lights, noise. There would have been no way they could disguise that something was happening in that facility which means..."

"Someone knows where they are," Agent Gordan said as he rose from the chair.

I nodded, stifling a yawn. "There are dozens of potential ironwork factories, but not so many that we can't check them if we hurry. We should start by scouring Admiral's Hill, then move on to Chelsea and Central Square. Keep near the waterfront and see if anyone remembers seeing a factory running during the blizzard. If so, then it's a good bet we've found their safe house."

"Brilliant," Agent Gordan said.

I took two steps nearer to the door and reached toward my coat, stifling another yawn. "If we split up, we can cover more ground. Radio in if you hear anything and I'll—"

"No," Agent Gordan said.

He reached out and took my coat from my hand, setting it back on the desk chair. "Not you."

I blinked. "Excuse me?"

"You need to sleep," Agent Gordan said and turned to the side. "You've been going all day without a break. You haven't eaten anything but pizza, and the only thing you've had to drink came from a police station instant coffee machine." He shook his head. "Going door to door isn't in the cards for you right now. You need food and rest. The three of us," he motioned toward Hilary and Basic. "Can do the legwork."

"You think I'm going to stay inside, warm and safe, while you three are out hunting? These people are dangerous."

"Which only emphasizes my point," he said. "When we find their safe house, we'll need someone to lead the strike. We've already established that my talents lie elsewhere and your lieutenant's aversion to firearms is well known. Since you're the only other law enforcement officer here, that means you'll be in command. And in order to do that we need you rested."

I stared at him for a long moment, a voice inside whispering that what he said made sense, even if I didn't like it. I glanced over at Lieutenant Kermit.

"It's your call, Sergeant," he said. "But a good commander knows when to listen to her troops."

I held on to my jacket for a moment longer, then reluctantly let my hand fall away. "You'll be careful?" I asked.

Agent Gordan's mouth quirked up into that boyish smile. "Of course."

"We've done this before," Basic said.

"Not really," Hilary said, then seemed to realize his mistake. "But yes, we'll be careful."

232

"Robbie here can help to coordinate our efforts," Agent Gordan said. "Create a grid pattern for us."

"Oh, goody, just what I always wanted," Robbie said, but there wasn't much fight in him.

"Sleep," Agent Gordan told me. "Eat. We'll be in touch soon."

He nodded toward the boys, and the three of them gathered their coats and began shuffling out the door.

"Alex," I said, as Agent Gordan neared the doorway.

He paused and glanced back. "Yes?"

"It's not just about building credibility," I said. "They're giving them a taste. Like a drug dealer offering a free sample bag. The next batch will be bigger. And people will know they're for real. Whatever comes next, every person in Boston who ever dreamed about being rich is going to go for it. The cops won't be able to stop them. People could get hurt."

"We won't let that happen," he said, and then slipped out the door.

I watched them go, feeling a hollow ache in my chest that had nothing to do with the pizza.

"Out of curiosity, how much bigger do you think the next batch might be?" Robbie asked.

I shook my head and didn't answer, but inside, a small voice whispered that it might be big enough to tear this entire city apart if we didn't put a stop to it first.

All Out of Advice. March 15th 2137hrs

I LET AGENT GORDAN take the loaner car, and Lieutenant Kermit gave me a lift back to the Prudential Center, where I retrieved my car from the valet lot. The night's temperature had dropped, and I pulled my jacket tighter, relieved to see that there were no outstanding parking tickets lining my windshield as I lowered myself inside and brought the engine to life.

First stop was a late-night dumpling joint located in Chinatown, where I ordered a large portion of their Chinese Chicken Noodle Soup. I wasn't actually hungry, but the pizza we'd consumed back at the office had settled badly, and I was hoping that the shredded chicken and rice noodles would help soothe my stomach. The steam warmed my hand through the bag as I drove, and the aroma of salt and shredded vegetables filled my car, banishing away the seemingly ever-present aroma which, now that I'd had time to dwell on it, did seem a bit rodent-ish in nature.

My apartment was located in the South End neighborhood, near Union Park and the Speakeasy Theatre. Parking can be difficult at times, but people were evidently still out taking advantage of the freedom denied to them during the blizzard, and I found an available spot along the side street near my front door. I killed the engine and grabbed my bag from off the floor. As I did, I inadvertently knocked free a section of the floor mat, and something small and dead came tumbling loose.

It was a rat, or so I thought at first. Once I stopped cursing, however, I noted a couple of things. For one, it didn't have much of a tail, which was usually a sure sign of the species, and two, it had something stuffed in its cheek pouch. I drew a pen from my pocket and used the tip to peel back the creature's mouth, tapping gently until the debris, which consisted of seat stuffing, fell out.

A flash of pity swept through me when I assumed the thing had failed in a last-ditch attempt to find substance and subsequently starved to death. Then it gave a little shudder and drew in a long breath, exhaling with a whoosh. I stared at it for a long moment, fighting against the call of my front door and the soup in my hand beckoning me inside. I really, really didn't want to do what I did next, but I'm a firm believer that no one, especially an innocent animal, deserves to die alone in the cold.

I scooped the hamster off the floor, and clutched him to my coat as I exited the vehicle and made my way up the sidewalk toward my door. I didn't notice the figure lingering in the shadows until she stepped out into the light.

"Hey, girlie" my sister said.

"Gah." I gave a start and nearly dropped both my soup and the hamster before catching myself. "Jesus, Cambrie. You scared me to death. What are you doing here?"

"I was hoping we could talk," she said and narrowed her eyes. "Where have you been?"

"Work," I said slipping the keys into the front door. "You can come inside, but fair warning. As soon as I finish my dinner I'm headed for bed."

I opened the door and led the way inside, the welcome warmth of the heater washing over me. I set my soup down on the table, then removed my boots and tossed them in the general direction of the doorway.

Cambrie followed me in, settling herself down on the edge of the couch. "Long day?"

"You can say that again."

"Is that a rat in your hand?"

"Actually, I'm pretty sure it's a hamster."

"Is it dead?"

I shook my head. "Temperature's dropping fast out there. I think he got caught out."

I made my way into my room and found an old shoe-box in my closet. I emptied the contents, two black leather heels, onto the floor, then returned to the kitchen, set the box on the dining room table, and gently laid the hamster down. He felt very small, and very stiff in my hands, but he shivered slightly when I released my grip.

Now that I had some light, I could see his fur was auburn colored, with two large white patches, rising on opposite sides like twin rock formations. It reminded me of one summer when I'd gone hiking in California, and had spent three days trekking through Yosemite Valley.

"Yosemite."

I said the name aloud without thinking, but something about it rung true.

I retrieved a small kitchen wash towel, bundling it up and using it to cover him. Then I filled a Tupperware container with fresh water, and opened my soup, spooning out a small portion of the shredded chicken and a couple of rice noodles. I laid them down on a bit of plastic and set them inside the shoe-box along with the water.

I wondered for a moment if I shouldn't take him to a veterinarian, but most of them had closed hours ago, and I was pretty sure that if I brought him to the animal hospital they would just put him down. It seemed a shame, not to at least give him a chance. If, in the morning, he hadn't taken a turn for the better, then I would see about doing what needed to be done.

"Soup smells good," Cambrie said, her voice hopeful.

"Don't even think about it," I warned.

"You'll share with a dead hamster but not me?"

"He's not dead," I said. "And if you want soup, then get one of those guy friends of yours to spring for it."

"Speaking of guy friends, that's actually why I'm here." She shifted on the couch, then cleared her throat. "He asked me out."

I hesitated, with the spoon near my lips. "Who asked you out?"

"Jimmy?"

"Jimmy as in Deputy Bulwark?"

I left the *as in my boss* bit unspoken.

Cambrie nodded.

"On a date?"

"I mean, he didn't exactly word it that way, but I've been around the block enough to read the subtext," she said.

"Huh."

"That's all you've got to say?"

"What else would you like me to say?" I asked.

"I don't know," she said. "I came here to get some advice. I mean, having someone like that in my corner could really help my career."

"Uh-huh," I said.

"And it's not like I'd have to *do anything* with him, after all. I mean, it's just dinner."

"Right."

"And, really, after all the time he's spent, it would almost be rude not to accept."

A hushed silence fell over my dining room, the chicken soup having been robbed of its flavor by the image of my boss and my little sister sharing a meal in a cozy, intimate environment.

"Chloe?"

"Yeah?"

"Don't you have anything to say?"

I was quiet for a long moment before I shook my head. "I think maybe you were right."

"About what?"

"About what you said back at the station. This is your career, Cambrie. Through the good times and the bad. You can listen to all the advice in the world, but at the end of the day, it's going to be what you make it. So, you do whatever you think is best, and then try to do it again the next day. As for me..." I shook my head and set my spoon down before rising from my chair. "I'm all out of advice."

Avant-Garde Financial Securities. March 16th O545hrs

AFTER I LEFT THE table, I went into the bathroom and treated myself to a hot shower. Cambrie was gone by the time I got out, and I combed the knots out of my hair, locked up the apartment, and went to bed.

Despite my fatigue, I slept poorly, plagued by nightmares of gunfights, sword-wielding swans, and leprechauns with gold coins that burst into flame when thrown. It was somewhat of a relief when my alarm finally went off, and I rose quickly and dressed in the dark.

The sun wouldn't be up for another half an hour, and I made my way into the bathroom, splashing cold water on my face before heading into the kitchen and placing the teakettle on the stove. I didn't have it in me to work out. The lack of sleep combined with the poor food choices pretty much guaranteed that I wouldn't be hitting any personal bests today. So I settled for a short stretching routine while the tea water came to boil.

Yosemite was sound asleep when I checked on him. I was no animal doctor, but his breathing seemed easier, and there were bits missing from both the chicken and the rice noodles. As I stared down, a small warmth spread through my chest. I'd never considered owning a pet before, my work hours were too sporadic for anything requiring much care, but I couldn't deny that he was a cute little fellow. If this was going to become a more permanent thing, then I would need to stop by the pet store today and pick up a few things. A cage for starters. Also, some bedding material. Probably some food too. He could survive for now on cold Chinese chicken noodle soup but he would probably need something resembling more of a balanced diet in order to make a full recovery.

I could make my final decision regarding Yosemite later. For now, I had more important things to worry about. I stepped away from the table and over to where I'd left my cellphone charging. I had a message from Agent Gordan. He reported that they hadn't found anything so far and were going to call it a night, but that they would resume their search at first light. I winced when I read that last line. Bostonians weren't known for their warm hospitality and going door to door at the crack of dawn is a good way to get expletives hurled at you, if not worse.

None of which is to say that I wasn't grateful for their efforts, especially since I had my own lead to run down. I poured myself a cup of tea and popped a piece of bread into the toaster. Once it was finished cooking, I slathered it with peanut butter and jelly, and folded it in half, making a poor man's sandwich. As I ate, I used my cell phone to peruse the news, focusing on the financial pages and taking notes as I went.

Once I finished eating, I piled my dishes into the sink and donned my coat, reaching into the pocket and drawing the business card I'd taken off the Swan-Sister from the pocket.

The indented text identified it as belonging to one Gerome Reed, whose title was listed as the Managing Director of Client Services at none other than Avant-Garde Financial Securities. The very financial institution who the leprechauns had stolen their gold from.

There were a lot of reasons why one of the Swan-Sisters might have Gerome Reed's card. If they were searching for the gold, then it made sense that they might be curious to discover where it had come from. Heck, they might even have made an appointment to speak to Mr. Reed in person. It was a loose theory, but I hoped it would prove correct, since that would mean there would likely be some sort of meeting log, or even a sign-in sheet that could help me identify who they were and, more importantly, what they wanted.

I dialed the number for the receptionist, and was directed to an automated system that informed me they were currently closed and would open in little more than an hour. I debated waiting inside my apartment, the allure of more peanut butter toast and hot tea combined with some morning television appealing to my more slothful side, but

I eventually pushed such thoughts aside and slung my boots on, tying the laces tight before heading out the door.

I walked over to my car and opened the driver's door, peering around for any sign of movement in case Yosemite had any brothers, sisters, or first cousins lingering around. I didn't find any, and the memory of my first trip, when the hamsters had fled the vehicle in force, made me think that Yosemite must have been left behind, a little hamster orphan, as it were.

I dropped into the driver's seat and brought the engine to life before pulling away from the curb and heading toward the city. I drove slowly, enjoying the sunrise and stopping by a coffee shop drive-through on my way in to the financial district. I ordered four coffees, and then asked for one of those cardboard cup holders, balancing it precariously along the floor of the passenger's seat as I drove.

Avant-Garde Financial Securities was located in the financial district, on the twenty-seventh floor of the 100 Summer Street Building. I'd tried to set up a meeting with them when the case was first assigned to me, but I'd run into the same problem that I had when trying to research the vault. According to the FBI, speaking with Avant-Garde's upper management didn't fall within the umbrella of Blue Moon division's prerogative.

The building boasted a unique U-shaped design, and the mirror windows cast the city's reflection with a noticeable bronze tint. Getting inside was actually easier than I expected. My badge got me through the lobby security, and the coffee allowed me access to virtually any floor, since all I had to do was enter the elevator behind someone and politely ask them to scan their keycard. I made a point to mention how I'd do it myself, but my boss would kill me if I spilled his coffee. Sometimes it pays to look flustered and helpless.

The elevator pinged open on the twenty-seventh floor, and I mouthed a big thank-you to my good Samaritan before stepping out. He looked as if he wanted to say something else, but I turned my back and the elevator door closed a moment later, cutting off any clumsy attempts at conversation.

A handful of steps carried me to Avant-Garde's waiting room. The windows were made of frosted glass, with delicate wood paneling and a soft blue rug meant to mimic the nearby harbor waves laid out across the spacious floor. The furniture was sleek and modern, modeled more for efficiency than comfort. A young woman dressed in a dark pantsuit with short-cut hair was already seated behind the long reception desk, the company's mast proudly adorning the wall behind her.

"Good morning," she greeted, her voice prim and professional. "How may I help you?"

"Chloe Mayfield," I said. "Here to see Gerome Reed."

"I see," the woman said, her brows scrunching in confusion. "And, do you have an appointment?"

I gave her a flat look. "You think I'd have lugged all this coffee up twenty-seven floors if I didn't?"

It wasn't really an answer, and I could see the receptionist debating her options. I'd purposefully avoided flashing my badge or using my rank, saving them just in case I needed them. Thankfully, the receptionist decided to kick it up the food chain, and she lifted the phone and dialed three numbers, speaking softly for thirty seconds before returning it to its cradle. "Go ahead and go on back. Mr. Reed will meet you in conference room C."

I nodded my thanks and walked around the desk, making my way down the hall. The doors were clearly labeled, and I found conference room C without difficulty, opening the door to reveal an elongated table made of rich cherry wood and surrounded by soft leather chairs. The windows were clear glass, offering a breathtaking view of the Boston skyline. I lowered myself down and let out a soft, contented sigh, sipping from my own coffee. I didn't have to wait long, two to three minutes at most, before the door opened to admit two men.

The first man was in his late thirties, dressed in a tailored suit with reddish-copper hair clipped short on the sides. His eyes were a shade too wide for his face, and his lips were narrowed, his cheeks sunk in, as if someone had stretched his neck when he was a child and he'd never recovered. He stepped into the room holding a rich leather satchel bag, and immediately turned and held the door open for the next man.

Gerome Richard was younger than I expected, based on his title. I put him at roughly thirty, or roundabout. A few inches shorter than average, his dark hair was cut short and neat along the back and sides, with the top left long enough to create a layered wavy look. He wore a tailored navy suit with a matching pinstripe tie. Large dark shades sat comfortably on his face, and he held a white cane in his left hand, gently casting it back and forth as he entered the room.

"Miss Mayfield?" he said. "I'm Gerome Reed."

"Pleasure," I said. "Thank you for, agreeing to—" I was going to say see me but I stopped myself at the last moment. "Meet with me."

I was pretty sure he'd noted my slip, but was polite enough not to give any outward sign as he lowered himself down into the chair. His associate laid his bag down in the chair adjacent to him, tapping his hand once to signal its location before lowering himself into the next chair.

"Well, I've always had a soft spot for a woman offering free coffee."

"By all means," I said.

I set the coffee down in the middle of the table, and Gerome reached out, his fingers tentatively exploring before lifting the cup and pointedly placing it down beside him. Watching him work gave me some insight into his vision, as most people who are labeled as legally blind don't always dwell in darkness. He evidently had retained some level of sight, though the extent of which was unknown, and it probably wasn't polite to ask.

Gerome lifted the cup to his lips and took a delicate sip, letting out a pleased sound. "Very kind of you, Miss Mayfield. Allow me to introduce my associate, August Varice, who specializes in client services."

"Pleasure," I said to August, as he helped himself to his own cup. He offered me a sharp nod and didn't even bother to smile.

"Forgive me for asking," Gerome said, "But are you the same Chloe Mayfield employed with the Boston PD?"

I blinked and straightened in my chair. "You researched me already? Fast work."

"No need," Gerome said. "I recalled hearing the name before. I believe you were the officer who discovered our ex-mayor Cherri during her indiscretion. You were, as a result, subsequently transferred to the city's Blue Moon division. Is that correct?"

"Two-for-two," I said. "You certainly seem well informed."

"Fascinating thing, that Blue Moon division. I've never heard of anything quite like it."

"Not sure anyone has. It's something new we're trying, and so far, we've had good results."

"Brilliant. I always enjoy a good underdog story. Especially when it's local. But of course, you didn't come all the way here just to chat. What can I do for you?"

"I was hoping I could ask you some questions about the recent heist at the Federal Reserve."

"I see," Gerome said. "I was under the impression that the FBI was handling the case?"

"They are," I said. "Blue Moon is assisting."

"Of course," he said. "In that case, ask away."

"Thank you," I said. "We've encountered a couple of peculiarities in the investigation that I'm hoping you can expand on. Firstly, why do you think the thieves targeted Avant-Garde?"

"I really have no idea," Gerome said. "Money, I suppose. We are a financial services organization after all."

"True," I said. "But there were lots of alcoves in the Reserve vault. Some of which had a lot more gold in them. Yet the thieves specifically went after yours. You've no ideas as to why that might be?"

"I'm afraid not," Gerome said. "Are you suggesting this was some sort of personal vendetta against the company?"

"I guess that all depends. Does the company have any enemies that you're aware of?"

"Sergeant," August spoke up suddenly. "We've gone through all this before with the FBI. Surely you didn't come all the way down here just to waste our morning rehashing questions that were answered within the first few hours of the investigation?"

"We've had a few new developments since the investigation began," I said. "I'd ask you to bear with me."

August's mouth tightened, and he looked like he wanted to protest more, but eventually he leaned back in his chair.

"Enemies, Mr. Reed?" I asked.

"I really can't say."

"Because you don't know or because you're not allowed?"

He shrugged and spread his hands. "Finance is an emotional business, Sergeant. Markets can rise and fall like the ebbing of the waves, and those who fail to prosper are bound to harbor hard feelings. If you're asking me if I know of anyone who might be angry enough to risk breaking into a vault as secure as the Federal Reserve? Then I would say no."

"I assume you—"

"Reed!"

A man's voice erupted from the hallway, its gravelly cadence carrying through the room a split second before the door banged open and a suited man stepped inside. He was in his late seventies, with steel-blue eyes and soft wisps of white still clinging to his head. His collared white shirt hung loose around his wrists, and the cologne he'd applied didn't quite cover the aroma of Scotch on his breath when he spoke.

"Youngman isn't returning my calls," he snarled, his coarse voice suggesting he'd indulged his fair share of tobacco over the years. "Send a driver to her house. Tell her I want her down here in the next hour. If I have to ask again, there will be hell to pay."

Gerome didn't blink. "Yes, Mr. Crosier."

"One hour!"

"Would that be Maura Youngman?" I asked, picturing the chief financial director of the Federal Reserve.

"Eh?" Mr. Crosier narrowed his eyes. "Who the blazes are you?"

Gerome answered before I could. "Mr. Crosier this is Sergeant Mayfield with the Boston PD."

"Boston PD? What the hell is she doing here? I thought we were working with the FBI."

"I'm part of a special division currently assisting the Bureau."

"Is that so? Well, good for you. Fact is, Mr. Reed here only bothered to introduce you because he thought it would make me watch my mouth. But I'm too old to give a fig what people think, and I'd guess that, in your line of work, you've heard worse than even I could imagine."

"Very true, sir."

"Excellent," he said. "In that case, I wish you the best of luck, Sergeant. If you should find my gold, bring it straight to me. I'll reward you with a trip."

I raised an eyebrow. "What kind of trip?"

"Anywhere in the world you want to go. Just so long as there's a bikini involved."

"And which of us would be wearing that?"

Mr. Crosier's eyes widened in surprise, then he let out a coarse, wheezing laugh. "Well, I'll be. You've got quite the mouth on you, young lady."

"So I've been told. It gets me into trouble more often than not."

"Well, have no fear on that account with me," he said. "Young people today are made of steamed horsecrap. You so much as blow on them wrong and they crumple to pieces. Nice to meet one with some fight in her."

"Nice to meet you too, sir."

Crosier raised a lone finger into the air toward Gerome and August. "One hour! And as for you. I'm deadly serious. Find my gold, and depending on how long that bikini stays on and what else you can do with your mouth, I'll make you a millionaire faster than you can believe."

"That's a tempting offer, sir. I'll have to think about it."

He snorted, turned and lumbered back down the hall, making it halfway down before he began screaming again.

Gerome turned to August and whispered something that made the other man nod. I gave them a second to recover, then gently cleared my throat.

"Uh, and that would be?"

"That was Mr. Walter Crosier. Head of Avant-Garde Financial Securities."

"Quite the fearless leader," I said.

"I would ask that you not take anything he says personally. He's under a great deal of stress."

"Perfectly understandable, given what's been happening. I assume you gentleman have heard the news regarding the coins circulating throughout the city? I imagine that has to sting a bit. Knowing that your gold is out there."

"There's no proof that those coins are in any way related to the Federal Reserve heist," August said, his face darkening.

"That's true," I said. "But it's a heck of a coincidence, wouldn't you say?"

August abruptly rose from his chair. "I think we've heard enough. There's no reason to sit here and listen to this drivel, Mr. Reed."

"Now, now," Gerome said. "No reason to get angry, August. Sergeant Mayfield is merely doing her job." He turned his head back to me. "In regards to your question, Sergeant, we don't deal in coincidences. We deal in facts. Furthermore, our company has excellent insurance, and all of our losses were fully covered."

"The current losses maybe," I said. "But what about future losses?"

Gerome tilted his head to the side. "I beg your pardon?"

"I was flipping through the Financial Times this morning. According to what I read, your company's reputation has taken a pretty heavy hit as a result of this theft. Investors are spooked. After all, this sort of thing doesn't happen every day, and having your company's name attached to it can't be good for business."

"Like I said, Sergeant. Ebbs and flows."

"Seems like more ebbing than flowing lately. Avant-Garde may have strong liquidity, but according to the Times, your stock has plummeted to the point where it might take years to recover. I'm curious, can Avant-Garde really afford to wait that long?"

"That's enough," August snapped and slammed his fist down on the table. He started to grab for the bag, but Gerome halted him with an upraised hand. The red-headed man regarded Gerome for a long moment, then took a step back from the table.

Gerome waited to see if he would say anything, and when it became clear that the other man was going to settle for a sullen silence, he turned back to me. "Sergeant, it's obvious that you're here for something specific. How about we save ourselves some time and you tell me what it is you're actually after."

"Alright, fine." I leaned forward in my chair. "Has Avant-Garde taken to hiring mercenaries in order to retrieve their gold?"

The corner of Gerome's mouth twitched, so fast I would have missed it were I not looking. "Why would we do such a thing?"

"Well, let's see. It's been three months since the FBI began investigating this theft, and as of right now, no suspects have been caught and not a single dollar recovered. Your investors are spooked, your stock is in the toilet, and your fearless leader is drinking himself silly and offering million-dollar blowjobs to anyone with a set of tits. All in all, you're in quite the unenviable position, like a ship that's run afoul of the rocks and is taking on water fast."

"Well, when you put it like that…"

I dipped my hand into my pocket and drew out his business card, sliding it across the table. I couldn't say if he saw the shifting shadow or just heard the sound, but he lifted it from the table, using his fingers to explore the indented words. "Where did you get this?"

"I took it off a mercenary after I spiked her head into the pavement for the *second* time."

"Truly?" he asked. "Remarkable." He drew in a breath and then let it out in a long huff. "But also inconsequential, since I can hardly be expected to account for every business card in my possession."

"That's not really an answer."

"You're a smart lady, Sergeant. It seems to me that you've got a firm understanding of the situation. If things are truly as bad as you say, well, you can hardly fault us for exploring other avenues. After all, as you so keenly pointed out, the FBI has been entirely unsuccessful in their investigation so far. Surely you wouldn't begrudge us seeking outside counsel."

"Outside counsel isn't the same as sword-wielding mercenaries."

"I'm afraid I can't speak to that," he said. "I will say this though, for the record. Avant-Garde, while it may choose to exercise its constitutionally protected right to bring in outside security expertise in an effort to return our stolen assets, would never endorse nor allow any individuals to knowingly break the law either in our employment or for our benefit."

"Noted," I said. "Now what about unofficially?"

Gerome spread his hands. "Plausible deniability is a powerful tool, Sergeant. We don't question our contractor's methods. Only their results."

"That's a weasel answer."

"I'm afraid it's the only one you're going to get. Now, if there was nothing else, I'll have to ask you to excuse me. We have to get back to bailing out our sinking ship."

"They're dangerous, Gerome," I said. "Those sisters. They're not playing by the rules. It's only a matter of time until someone gets hurt."

"I'm afraid I don't know what you're talking about, Sergeant."

"Then I'd suggest you figure it out," I said as they rose from the chairs. "Because if even one civilian gets hurt, and I find out you were responsible, it won't be their head I'll be bouncing off the concrete. It will be yours. Understand?"

Gerome paused, then his head slowly turned, and he speared me in his sightless gaze, causing me to shiver. "I understand more than you know, Sergeant."

Collateral Damage. March 16th O95Ohrs

I LEFT THE OFFICES of Avant-Garde and made it all the way back down to my car before I exhaled. Going up, I wasn't really sure what I'd been expecting to happen, but now I felt certain that Avant-Garde had enlisted the Swan-Sisters to retrieve their gold.

Which, if I was being honest, wasn't a complete surprise, but it definitely made things more complicated. Especially since I didn't know who'd done the actual hiring. Most likely it was someone higher up in the company, since I couldn't really see Gerome entrusting the retrieval of the gold to the two sisters. Masked women wearing leotards and wielding swords struck me as too flashy for his tastes. I got the sense that he valued efficiency and discretion over direct action, and it's hard to be discreet when you're flipping around parking garages, getting into sword fights or stabbing holes into pawnshop flunkies.

Mr. Crosier was a different story altogether. Based on what I'd seen, a couple of dark-haired gymnasts would be right up his alley. Plus, he struck me as the kind of man who enjoyed being with someone dangerous.

I sat in the car thinking about it for several minutes before a tiny voice inside whispered that I was only prolonging the inevitable. At the end of the day, it didn't actually matter who'd hired them. All that mattered was what I was going to do about it, and that's where things got tricky.

I fished my cell phone out of my pocket and called the office. Robbie answered on the second ring, and, to his credit, greeted me with at least a sliver of enthusiasm.

"Welcome to Blue Moon division, your one-stop-shop for all your paranormal needs."

"Robbie, it's—"

"Do you suspect that your mother-in-law is actually in league with the devil? Are you wondering if your son's new girlfriend is actually a ghoulfriend? Are you convinced that your creepy uncle Charlie is still touching you from beyond the grave? Well, our skilled and seasoned investigators can help you touch him right back."

"Robbie—"

"Ask about our two-for-one special and let our officers get rid of any toasty ghostys haunting your fireplace."

"*Robbie!*"

"Uh, yeah?"

"It's Chloe."

"Oh, hey, Sergeant," he said. "How's it going?"

"Not well, Robbie. Not well at all."

"Ah, sorry to hear. Keep your chin up."

"Your concern is touching," I said. "I need you to do something for me."

"Oh, well, I guess I could be down for that. My mom doesn't get home until after five, so maybe if we—"

"What the hell are you talking about?" I snapped, cutting him off.

"Uh, what are *you* talking about?"

"I need you to run a search on Avant-Garde. They're a financial management company here in Boston. I also need you to run a background check for August Varice, Gerome Reed, and Walter Crosier. Everything you can find, and I need it fast."

"Right," he said, scribbling the names down. "Okay, sure thing. And listen, as for that other thing—"

"Time is of the essence, Robbie."

"Right," he said. "Probably one of those things that's better left unsaid."

I hung up the phone and let it drop into my lap. Then I rubbed my eyes and stared at the space in the dashboard where the digital clock should have been. The numbers had long since burned out, but my gut told me it was just before ten. Way too early for propositions involving million dollar blow jobs or unsolicited rendezvous in a teenager's bedroom. I needed some space to think. Unfortunately, I didn't want to head back to headquarters, and I couldn't risk using the police station for fear of running into Mack or Bulwark. I could have hit a coffee joint, but I already drank my fill this morning. Another cup would leave me jittery.

A quick glance down at my phone screen revealed that there'd been no word from Agent Gordan. Likely he was still out with Hilary and Basic, canvasing the areas and trying to find our leprechauns' safe house. I considered my next step for several minutes, then I turned and booted up the department laptop, signing into our dispatch system and perusing the morning's calls.

At a glance, it seemed like business as usual. There was a fight in the subway, as well as some vagrants sleeping in the bushes near the Commons T-line stop, and... well, hello there.

Apparently there had been some sort of incident during the night. Someone had called in a body, found lying in the gutters near the Constitution Wharf. On the surface, there wasn't much of interest about the call. The homeless have a habit of freezing in Boston, and last night's drop in temperature would have been enough to claim the life of anyone left out unprotected. But the mention of a red sweater caught my eye, and I debated for a long moment before curiosity won out. I brought the engine to life and headed that way.

There were more people out and about than usual, clogging the roadways and the sidewalks. It took me a minute to realize they were searching for more leprechaun gold. I watched them, peering around and into trees, checking the corners and nearby storm drains of the city buildings. There was a strange, sort of fevered energy, similar to the kind that had been around back when people started hunting Pokémon, except more visceral, since this time they were hunting actual gold.

I forced my way through traffic, honking when necessary and being yelled at or, more often than not, flipped off in return. Eventually, I crossed over the North Washington Bridge. Two blocks later, I spotted a squad car with its lights on, as well as an undercover silver sedan and a familiar Forensics van. I pulled in along the edge of the curb, and exited, making my way on foot.

The silver sedan was empty, but I recognized the officer sitting inside the squad car sipping coffee. It was the same one from the other morning. Officer Bill Thompson. He glared at me as I walked past, but didn't bother getting out of the car.

As crime scenes go, it was fairly bare bones. The body was still face down in the gutter, rigor mortis beginning to set in, and there was a familiar figure dressed in a black windbreaker with the word "Forensics" on it standing a few feet away, adjusting his camera lens.

"Hey Jerry," I said as I approached. "How are the boys?"

He glanced up, clearly surprised to see me. "Chloe. Oh, they're, uh, well to be honest I had to go to the emergency room last night to get them drained. The doctor said they're infected. He gave me some antibiotics and some pain pills though, so that's helping. The worst part is he said he doubted that the procedure was done correctly, meaning—"

"You're still fertile?"

He nodded. "Once the infection goes down, I'll need to go and see another specialist."

"That's a tough break, Jerry. And to think, this all could have been avoided with a simple little pill."

Jerry huffed out a sigh. "Tell me about it."

"You sure you shouldn't be home resting?"

He shook his head. "Rosie has her heart set on Hawaii, and come hell or high waters, I'm going to get her there."

I glanced at him, feeling the corner of my mouth rise. "You're a good man, Jerry. And you're tougher than you look."

He got quiet for a long moment. "Thanks, Chloe."

"So, what can you tell me about him?"

"Not much," he said. "Call came out about an hour ago. Jogger noticed him during their run."

"Mind if I take a look?"

"Just don't touch him."

I nodded, and slipped forward, ducking beneath the yellow police tape and choosing my steps carefully. It only took a few seconds for my worst fears to be confirmed. Dressed in dark pants with a red hooded sweatshirt, it was the same person I'd seen back inside the Prudential Center. Sullage's accomplice.

Someone had done a number on him.

There were markings along his neck, with signs of strangulation and ruptured blood vessels in his eyes. That alone would have been enough, but there were also lacerations along his wrists. Handcuffs maybe, or ropes. Dark wounds lined the back of his neck, and part of his left earlobe had been burned away.

"It looks like someone tortured him," I said.

"Oh, gee, I wonder why they would do that?"

The voice that spoke didn't belong to Jerry, and a quick glance back revealed the forensic tech retreating to his van as a pair of men approached. The first was Mack. The second was Detective Ruscutt. Further down the block, Officer Thompson had exited his vehicle, leaning on the doorway for a better vantage point to watch.

"Here to screw up another murder scene, Chloe?" Mack asked. "Or do you figure you've done enough damage for one day?"

I flashed a humorless smile and tried to hide the shiver that passed through me. "Last time I looked, I caught your killer for you."

Mack snorted, and Scutt stepped wide around the sedan, drawing a pack of cigarettes from his pocket and slipping one between his teeth. He lit the tip using an old-fashioned Bic lighter, then puffed contently as Mack came up beside me.

"One killer, maybe. But our friend here didn't die of natural causes. Someone got a hold of him and worked him over good. Now why do you suppose they would have done that?"

I shook my head. "How could I possibly know that?"

"Not even a guess? Well, try this on for size. Word on the street is that Sullage wasn't working alone. That our friend here was complicit in Ricky Brannon's death."

"I can believe that."

"Yeah, but it goes deeper than that. Rumor is you told Sullage he was already in custody. That he'd cut a deal, in fact, and was planning on ratting him out for a reduced sentence."

"Misdirection is nothing new in interrogations. Cops do it every day."

"Sure they do," he said. "But times are changing. Public opinion holds more weight than ever. If those rumors are true, and you convinced Sullage that our friend here was ratting him out, and he took it upon himself to call some of his friends from around the neighborhood and ordered them to silence our victim, well, you'd be looking at way more than just professional misconduct. You could find yourself facing aiding and abetting charges for capital murder."

It's a testament to my time in Blue Moon that I kept my face smooth, but inside, I was shaking. "Well, you know what they say about rumors, Mack. You can't believe everything you hear."

"That's a good line. I'll have to remember it." He took another step forward and lowered his voice. "I'll be honest, Chloe. I spent the last three months thinking about killing you, but now, I'm thinking I would rather see you locked in a cell, somewhere cold and dark, where you'll learn what the real monsters look like." He leaned back, just far enough so that I could see him smile. "Won't that be something?"

A Feather in the Cap. March 16th 1125hrs

THERE WASN'T MUCH ELSE that I could say, and lingering around watching Mack and Scutt work was enough to make my skin crawl. I headed back to my car, brought the engine to life and pulled away from the curb before turning back toward the city. I made it over the Washington Street Bridge, then I pulled over to the curb outside of a pizza joint enjoying a brisk lunch traffic. I shifted into park and let the engine idle, forcing myself to take a series of long breaths before rubbing the glaze from my eyes and struggling to think clearly.

Despite what most people believe, there is no law that prevents detectives or investigators from lying to suspects. Point of fact, we are encouraged to use any and all means of psychological manipulation, including outright deception, as a means of procuring a confession or uncovering evidence that might lead to a conviction. It may seem counter-intuitive to some, but you have to keep in mind that the goal is the application of justice, and seasoned investigators have learned to bend the truth in all sorts of interesting ways, both to build rapport and to convince potential suspects that confession is in their best interest.

Even if what Mack said was true, and Sullage had taken what I said to heart and murdered his accomplice as a result, then, legally speaking, I should be in the clear.

Mind you, *should* isn't always the same as *will be*. Law enforcement has changed over the past ten years, and officers were being held to greater amounts of accountability every day. Things that would have been allowed to slide in past years were being called into light, and the entire system was in a drastic state of overhaul, with no one sure exactly what would happen next.

Furthermore, even if I was on solid ground legally, there were other courts besides the criminal system.

The court of public opinion, especially around the department, was an equally volatile force, and if word got out that I had gotten careless and one of my suspects had been murdered as a result, then my days within the department and Blue Moon were numbered. That was to say nothing of any potential civil litigation. If Sullage's accomplice had any family and they learned about any of this, you could bet they would be filing a lawsuit against me and the department.

Mind you, I wasn't totally defenseless. If Sullage had arranged for his accomplice's death, then he must have done it from the jail. Those telephone calls are monitored, something he should have known by now. If he'd taken matters into his own hands, then there had to be a record of it. How that would play out in court, I didn't know. One thing was for sure, it would be messy with no quick end in sight.

I'd seen it happen before. Officers who stumbled into questionable circumstances could end up sacrificing years of their career stuck on paid administrative leave while lawyers argued endlessly over the smallest of minutia.

I'd already gotten a brief taste of that life these past few months, when I'd been cast aside by the rest of the department and forced in by the snow. The idea of living that way on a more permanent basis was almost more than I could bear. I cared about my job, and being forced to sit on the sidelines watching as months, or even years, passed by, was more than I could bear to think about.

Which, I imagine, is what Mack had in mind. He had to know that any threats of prison time were largely unfounded. He'd been trying to scare me (spoiler: it worked). Maybe he hoped I would go off and do something foolish, or maybe, more likely, he knew I was smart enough to work it out and then... what?

I thought about it for a long moment before it came to me.

Pressure.

He was turning up the pressure, hurtling another brick on to the load I was already carrying. He was trying to overload me, or else to distract me. Make me do something rash or stupid. I didn't know how far up the food chain Mack's influence went. I believed him when he told me he had Bulwark under his thumb, but who else? The chief? The district attorney's office? Where did his sphere of influence end?

I didn't know, but something told me I had better find out soon, and in the meantime, I needed to avoid any mistakes. Better yet, I needed a win. A big one. Something that would cast my name in a good light and earn me some goodwill within the department.

I needed to solve this heist.

I needed to, as Sullage had put it, find these "Irish-looking micks" and bring them to justice. Twenty-five million dollars worth of gold would be a heck of a feather in the department's cap. If nothing else, it would assure me a job for at least a few months more.

Unfortunately, that was easier said than done. I'd had three months to work this case, and I hadn't caught so much as a whiff of them, much less the gold. All I'd found was blood and death. Heartache and pain.

It happens like that sometimes.

Amateur detectives can inadvertently run a case into the ground, when all their leads and clues crumble into dust before their eyes, leaving them with nothing but more questions. Every detective has seen it happen, usually more than once. And those are the times that it pays to have a friend nearby.

I couldn't find the leprechauns. Not on my own. The city was too big, and they were too slick. But I had something that not everyone does. I had friends, people who were in this alongside me, who cared as much about justice and doing the right thing as I did. They were darn good at their jobs, and when we worked together, I truly believed there was nothing we couldn't accomplish.

The phone rang in my lap as I sat there in front of that pizza restaurant.

A quick glance down revealed Agent Gordan's number, and my heart skipped a beat as I brought it up to my ear.

"Alex?"

"We found them," he said, his voice buoyant. I could practically see his boyish grin, smiling back at me from across the city.

"Where?"

He told me. It was an older warehouse, west of Chelsea and Admiral's Hill, not far from the Exelon Power Station.

"You're sure?"

"Well, there are no signs of any leprechauns yet, but the neighbors are positive that the far building has been running steadily for months. We confirmed it with three different sources, all of whom found it strange, considering the shutdown, but none of whom bothered to tell anyone because—"

"This is Boston, and people know to mind their own business," I said. "Alright, I'm on my way. Don't make any moves until I get there. And Alex…"

"Yeah."

"Good job."

"Thanks," he said. "See you soon."

Planning on The Fly. March 16th 1207hrs

I PULLED AWAY FROM the curb and headed back north, driving through Charlestown and up Alford St before crossing over the bridge and into Everett. I wasn't as familiar with the streets up near this part of town, but all I had to do was head for the large row of warehouses lining the southern waterfront.

As I drove, I kept an ear attuned to the computer's dispatch screen. There were only three hours until the leprechaun's timer was set to run out, and distributing those coins in exchange for attention had clearly paid off. The gold hunters were getting antsy now, and our dispatch system was being inundated with calls for trespassing, traffic accidents, and, in several cases, fist fights. The upper brass had already called in the next shift, but they were having difficulty getting through the traffic. If the leprechauns intention was to overwhelm the police force and grind their response time to a halt, then it was safe to say they were succeeding.

It also meant that backup wasn't really an option.

Not that I necessarily would have called for it anyway. That was the trouble with having a two-man department. You're basically on your own for much of the time. I had a few favors I could call in, a friend or two on the force who would have shown up if I asked, but they were out of play, stuck responding to calls.

Which just meant that we would need to do it ourselves.

The Rover Street Ironworks Facility was located on the southern edge of town, lining the waterfront. It wasn't anything close to a picturesque part of town, but these places usually aren't. The building sat near the end of a long industrial road, flanked by the recycling station and a power plant. Two-stories tall and made of red brick, half a dozen shutter-style doors lined the western side, and heavy graffiti marred its roadway face. All the surrounding grass had long since died, and the air smelled of rust, exhaust and cold metal that could be noted as soon as you crossed over the bridge.

I pulled over onto the curb a few blocks away and spotted Agent Gordan as well as Hilary and Basic waiting for me. Agent Gordan had removed his jacket, loosened his tie, and rolled up his sleeves. I was glad to see the clear indentation of the Kevlar vest beneath his clothes, and he had his firearm holstered securely on his belt. Hilary and Basic stood beside him. They were both wearing the same clothes I'd seen them in yesterday, an ill-fitting off-the-rack gray suit for Hilary, and loose jeans and a simple long-sleeved cotton sweatshirt for Basic. Both had Kevlar vests wrapped overtop their clothes, and were armed, after a fashion. Hilary was clutching a large cannister of OC spray, commonly known as pepper spray, while Basic had found himself a heavy piece of rebar piping. He'd curled one end into a U shape to allow for a better grip, and was giving it several practice swings when I pulled up.

"How are we looking?" I asked.

"We've been watching it," Agent Gordan said. "There's definitely movement inside, but nothing definitive that we can see."

"Any sign of the gold?"

Agent Gordan shook his head.

"Okay," I said. "Gather up everyone."

Basic lowered his rebar club and Hilary stopped fiddling with the OC spray. They drew up in a loose huddle around me.

"First off, I want to say thank you. Neither of you have to be here. You could walk away right now and no one could blame you. That takes guts."

"S'no big deal," Basic said.

"Well, I appreciate the sentiment, Sergeant," Hilary said. "I've never been a soldier, but I've seen a few things, and, I guess what I'm trying to say is." He cleared his throat and shifted his shoulders. "Tempest wouldn't just walk away. So neither will I."

"Do we have a plan?" Agent Gordan asked.

"We go in quiet," I said. "Take a look and try to figure out what exactly we're dealing with."

"Then what?"

"If it's the leprechauns, we hit them hard and fast. Disable them quickly and get them in cuffs."

"Do you actually think there will be gunplay?" Hilary asked.

"They'll have the advantage if it comes to a shootout," Agent Gordan said. "We don't have the ammo or the manpower for a drawn-out battle."

I could tell he was remembering the black-and-white photo we'd seen, and the assault rifles strapped to their back. "All true," I said. "But we've got the element of surprise. If we stay on the offensive, we can take them down before they know what hit them."

"Any chance of backup?" Hilary asked.

"Not from the department," I said. "They're swamped answering calls."

"What about from the Bureau?"

I glanced at Agent Gordan, but he shook his head. "Most of our field agents are working hand-in-hand with the National Guard to prepare for tomorrow's St. Patrick's Day parade. Pulling them off would send up a lot of red flags, and if we're wrong..."

"That settles it then," I said. "We go in just us. Anyone want to change their mind?"

No one did, and I rolled my shoulders and loosened my gun in my holster. "Alright then. Let's move, people. We've got a job to do."

Rover Street Ironworks Facility. March 16th 1257hrs

GETTING INSIDE WASN'T AS complicated as I feared, although there were several things that needed to be worked out ahead of time. Starting with if the leprechauns had spotters.

The element of surprise wouldn't mean much if we were spotted tip-toeing our way up to the building. Caught out in the open, we'd be lucky to make it ten feet from the doorway. To avoid that, we spent the next half hour conducting our own surveillance, searching the windows and rooftops for a spotter. We didn't see anyone, nor did we note any obvious cameras. That didn't mean they weren't there, but a camera is only worthwhile if you have someone monitoring it. Likely the leprechauns had kept a close eye out in the days immediately following the heist, but now, three months later, they were letting things slide.

Or so I hoped.

Once we had the all clear, I led the way up to the ironworks building, cutting through the power station and approaching from the west. The building itself was only two-stories, but four people trying to move together would be cramped, and bound to draw attention. For that reason, we made the decision to split up. Hilary came with me, and Basic went with Agent Gordan. Neither of our visitors would be much good in a shootout, but my hope was that Basic would keep Agent Gordan from getting his head caved in.

We broke apart as we crossed the road, Hilary and I heading up a trio of stairs towards the doorway, while Basic and Agent Gordan circled around the building and attempted to gain entry through one of the garage doors. I watched them disappear from view, then slowly made my way up to the door, gently testing the handle. It proved to be locked, but the window beside it wasn't. I motioned to Hilary, and then did a slow half-circle, peering through the glass. Beyond the window was an entryway hallway. Fluorescent lights hung overhead, but only one out of every three lightbulbs appeared to be on. It was almost as if someone had purposefully wanted the facility dark. I debated a moment, then handed Hilary my gun. He accepted it as if it were a hot turd, grimacing slightly and holding it with the tips of his fingers away from his body. Clearly, he was not a fan of guns.

I ran my fingers along the bottom of the window, pressing gently until I felt it give. The rusted metal groaned softly as it rose, but not so loud that I thought anyone might be alerted. All the same, I retrieved my gun and held back, slowly counting down from ten to see if anyone came to investigate.

They didn't, and I grasped the windowsill and hauled myself inside, dropping into a crouch on the floor and covering Hilary as he followed after me. The wind had picked up outside, and the building creaked and groaned as it swept in after us. Once we were both inside, I took point, keeping my footsteps soft as we made our way down the hall. The building's interior was old, cracked, marred by scorch marks on both the walls and the floor. At the end of the hall was a pair of offices. The lights were off inside, and I drew my flashlight, keeping the beam low as we stepped through the doorway.

As offices go, it was dingy and cramped, the low ceiling oppressive over our heads. Metal was the prevailing decor, and included lockers, a pair of desks, a couple of chairs, and even a footlocker. The air smelled worse in here. Cold steel mixed with notebook paper, stale fast-food grease, and something else. Something sharp and sulfuric, that took me a minute to recognize.

Hilary noticed it too, and he raised his jacket, using the edge to cover his nose. "What is that?"

"Gunpowder," I said. And something else. Something I wasn't sure how to identify, but that caused the hairs along the back of my neck to rise.

"Come on," I said.

We exited out the office through the opposite side, moving deeper into the heart of the warehouse. Past the door we had two options. Either we could continue down the hallway, or we could take the stairs up to the platform, and the rooms beyond. I debated for a moment, then decided to head up. Moving down the hall like this was risky, and the lack of working lightbulbs meant our visibility was limited. Better to find an elevated position and see what we could see.

I took point and Hilary followed, the pair of us ascending the long flight of stairs to a wide balcony that overlooked the main floor below. There were stairs connected to the opposite side, and a door leading into a second set of offices. I could hear voices from the area below us, but I didn't dare move that way for fear of being spotted. Instead, I motioned for Hilary to follow, and we crept over to the second office and stacked up along the doorway. I tested the knob and found it unlocked. It gave way with a wheezing groan, and I inched it open only what we needed in order to slip inside.

The smell I'd noticed earlier was stronger, pungent and chemical. It smelled like burned metal, and it set my teeth on edge, but I ignored it, and pushed deeper into the room.

There were no working lights inside, and I kept my flashlight low to the floor, covering its opening with my pistol to minimize the beam as much as possible. The office looked like it had belonged to a foreman. There was a heavy workbench set against the far wall, and a pegboard lined the space above, filled with well-worn tools and other mechanisms. I risked a little light to illuminate the top of the bench, and a flash of fear swept through me.

A pair of plastic wire buckets sat on the bench, loaded down with cell phones. There must have been three dozen of them at least, all different makes and models, some with their guts opened to reveal the innards within. Spools of wire lay curled in the corner, and there was a soldering tool nearby, the sight of it giving explanation to the burned metallic smell I'd been noticing. There were other things. Black double-sided tape, stacked cans of epoxy adhesive and asphalt tar, a handful of large springs, and dozens of electronic bits that I didn't know enough about to be able to identify. I thought I might know someone who would though.

I motioned Hilary up beside me and whispered in his ear. "Does your phone have a camera?"

"Yes."

"Start taking pictures," I said. "No flash. Just do the best you can."

He nodded and fished his phone from his pocket. At the same time, I slipped over to the far wall, peering through the heavy windows and down to the main work area.

The facility clearly worked in materials other than gold, but the leprechauns had retooled it to suit their purposes. A heavy oven with mesh racks sat opposite three large workbenches and a rolling bin loaded down with white sand-like powder that I assumed was necessary for the smelting process. A thick furnace was mounted on a winding crank that could be tilted to pour the melted gold down into the waiting molds, and I could see the circular indentations in each container, identifying them as the ones used to create the coins.

Directly below us sat a large vat containing the molten castoffs, impurities removed from the gold, then left to cool on their own. There was also a water bath, lined with heavy black hoses, and a stamping press, capable of indenting its markings onto each coin mold as they passed through.

Four figures stood on the main floor.

The first was cloaked in darkness, giving me nothing but a flash of shoes and a bare silhouette of a slender man. The second figure wasn't much easier to see. He was dressed in a suit but he had his back to me, and I couldn't make out much beyond that his skin was pale.

The third figure was a woman. Dressed in a wool flannel shirt with the sleeves rolled up and dark hair, she had a rough face, aged by more than just the years. Tattoos adorned her forearms and fingers, their patriotic motifs suggested she was prior military, although there was a jittery, twitchy sense to her movements that I'd long since learned to recognize as someone in need of a fix. She was also the only one of the four who was armed, a well-worn assault rifle slung across her back.

The fourth figure was a man. I placed him near retirement age, the thick roundness to his shoulders and forearms suggesting he was no stranger to the forge. He was dressed in a thick wool shirt with a heavy leather apron covering his front and a face shield currently in the raised position. The four were discussing something, but the words were too muffled for me to hear. Not far from where they stood, I spotted a familiar-looking cargo van. Its back door was cracked open, and there were military style ammo carts stacked inside along with several dozen unmarked black crates the size of a fishing tackle box. A flash of movement caught my eye, and I glanced down to see two figures creeping between rows of stacked pallets.

Agent Gordan and Basic had evidently found their way inside. They were moving stealthily, creeping closer to the light and the four figures. I did some quick odds in my head and realized that we had the advantage. If we were smart, Agent Gordan and Basic could hit them fast and disable them while I covered them from above. The leprechauns had no way of knowing that Hilary was virtually unarmed. If he stayed in the shadows, they would assume we had two shooters, and by the time they realized the truth, Agent Gordan would already have them in handcuffs.

"Hilary," I whispered and motioned for him to take up position along the opposite doorway.

It was a good plan, all things considered, but it would require precise timing, and it was paramount that no one realize we were up here until it was too late. I tightened my grip on my pistol and slowly exhaled, readying myself as Agent Gordan and Basic took up positions not far from the foursome. Agent Gordan's eyes rose to meet my own, and I could see in his gaze that he had worked out the plan as well. I felt the corner of my mouth twitch into a small half smile, and I gave a soft salute which he returned. His gun came free of its holster, and I saw him draw in a deep breath, silently counting down from three.

A heavy footstep sounded behind me when he was still on two, and I suddenly realized that I'd been wrong.

Someone did know we were here.

The fifth leprechaun, as it turned out.

He came hurtling through the doorway, a feral scream tearing from his mouth and a heavy machete clutched in his grip. The blade was coated with rust, and something else that I didn't want to dwell on. The wisps of his red beard did nothing to hide the twisted smile of his character's visage, or the naked bloodlust gleaming from behind his eyes as he drew back his arms and swung toward my head.

Somewhat of an Impasse. March 16th 1311hrs

THERE'S NOT MUCH TIME for conscious thought when someone is swinging a machete at your head. I'm surprised it had taken me until this moment to realize that.

I cursed and threw myself to the side, feeling the blade slip past my head an instant before it bit into the guard railing. Sparks erupted, and I slid on my knees, turning in a quick circle just as the leprechaun grimaced and ripped his blade free. I brought my gun up, but he was a hair's breadth faster, and he swung his arm around, his blade striking the tip of my pistol and ripping it free from my grasp. I watched it spin off into the darkness a split second before he brought his opposite arm around and slugged me in the side of the face. I had enough time to note the tattoos on his knuckles, but not enough to make out what they said before dark stars flashed in front of my face, and the world tilted, the floor rushing up to meet me.

I hit hard and lay there, stunned. Shock hid the worst of the pain, but only for a moment. Then it came crashing down in a great *whoosh*, my head and chin throbbing. I tried to scramble back to my feet, but the leprechaun saw me coming, and his foot slammed into my side, his heavy-toed boots catching me under the rib and sending me in a full spin before I crashed down beside the guardrail.

I landed with my face forward, peering down toward the main floor as the ex-military junkie shrugged her rifle from her shoulders. Her eyes met mine, and she raised her weapon, but a gunshot rang out before she could set me in her sights, and a bullet whizzed past her head, striking the furnace and ricocheting away. She cursed, sputtered, and dropped to one knee, bringing her rifle around and catching sight of Agent Gordan as he ducked behind a stack of heavy metal crates. She opened fire at his retreating figure, blasting rounds into the darkness using short controlled bursts.

The sight of her shooting at my friends stirred me to action, but my body hadn't quite caught up with my resolve, and the leprechaun caught me as I rose to one knee. He seized me by the neck, turned me around and slammed me against the rail, placing my head so that my neck was directly on the middle guard railing. He held me there with one hand, while his sword-arm drew back. Realization that he intended to behead me hit all at once, and the second I saw his arm draw back, I knew I wasn't going to be able to avoid it. I didn't have the strength, or the leverage. I seized his arm, shook myself like a dog, but his grip didn't slacken, and a scream that was part rage and part fear tore from my throat. The sword came down, and I waited for the moment I would feel the metal bite into the back of my neck. I hoped it would be clean, but something told me it might not, and fear made me brace for impact.

The machete never landed. Instead, Hilary threw himself forward with a warbling scream, crashing into the leprechaun and pounding his fists against the man's chest. It was a brave effort, but the machete-wielding leprechaun was no stranger to violence, and he redirected his strike and batted Hilary's arms aside with ease, seizing him underneath the throat and lifting him into the air. A half-turn and he hauled Hilary over the guardrail, holding him with legs suspended directly above the large vat filled with molten castoffs, still smoking and glowing in the dim light.

The leprechaun held Hilary, laughing softly to himself as the smaller man struggled, his feet kicking out into nothingness. His movements were panicked, fearful, but there was something else. A stubbornness, and a sense of pride. I couldn't say for certain where it came from, but all of a sudden, Hilary stopped squirming, brought his hand up, and depressed the trigger of his OC spray, casting the burning liquid directly into the leprechaun's face.

The leprechaun's head snapped back, and he screamed, shaking his head against the sudden burning but unable to wipe at his eyes. Realization of what was about to happen struck me hard, and I acted quickly, jerking away from the guardrail and seizing the leprechaun around one leg. My hands closed around his thigh, locking in place just beneath his groin, and I pushed up with all my might.

I couldn't have lifted him, but blinded as he was, he didn't see me coming until it was too late. His feet left the floor and his waist went over the guardrail, his sword slipping from his hand and clattering down an instant before he toppled head over heels. As his balance shifted, he released Hilary, and my heart stopped as I watched the smaller man start to plummet. He was faster than I expected, fueled by the stubbornness and pride that had lain dormant, and he reached out, seizing the edge of the balcony as the leprechaun toppled past.

I watched his body plummet and heard the moment his head hit the side of the vat. His neck broke with an audible *crunch*, and his body flopped down onto the molten bits, his suddenly boneless form sizzling and burning.

Hilary held for a long moment, then I saw fear enter his eyes, and his grip slipped. He tried one last time to pull himself up, but his strength was spent, and his fingers slipped away from the metal's edge and he plummeted down with a cry.

I threw myself over the balcony's edge, catching the guardrail with one hand and using the crook of my elbow to brace myself even as I cast my other hand out into the air. I stretched for every ounce I could manage, and I felt Hilary's hand catch mine a split second before he would have plummeted into the vat below. Our hands locked, and I tried my darndest to hold, but the weight discrepancy between us was just too much, and I realized in that moment that I couldn't save him.

Pulling his weight up was beyond me, so I shifted my grip and let my arm relax, using the momentum of his fall to swing him out wide, past the edge of the molten vat. The pendulum motion reached its climax, and I released my grip, watching as Hilary fell to the ground below. Landing wasn't fun, but it was better than dropping into a vat of molten metal, or breaking his neck on the jagged edge of the vat, like what had happened to the machete-wielding leprechaun.

Unfortunately, I wasn't the only one to notice. The ex-military junkie let out an ear-piercing scream a split second before she brought her rifle around. I threw myself back over the guardrail and away from the balcony's edge a split second before she depressed the trigger. The gun's report echoed through the building, and brass flew in a circular arc from the weapon's chamber even as her bullets tore through the balcony, ricocheting around in a firework's display of sparks.

In that moment, I learned a very valuable lesson. There is such a thing as being too prepared. Efficiency is good, but sometimes, vigorous execution can backfire on you in all sorts of interesting ways. For example, if you're going to open fire on someone standing on a balcony hanging suspended above your head, you probably shouldn't use armor-piercing rounds. Because you might get lucky, or unlucky in this sense, and blow apart the support beams.

Which is basically what happened.

Sparks flashed all around me, as bullets tore through the balcony. The first inclination I had that something was amiss was when the floor shimmered. Realization dawned, followed by a heavy groan that still echoed in the air when the entire thing came crashing down. I'd love to say I surfed it down, like Thor or Tom Cruise, but the truth is, I was scared out of my wits and I just sort of clung to whatever was available. I fell for a subjective eternity and the ricochet when it hit bounced me back into the air, cutting off my scream and sending me head over heels to the hard concrete.

The female leprechaun wasn't so lucky.

When the balcony came down, all of its weight came with it. The metal beams and broken bits crashed down on top of her, crushing the life from her in less time than it takes to describe.

I lay still on the concrete, noting with some dismay the pool of blood expanding from underneath the wreckage and onto the floor from where I'd last seen her. A sort of mindless desire to not have her blood touch me stirred me to action, and I struggled into a half-sitting position, turning my head just in time to see the van's brake lights come on.

Its engine started up, and the shuttered garage door ascended, casting traces of sunlight beneath its frame. The sudden light revealed the elder leprechaun, still wearing his leather apron and welding helmet as he raced across the warehouse floor. I started to rise, intending to pursue, but Basic beat me to it. He stepped out from behind a row of metal crates, placing himself directly into the elder leprechaun's path and raised his rebar club.

The elder leprechaun saw him and changed angles, circling wide to his workbench. He seized a heavy pipe wrench, gripping it tight as he threw himself forward, the pair coming together with a heavy crash.

Basic had the youth, but there's no substitute for spending four decades hammering metal into all manner of shapes and sizes. The elder leprechaun swung his pipe wrench around and slammed it against Basic's rebar, the force of the blow knocking the younger man off-balance. Then, before Basic could react, he lifted his foot, and drove his heavy work boot into his chest. A heavy gasp of air escaped Basic's throat as he was sent backward. He hit the edge of the pallet and tumbled back, crashing to the floor as the elder leprechaun raced to the van.

I staggered up to my feet, angling across the broken balcony wreckage before catching sight of the female leprechaun's rifle on the floor. A handful of steps carried me clear, and I seized the rifle and brought it up to my shoulder, angling my feet into a shooter's stance just as the elder leprechaun seized the van's back doors. I depressed the trigger, and the back windshield blew apart, spraying glass everywhere and sending the elder leprechaun stumbling back. It was age and arthritic joints, more than the glass shards, that sent him crashing to his knees. He caught himself, then slowly turned around. I watched him judging the distance between us as I approached, weighing his chances of crossing and hitting me with the pipe wrench before I could fire. His eyes were speculative for a moment, but age and the laws of physics were not on his side, and I saw them harden, as a bitter gleam took hold.

"Well, guess that's that," I heard him mutter.

"Hands up, fingers spread apart," I said. Then louder. "Driver! Turn off the engine and exit with your hands in the air. That car moves so much as an inch and I'm going to punch your ticket once and for all. This is your first and only warning."

"That would not be advisable," said a voice from within the van.

"Oh, no?"

Footsteps sounded behind me, and I glanced back to see Hilary and Basic. The smaller man was limping, and Basic was clutching his ribs, but neither seemed to be in any danger of expiring anytime soon.

"Yes," the voice said. "You see, by 'punching our ticket,' you will be condemning Agent Gordan to death as well."

A cold, sickly feeling took form in my stomach, and the barrel of the rifle dipped before rising.

"Alex?" I asked.

There was the sound of a gun being prodded into flesh, followed by a curse. Then his answer came from inside the van. "Yeah, it's me, Chloe. Sorry."

"Nothing to be sorry about," I said. Then to the leprechaun. "Let him go."

"Happily," he said. "Just as soon as you safety that rifle and discard the magazine."

"I can't do that."

"Then he will die alongside us."

"No!" I said.

Several seconds passed before the leader of the leprechauns spoke again. "It appears we are at somewhat of an impasse. Wouldn't you say, Sergeant?

The cold feeling that had taken root began to spread through me. "You know me?"

"Indeed," he said. "After all, you've been working so diligently trying to find us. It seemed the least I could do was to learn your name. It wasn't difficult, especially given your recent rise in popularity."

"Who are you?" I asked. "Let me see your face."

The lead leprechaun debated for a moment, then he appeared at the back of the van. He'd taken time to don the leprechaun mask and was dressed in a close-fitting suit with leather winter gloves. I couldn't see his eyes behind the mask. They were hidden, covered by dark material which prevented the light from seeping through.

"You got a name?" I asked.

"Halfcrown," he said, and inclined his head. "I hope you'll forgive me for not shaking hands. Seems best not to get too familiar, circumstances being what they are."

"Why are you doing this?"

"Ask me again sometime, and perhaps I'll tell you. For now, it's best you stay focused on the matter at hand. You've quite a difficult choice in front of you. Tell me, Sergeant, which will it be?" He turned his arms up so that his thumbs were facing outward and opened his palm, spilling two piles onto the floor. "The gold or the brass?"

"The minute I drop this rifle, you'll open fire on us."

"Likewise, the minute I hand over Agent Gordan, you will do the same."

"Hence the impasse."

"Indeed," he said. "The only way out of this, it would appear, will require some trust on our part. Should I begin the negotiations?"

"By all means."

"Keep the rifle, if you must, but discard the magazine. You'll still have one in the chamber should we double-cross you."

"And in return?"

"I will allow Agent Gordan to go free and you will allow us to drive out of here."

"That's not good enough."

"No? How about this then. I will even throw in Agent Gordan's pistol, minus the magazine of course. Now you have two shots in which to defend yourself."

"While you have virtually unlimited ammunition."

"I did say some trust would be required," he said.

"No," I said. "Even if you were serious, which I don't believe for a moment."

"And why is that? Were my fingers crossed? Perhaps you require a scout's honor?"

"Even then," I said. "You're smarter than this. You have to know that the moment you drive out of here I'll have every cop in Boston looking for you. A white cargo van with the back windshield blown out? You won't last ten minutes out there."

"That's true," he said. "If only there were some way to ensure that the police department was kept busy."

A tremor went through my chest. "Don't even think it."

Halfcrown reached into his jacket and drew out a small iPad. He turned the screen to face me, revealing the timer for the website. "I'm afraid you've left me no choice, Sergeant," he said. "My original plan called for an additional two hours until the timer went. But we'll need to accelerate that. Let us say, oh, how about twelve minutes? Wouldn't that send them all into a tizzy?" He turned back toward me. "I'm afraid time is up, Sergeant, and I must request an answer. Either remove the magazine, or poor Agent Gordan will be one of the last in a long line to perish within the line of duty. That will be three... two... on—"

"No!" I snapped. I cursed, and removed the magazine, casting it off into the darkness. "There. You see? I did what you asked. It's out."

"Very kind of you," Halfcrown said. He reached back into the van, and dragged Agent Gordan out a moment later. The driver handed over his pistol, and Halfcrown removed the magazine, then shoved it down into Agent Gordan's holster, keeping the pistol for himself as he shoved him toward me.

"That wasn't the deal."

"To be fair, you chose not to accept the deal I offered. We're making this one up on the fly." He turned toward the elder Leprechaun, who hadn't moved during our conversation. "Come along, Sixpence."

"I can't," the aged ironworker said.

"Excuse me?"

"She's seen my face," he hissed. "If we leave her alive, then she can identify me."

"That's true," Halfcrown said. He considered it for a long moment, then let out a regretful sigh. "How unfortunate."

Sixpence's eyes shifted, and realization came an instant before Halfcrown raised his arm and levied Agent Gordan's pistol at the back of his head.

"Boss, no!"

The gun went off, and Sixpence dropped like a ton of ore, his heavily muscled body crumpling into a boneless heap at the base of the van.

"Very unfortunate," Halfcrown repeated before he turned and inclined his head to me. "This is where we say goodbye, Sergeant."

"Not for too long," I said. "I'll be coming for you."

"I'll keep a close eye out."

He stepped back inside the van, closing the doors behind him, and the vehicle came to life, passing through the shutter door and into the lot. It made its way to the street, accelerating and disappearing from view.

Regroup at the Hobbit-Hole. March 16th 1919hrs

I was still at the ironworks facility twelve minutes later when the timer reached zero.

As the countdown expired, the timer was replaced by two items. The first was a picture of a pot of gold with the numerical amount, seven million dollars, above it. The second was a pair of coordinates that corresponded to the Massachusetts State House.

The officers standing guard nearby never had a chance.

As the mob swarmed, the calls for aid went out, but it was too late. The crowd, numbering several thousand strong, pushed through the fence and into the grounds of the state capital. There wasn't enough room for everyone, but for those who made it through the doors, a frantic, desperate hunt ensued. Almost immediately, videos began popping up online, showing people running through the corridors, pushing and shoving with their phones out, using their GPS applications to search for the matching coordinates. Several of them reached the gold at the same time, and the videos showed them bursting into a bland office belonging to a low-level assistant. There, sitting proud between cubicle walls, was the promised treasure.

It was, in fact, a literal pot of gold coins.

What came next can only be described as chaos.

The leprechauns had given away nearly one third of their stash. Four-hundred pounds, give or take. All broken down into tiny, one-ounce coins. No single person could carry that much out, not that they didn't try. Treasure looters shoved and grabbed for what they could, filling their pockets and bags, not realizing that they had virtually no hope of being able to escape the grounds with it. The pot ended up on its side, its contents spilling out across the floor, and all the while, chaos reigned throughout the city.

I watched it from my phone, monitoring our dispatch radio as events unfolded. Neighboring police departments were called in to assist, along with the National Guard. Those officers already in the city were eventually forced to fall back, regroup, and return in force, deploying tear gas and non-lethal rounds to clear the grounds. It took hours to empty out the statehouse, and hours more to see to the wounded. There were no fatalities, thank the Lord, but there were dozens of arrests, and all reports seemed to agree that at least some part of the gold had been recovered, though no one could give an accurate estimate of how much, or where it was.

Abandoning the leprechaun's crime scene, not to mention the bodies of three of their number, would have been unconscionable, not to mention outright criminal. Unfortunately, every officer, including the forensics team, was currently regrouping south of downtown. There was no one but me to secure the crime scene, and no one to even answer my call, had I bothered to make one.

Agent Gordan had better luck. It took three hours and a dozen phone calls, but he eventually managed to put together a federal forensic team to come out and secure the scene. They arrived just as the sun was going down, and promptly took over, muttering and grumbling as they set up their perimeter. I waited for them to get settled, then headed back to the car with Hilary and Basic trailing behind me. Agent Gordan had elected to remain behind and help direct the team. The wreckage inside the building was severe, and everything would need to be collected and catalogued. Bodies, bullets, even the equipment used to make the gold. The federal agents were looking at several weeks' worth of work, if not more.

I dropped Hilary and Basic back off at their apartment near the airport so they could clean up. Both bore wounds, but neither wanted to go to the hospital, a fact for which I did not blame them. I had no doubt that the emergency rooms were currently overrun with people injured during the State House catastrophe. Better to tend to it themselves. They exited the car and promised to get back in touch once they'd had a chance to find some food and get some rest. I waved goodbye, and took the long way back to headquarters, steering clear of the State House and downtown area and approaching from the south.

I parked in the Government garage and descended down to our hobbit-hole, opening the door to find Robbie still sitting in Topher's old seat with his feet up on the desk. He had the television on and was watching the newscasters as they replayed footage.

"This is bad," he said by way of greeting.

There wasn't much that I could say, and I made my way over to my desk, removing my jacket and then peeling my Kevlar vest away before laying it overtop my chair.

"Someone screwed up," Robbie said, his eyes still glued to the screen.

"Big time," I agreed.

"Was it us?"

I honestly didn't know how to answer that, and in the end, I said nothing.

There was no food inside our hobbit hole, and I didn't dare sneak across the lot to the police station in search of coffee. Based on the dispatch radio traffic, things were largely calmed down, but there were a lot of angry people out there tonight, civilians and officers alike. It wouldn't do me any good to run afoul of them right now, so I stayed inside our headquarters with Robbie and watched as the newscasters provided round-the-clock reports, playing video footage scrubbed from the internet and continually rehashing the Federal

Reserve heist. Somehow, they'd gotten hold of the black-and-white photograph showing the leprechauns in action. I'd bet my last dollar someone at the Bureau leaked it, but it didn't matter. Done was done.

There was no mention of Blue Moon, thankfully, but I knew it was only a matter of time. Most of Boston didn't even know we existed, but all it would take was one reporter hearing a rumor, and we'd be thrust out into the public eye soon enough. The police department was a state-funded organization, and open to public auditing. If someone were inclined to look hard enough, they'd be able to find Lieutenant Kermit and me on the books, and the upper brass would be forced to admit, not only our existence, but our purpose as well.

I was still mulling it over in my head when Lieutenant Kermit arrived. He came in softly and closed the door behind him, removing his jacket and placing it over the chair in his office before dropping down into the seat beside me.

"Are you alright?" he asked.

"A little banged up, but nothing that won't heal," I said.

"Agent Gordan?"

"Still at the ironworks facility, so far as I know."

He nodded. "I understand there were some fatalities."

"Three. All bad guys," I said. "Two of them got away."

"Unfortunate, but understandable," he said. "Do we know the identities of our thieves yet?"

I shook my head. "None of them were carrying any identification. We'll have to rely on the federal team to identify them, and then hope they share it with us."

"I don't think that will be a problem," he said. "I've just come from a meeting at the station. The mayor had an emergency sit down, both with our own chief of police and the FBI regional director. He's ordering both parties to work in unison to find the men responsible for this."

"Halfcrown," I said.

"Is that a name or a title?"

"A name," I said. "It's not much, but it's a start."

"Indeed," Kermit said.

I groaned, and stretched in my seat, rubbing my eyes and running my hands through my hair. "At least there's some good news. Do we know when they'll make the announcement cancelling the St. Patrick's Day Parade?"

"They won't."

I blinked. "What?"

"That was one of the talking points of the meeting. The parade will go on as planned."

"But what about all the damage to the State House?" I asked. "What about the fact that there are two of them still out there?"

"It is the mayor's opinion that the culprits responsible most likely used the day's events as cover in order to flee the city, and that the public has nothing more to fear."

"B-but that's idiotic."

"I happen to agree. But the mayor's word stands. The parade will go on as planned, albeit with extra security from both the police and the National Guard."

"Uh-huh," I said. "And I suppose the fact that any mayor who cancels a St. Patrick's Day parade in the most Irish city in America is basically begging not to be reelected has nothing to do with it?"

"I'm sure it does," Lieutenant Kermit said. "But the fact remains that it is out of my hands, Sergeant. And yours."

He was right about that, and I leaned back in my chair, thinking. The mayor might have preferred to believe that Halfcrown and his accomplice had used the gold as a distraction to make their escape, but I knew better. As it stood, they'd given away nearly half of their haul. Twelve million and change, such as it were. Which begged the question, why?

Why go to all the trouble of stealing it, only to turn around and give it away? I turned it around and around in my head, but no matter how I looked at it, I didn't make it make sense.

Not until I considered one thing.

Suppose for a moment that the leprechauns' intention had never been to keep it? Suppose they'd enacted their entire plan, knowing full well that they were going to give it all back? Why then, would they parcel it out such as they had? What did they hope to gain?

I thought about it for a long time, then realized I'd already answered that question.

Credibility.

Attention.

They had them both now. The bags of coins could have been overlooked, but the pot of gold was too much to be ignored. Granted, some might call foul because of the timer, but they would be among the minority. Most people would have seen enough to be convinced of the leprechauns' intentions, which, I quickly realized, was exactly what they wanted.

A sudden cold overtook me, causing goosebumps to appear along my arms.

The parade would go on. The leprechauns would still have their chance to do whatever it was they were planning. They'd spent half of their haul, but they had the eyes and ears of the city fixed firmly on them. All they had to do now was to deliver their message. Loud enough where everyone could hear.

I stood up suddenly. "I need to make a phone call."

I grabbed my phone from the desk and made my way into the conference room, closing the door behind me. Point of fact, I needed to make two phone calls. The first one was to Hilary. He answered on the third ring, rubbing the sleep from his voice.

"Sergeant Mayfield?" he asked. "We were just about to get up and head back your way. Is everything okay?"

"It's..." I was going to say fine, but that would have been a bald-faced lie. "It's complicated," I said. "Do you still have those photos you took today?"

"You mean from inside the ironworks facility? Yes, of course."

"I need you to send them to someone."

"Who?"

I told him.

"A-are you sure?" he asked. "Maybe I should call Tempest instead?"

I glanced at my watch. "It's after midnight where he's at. From what I understand he's an early riser. Likes to get his workout in."

"That's true," Hilary admitted reluctantly.

"I don't have time to wait for a callback. I need someone who we know is going to be awake at this time. Someone who can think clearly."

"Alright," Hilary said. "I'll send them right over."

I hung up, then counted to thirty in my head, and dialed another number, one I never thought in a million years I would call.

Big Ben answered on the fourth ring. "Hello?"

"It's Chloe," I said.

"Chloe," he said, drawing out the vowels of my name. "I wondered when you'd be calling me. You're just lucky I hadn't gone out yet."

"I need a favor," I said.

There were only a couple of guys I know who'd served time in the military, and only two I was certain had real world combat experience. The first was Tempest Michaels. The second was Benjamin Winter, his six-foot-seven, womanizing counterpart, who went by the nickname of Big Ben. I'd met him last year, when he and his friend, a bookstore owner by the name of Frank Decaux, came to town in search of an old manuscript. He'd come close to shagging my sister, but I'd put a halt to that, and he'd ended up redirecting all his sexual mojo toward two of the witches who'd been intent on killing us.

"Say no more, love. This time of night, I can get you wherever you need to go. Should we use zoom, or do you want to do this old school, with photos?"

"Photos," I said. "Hilary should be uploading them to you now."

"Uh, Hilary is involved? I wouldn't have expected this from him, but if he's…" he trailed off, and I could hear the after-buzz of his cellphone as the pictures began to arrive.

"Uh, Chloe, what am I looking at?"

"I'm hoping you can tell me," I said. "What do you see?"

"Uh, well, it's hard to say for certain. The lighting isn't great, and without some context..."

"Help me, Big Ben," I said, and really hated myself for completing the sentence. "You're my only hope."

"Chloe, I think you may have a problem."

"I've got more than one," I said. "But go on."

"Well, the cellphones are a dead giveaway. Someone's been stripping the guts from them."

"Why would they do that?"

"Well, at their core, a telephone is just a way of sending and receiving signals. They're useful, but not overly dangerous by themselves."

"I sense a 'but' coming."

"But, some of the other items are concerning," he said. "The wire and taping, not to mention the adhesive spray and springs, combined with the asphalt tar. I almost hate to ask but are you guys building a bomb over there?"

My heart dropped, and my stomach curdled. On some level I'd suspected it was coming, but hearing it confirmed struck me at the core.

"Chloe?"

"I've got to go," I said. "Thanks, Ben."

I hung up and exited the conference room, catching sight of Lieutenant Kermit in his office. I knocked twice, then opened the door and stuck my head in. "Call everyone back," I said.

He blinked. "Sergeant?"

"This isn't over yet," I said. "Not by a long shot."

I closed his door and made my way back to the main area, where Robbie sat watching television. I glanced past him to my desk, where his gadget still stood.

"I need you," I said.

He blinked. "Uh, here?"

"And now."

"Okay," he said and took his feet off the desk. "I should probably mention that I've never been with a wom—"

I scooped his machine off my desk and dropped it down in front of him. "How well does this thing work?"

"Uh, it works just fine."

"You're sure?"

"Positive."

"And what's the effective range?"

"Depends how fast you want to drain the battery," he said. "Five hundred yards is the max, but you won't get more than an hour or so. Less range means more time."

I nodded, already working the math in my head. "Can you make any more?"

"Sure. I mean, I guess. I'll need some things from the hardware store."

I fished my wallet out of my bag and removed my credit card, handing it over. "Get what you need and then get back here pronto. And swing by and pick up Hilary and Basic on your way back."

"Okay," he said. "Mind telling me what we're doing?"

"We're getting even," I said. "This isn't over. Not by a long shot. And this time, it's our turn to have the upper hand. Now go."

The Missing Piece. March 17th 0714hrs

We worked through the night.

I tried to help Robbie as best I could, but it quickly became apparent that it was going to take twice as long with my assistance than if I just left him alone. Likewise with Hilary. Basic, of all people, showed a surprising aptitude for the work, and Robbie watched him warily until it became apparent that he was more than competent.

Robbie had compiled his preliminary searches on Avant-Garde, as well as Gerome Reed and August Varice, but there was too much information missing for me to come to any conclusions, so I set Hilary on the task. He seemed to understand computers, and how networks connected together, and I hoped that he would have more success.

I spent several hours poring over maps, working my way through the parade route and studying the surrounding buildings. I knew what I was looking for, or at least I suspected I did, but finding it was like trying to play chess without seeing the board. I could anticipate all I liked, but at some point, it just became guesswork.

Basic made a food run a couple hours after midnight. There wasn't much open, but he found an all-night drugstore, and loaded up on eggs, milk, bacon and bagels. He also purchased an electric frying pan to cook them in, which was forward-thinking on his part, since our kitchen area was decidedly void of them. Once he arrived back at headquarters, he disappeared into the kitchen. There was some initial confusion in which the fuses kept blowing, but he was eventually able to finagle the pan to life, and the smell of breakfast quickly filled the office.

I ate methodically, not really tasting but enjoying the warmth it provided, and then settled in, running the numbers as well as double checking our weapons for the umpteenth time. I was still there when the sun crested the horizon, and shortly after that was when Lieutenant Kermit came walking back through the door. He motioned his head, and I followed him into his office, closing the door behind me.

"How did it go?" I asked.

"About as you'd expect," he said. "Both the mayor and Deputy Bulwark listened politely, and then immediately disregarded everything I said."

"That's the bureaucracy for you," I said. "Highly averse to hearing anything that might conflict with their wishful view of the world."

"So it would appear," he said.

"Guess we're on our own for this one."

"Not entirely. I did manage to convince them to assign additional security for the parade route. There will be plenty of officers standing by, as well as National Guardsmen."

"They'll need them," I said.

I'd been checking the leprechaun's website every hour or so, and so far, there was nothing new, but I knew them too well to believe that whatever they were planning wouldn't come to fruition during the parade. And I wasn't the only one. The entire city would likely be turning out, some in search of gold, others just to see what might happen.

"I also found these," Lieutenant Kermit said. He handed over a pair of badges, along with two police IDs, showing Hilary and Basic's face.

"Special investigators," I said. "Nice touch."

"It seems fitting."

"Bulwark finds out about this and you'll have some serious explaining to do."

"Best he not find out then," Lieutenant Kermit said. "Either way, we require all hands on deck for this one, and these should be enough to allow them to pass freely through the checkpoints with their bags in tow."

I nodded. "Makes sense."

"Have you heard any word from Agent Gordan?"

I shook my head. "Nothing yet. Might be he's still wrapped up at the ironworks facility. Or else he went home to get some shut-eye."

There was another possibility, one I didn't want to think about. During our raid, Agent Gordan had been disarmed and taken captive. He'd escaped unharmed, but his gun had been used to execute the elder leprechaun. Forensics would show where the bullet came from, and the fact that it had gone through the back of the leprechaun's skull. Agent Gordan would have some explaining to do, and he wasn't the type to lie or try to spin the truth to make himself look better. There was a very real chance that he could find himself being terminated, or at the least reassigned, which would spell disaster for us. Without Agent Gordan, we had no bureau support, and no time to bring whoever they decided to replace him with up to speed.

All this flashed through my mind in an instant, and Lieutenant Kermit read the expression on my face. "We'll make do."

"Yeah," I said, my voice low. "It's just... this isn't some case of a greedy landlord trying to scare his tenants, or a crazy cat-lady convinced her mother-in-law is haunting her shower. Halfcrown is serious. He's got a mind to hurt people, and he'll succeed if we don't stop him."

"Perhaps it has slipped your notice, Sergeant, but we're serious as well, and we have something he doesn't."

"What's that?"

"Truth, justice, and the American way."

"In that case, should I send out for some red capes?"

"Heavens no," Lieutenant Kermit said. "We'll all end up looking like Vermont Wensdale."

I had a flash of our team dressed in red capes with thigh-high boots and musketeer swords on our hips, and I couldn't stop the soft chuckle that escaped out. It felt good to laugh, all things considered, and I savored the moment.

"There now," Lieutenant Kermit said. "Things will work out alright. You'll see."

I started to respond, but a tentative knock came at the door before Hilary stuck his head inside. "Uh, Sergeant? I've found something you're going to want to see."

He stepped into the office and handed me a small stack of papers. I laid them down and scanned the pages, feeling my stomach tighten as I reached the end of the first page.

"What's that?" Lieutenant Kermit asked.

"The missing pieces," I said and glanced up at Hilary. "You're sure these are correct?"

He nodded. "Positive."

"Okay," I said. "Tell everyone out there to gear up. I know where we're going now. And I know what we have to do. Move out in ten minutes."

Race to the Finish. March 17th 1237hrs

"WE'RE BEING FOLLOWED," HILARY said from the passenger's seat.

I glanced up and into the rear-view mirror, searching the vehicles behind us. "How can you tell?"

"I don't know," he said. "I can just feel it."

"You've got a spider-sense now?"

"He's been like that ever since the witches," Basic offered from the backseat.

"I thought we agreed not to talk about them," Hilary said.

"Sorry."

"No judgement here," I said. "Lord knows I've had my share of bad experiences with witches too."

"What do we do?" Hilary asked.

I considered it for a long moment as we passed over the train tracks along South Hampton Street.

The parade was scheduled to begin in little over half an hour, and would follow a two-mile trek through the streets of South Boston. At last count, there were over one hundred different groups making up the line, including student representations, marching bands, parade floats, and dance groups, along with city officials, including the mayor. I spotted Titus Broggart on the list, as well as the Sons of Liberty, who would be dressed in their historical regalia. I hadn't spoken to him since the events of the previous year, when he'd led the defense of the city against an imaginary leviathan. The National Guard had also reserved a spot, and would be driving a trio of light combat vehicles, decked out in green with sparkling clovers along the side. A show of community spirit, or so it appeared, but I knew they were more than just decorative.

"Chloe?"

"We stick to the plan," I said. "You both know where you're supposed to be?"

They both nodded.

"Okay then," I said. "Stay focused.

The streets surrounding the parade were closed off for three blocks in every direction, uniformed officers redirecting traffic away from the crowds. I got as close as I could before I pulled over onto the curb, slowing to allow them to exit.

"Be careful out there," I said. "And watch your backs."

They both nodded, and slung their respective backpacks over their shoulders, tucking the official identifications that Lieutenant Kermit had forged for them beneath their collars. Backpacks were dangerous within the crowds, ever since the Boston Marathon bombing back in 2013. Guardsmen and officers were trained to specifically target those with large packs on their backs, and they might need those IDs if they came under scrutiny. Not for the first time, I wished Agent Gordan was here. He could have added any additional credentials we needed, but so far he'd been silent since the ironworks facility. I'd called and left him a message, detailing the basics of our plan but not so much that it could be used against him, or us, later down the line. I hadn't heard back yet, and it bothered me.

They exited the vehicle, and I pulled away from the curb, casting continual glances up toward my rearview mirror. I didn't see anyone, but I trusted Hilary when he said they were back there. Unfortunately, there wasn't much I could do about it. Most likely it was just Mack or one of his guys, watching me in the hopes that I would screw up and they could somehow document it. It was annoying, for certain, but not overly dangerous, considering all the other threats I might soon f ace.

I took the next detour and headed east, away from the parade's starting location. As I drove, I caught flashes of the parade route. Safety barriers ran the length of the streets, directing the foot traffic away from the parade route, and marked police vehicles blocked off the intersections.

Thousands of people had come to watch the parade, young and old, desperate for a touch of the emerald isle and, I suspected, more gold. They swayed together, a sea of green top hats and four-leafed-clover ears, sporting festive jackets, sweaters, and scarves. According to the news, spirits were up, and the Guinness was flowing, the collection of green beads and matching plastic cups already filling the street gutters, even as the scent of sweat, beer, and fried food filled the air.

On the plus side, Bulwark and the mayor hadn't been lying. There was a noticeable markup in security. Officers wearing fluorescent jackets were stationed every twenty feet, and National Guardsmen walked the routes, wielding heavy rifles and leading dogs on leashes.

I came to the intersection just as the traffic light turned yellow, and I accelerated forward, crossing over the line just as it changed to red. A little thrill went through me at the sight of the cars drawing to a halt behind me. Whoever my tail was, he'd need the luck of the Irish if he was going to catch up now. I beat my hand against the steering wheel and allowed myself a small smile as I drove. Two blocks later, no one had caught up, and I turned off the main roadway and pulled into a driveway alley between two brownstones.

I was fairly certain that Halfcrown's intention was to set off an explosive device along the parade route. The problem was, I didn't know where.

That's where Hilary came in.

The sheet of papers he handed me had provided the missing piece. The one thing I'd needed to link Halfcrown to the area, as well as to provide some reasoning behind his motivation.

I put the car into park and killed the engine. Then I turned in my seat, making sure my Kevlar straps were tight and my pistol loose in its holder. Once that was done, I cast one final glance into the rear-view mirror, and it was that last second move that saved my life.

Headlights flashed into view, and I had all of a second's warning to brace myself before a large black van crashed into my rear bumper. The sound of metal impacting against metal rang out, intermingling with crunching plastic. The force of the blow cast my vehicle forward at an angle, causing it to clip the edge of the brownstone, shattering brick across the front bumper even as my forehead hit the windshield.

Things got a little fuzzy after that.

I wasn't sure how long I was out. No more than a few seconds, and I came to just as a figure moved up beside my door. My vision was blurred, and I was seeing double, but some part of me recognized the gunman from the pawnshop. The one wearing the Boston Bruins's hockey mask. Alarm bells started ringing, and I reached for my gun, but nothing was working right. The gunman tore my door free, then reached inside, seized my wrist with a *tsk,* and yanked me from the car.

The cold air slapped my face, carrying along a familiar scent that barely had time to register before I hit the pavement. Strong arms scooped me up, lifted me from the ground and carried me half a dozen steps backward. I briefly glimpsed the back of the van as the doors opened, then I was pitched face first, sent rolling across the hard metal floor. My attacker followed me in, slamming the door shut behind him and casting us into darkness.

Inside the Van. March 17th 1249hrs

I OPENED MY EYES expecting to find a gun in my face.

Instead, I found a spoon.

Cloudy liquid burned along the brim, shivering as the gunmen lowered the needle tip inside and began to draw it in. He noted my stirring, and I could hear the smile in his voice when he spoke. "You back with us, Sergeant?"

A low groan slipped out past my lips, echoing off the cold metal of the van's floor. I clamped my teeth shut after a moment, stifling the sound as I pushed myself into a sitting position. A quick glance around revealed that I was still in the back of the van, and we were driving down a residential street. I could hear the sounds of the parade in the distance, but the back windows were covered over, and I couldn't see much through the windshield. I did a quick check of my person, and found that I still had my handcuffs, but my pistol was sitting snuggly inside the gunman's waistband,

"I'll take that as a yes," the gunman said.

"You know my name, Scutt," I said.

The gunman froze for just a moment before he lowered the spoon, its chamber empty, and lifted his mask, revealing the worn face of Detective Collum Ruscutt. His broad nose and hollowed cheeks seemed even more out of place in his tactical gear, and his beady eyes regarded me, hints of anger and curiosity shining back.

"Worked it out, did you?"

"Seems that way."

He grunted. "How long ago?"

"Shorter than I'd care to admit," I said and glanced toward the driver. "That you, Thompson?"

Officer Bill Thompson pointedly didn't acknowledge me, but I took that to mean my guess was right on the money.

"What gave it away?" Scutt asked.

"You did," I said, and wrinkled my nose. "You stink."

He snorted, the side of his mouth curling up into a smirk. "Might be I do after all this time. Nasty habit, tobacco. Never have been able to kick it. The dip or the smoke. I love it all."

"From the looks of it, tobacco is the least of your problems." I motioned toward the needle. "You might want to consider getting some help for that."

"What, this?" he asked and pointed toward the needle in his hands. "On no, lass. This isn't for me. It's for you."

My heart started to hammer in my chest. "Me?"

"Aye," he said. "A crying shame. You had so much potential, or so we'll all lament."

"No one will ever believe it."

"Won't they?" he asked. "People hide the truth from others all the time. And your behavior these past few months has been nothing if not erratic. Oh, I think they'll believe it just fine."

"No," I said. "I have friends who'll know the truth. They'll come for you."

"Will they now?" he said. "Well, maybe we'll deal with them too." He leaned forward, and his voice dropped. "Don't be scared, darling. I've done it a time or two myself. There's no pain. It'll be just like slipping into a nice warm bath. One minute you're here, and the next—" He snapped his fingers. "It's over. Just like that."

"Just like that," I said.

"Don't knock it, lass," he said. "There are worse ways to go."

"If you like it so much, how about you go in my place?"

"I expect I will, but I've got some years yet. You, however, are unfortunately out of time."

The van pulled into a familiar-looking alley, and I caught sight of my own battered car as they pulled up alongside it. Fear rose up within me, tightening its grip on my throat as their plan became clear. I could practically see the headlines. An officer in need of a fix pulls over and accidentally overdoses, causing her car to crash. I had no doubt that once I'd expired, they would place me back within my battered vehicle, and it would be up to the citizens of Boston to call it in, if and when they got around to it.

Such a death would serve as a stain on my record and an embarrassment to the department. I had no doubt that Bulwark and others like him would take steps to try to keep it quiet, sweeping my memory under the rug as swiftly as possible. Those who knew me would know something wasn't right, but any official inquiries would be met with swift blowback, up to and including termination.

I had to hand it to Scutt, and Mack, I suppose, since I was convinced that he was the brains behind all this. They'd planned it out well, near perfect in fact, except they'd forgotten to account for one thing.

"Funny that you mentioned that," I said. "You might not have as much time left as you think."

"Is that so?" Scutt asked. "What are you on about now? You hoping against hope that one of your little friends will be along to save you? I wouldn't bother. No one knows you're here."

"Actually, someone does," I said. "But they're not my friends. And they're sure as hell not yours."

Scutt frowned, and opened his mouth, but something landed on the roof before he could speak, and a moment later a blade shot down, punching through the van's roof and stabbing Officer Thompson in the space where the neck meets the shoulder.

People think scalp wounds are bad, but trust me when I say that neck wounds are where the blood really flows. Thompson screamed, or tried to. He only made it half a second before the blood began to choke him. His hands flailed, and he got his door open, stumbling out of the car and drawing his pistol just as the first Swan-Sister came down beside him.

He raised his gun, but she swept her blade around, sending his pistol along with two fingers flying off down the alleyway. Her reverse strike caught him across the neck, and Officer Thompson hit the floor, slouching down into a kneeling position before expiring.

"What in the hell?" Scutt snarled.

"Look alive, Scutty-boy," I screamed, my voice tinged with mad panic. "You are so freaking boned!"

Scutt's eyes, already beady, somehow grew even smaller, and he snarled something and threw himself forward. There was a desperation in his eyes, and a fury, born of a lifetime of bitterness that told me, no matter his fate, he was going to try his darndest to take me with him.

I brought my hands up, and caught his arm, relying on a two-on-one grip for wrist control. He snarled, sour spit spraying from his lips as he cursed and shoved. Even with both hands, Scutt was not a weak man, and I felt myself being pushed back into the wall. Panic slipped through me, and I raised my knee, shoving it between us as we struggled. I could feel him looming over me, and my hands were weakening. Any second now, they would give way, and the needle would come down into my face. From there...

The van's rear door came open with a loud crash, and I glimpsed the other Swan-Sister a split second before she thrust her sword inside the van. The blade pierced Scutt's back, sliding below his tactical vest, and he jerked up, a low, breathless noise escaping his mouth.

Some people might have been hesitant to attack in that moment, but I wasn't one of them. The moment I felt his grip weaken, I pushed my arms up, thrusting out with all my might and driving his hands back. The needle entered his neck, and his beady eyes widened a fraction of an inch, realization giving way to anger. His eyes went glassy, his jaw tightened as he struggled to maintain control.

"Don't fight it," I said. "Remember what you told me? Just like slipping into a warm bath."

Scutt died without a word, his body slumping over in the van and remaining still. I watched him for a moment to make sure he wasn't playing possum, then turned to regard the Swan-Sister.

"I suppose it's too much to hope that you've suddenly seen the light and are now on my side?"

Her fist snapped up, striking my face and sending me over backward. Dark stars flashed across my vision, and she seized my ankle. My hand shot out, grabbing my pistol and yanking it free of Scutt's belt a split second before she tugged me out.

I didn't try to fight her momentum. Instead, I went with it, sliding out of the van and swinging my arm around. The butt of my pistol impacted the Swan-Sister's face, smashing down onto her cheek and crushing the hard exterior of her mask. It was a good shot, and I wish I'd had time to savor it, because it was the only one I got.

Her sister stepped up beside her and kicked my leg, driving her shin into the crook of my knee and sending me down to one knee. What happened next was essentially a beatdown, with strikes coming from every direction, flattening me down onto the pavement. I dropped my pistol somewhere along the way, and they didn't even bother to pick it up. Eventually, the beating ceased, and I was left as a quivering, bloody mess.

"Surrender the leprechaun to us," the first sister said as her sword came around. She tapped my cheek with the flat of the blade, the cold metal at stark odds with the warm blood leaking down my face.

"That's why you're doing this?" I sputtered. "I thought you were looking for the gold."

The sisters glanced at one another, then the nearest one reached down and seized my hair, forcing my head back and laying her blade against my throat.

"No more games. We know you know where he is. Tell us, and we shall let you live."

"Tell you? Hell, I'll freaking draw you a map," I said.

"That won't be necessary," the one to my left said.

"He won't lead you to the gold," I said. "He's not keeping any of it."

"How do you know this?"

"It's never been about the money," I said.

"Then what is it about?"

"It's about people," I said.

The sisters considered my words, sharing a long meaningful look before reaching their decision. "If what you say is true, then it appears our time in this city has reached its end."

"All that is left is to clean up," her sister replied.

"Regrettable."

"But necessary."

"Agreed." The sister to my left looked down at me. "I am sorry, officer. You have conducted yourself with bravery and honor, but we cannot leave you behind to hunt us."

Realization hit me like a slap, and I shot my hand out toward my pistol, knowing even as I did that it was going to be too late.

Too late for me, and, ironically, too late for the sister to my left.

There was a flash of motion, and then something struck her from behind. It hit hard, hard enough to knock her senseless, and I caught a brief flash of a brownstone brick, the same kind that had been knocked loose when my car crashed, as she crumpled to the ground.

The second sister spun around, bringing her sword to bear just as another brick flew through the air. She jerked her arm, and the blade sliced cleanly through. Too cleanly, in fact. The brick separated, both ends continuing on in their path and striking her in the face. The slash of her blade had slowed their flight, but even at moderate speed, a severed brick to the face still hurts.

Her head snapped back, and she crashed against the van. She caught herself before she could fall, and forced herself back up to a standing position. Footsteps drew her attention, and she turned, raising her sword just as Hilary came into view.

I think the vision of the mild-mannered man in the ill-fitting suit wasn't what she'd been expecting, and it caused her to hesitate, just for a moment, which was all Hilary needed.

He raised his can of OC Spray, and depressed the trigger, casting a steady stream of burning, orange liquid right into her face. The stream found its way into her eyes and the cuts along her face, and she screamed and jerked back, pain overriding any conscious thought.

Kneeling down at her feet, I caught some of the spray's offshoot, the burning liquid causing my eyes to water and my nose to burn.

Experience told me that it would only get worse the longer I remained, so I pushed aside the pain, seized my pistol, and smashed the butt into the back of the sister's head. Her body went stiff, and she crumbled like a board, hands extended out as she hit the ground behind her sister.

Hilary lowered his arm, ceasing the spraying as Basic appeared around the corner. His hands were stained with brown dust, and he seized me around the waist and carried me halfway down the block before setting me down.

I'd inhaled some of the pepper spray, and it took a few minutes to clear my windpipe. Eventually, the burning and the flow of mucus subsided enough that I could speak. "What are you two doing here?"

"We knew you were being followed," Hilary said. "I couldn't stop thinking who would be doing that."

"Worried about you," Basic said.

I swallowed and felt a warmth in my chest that had nothing to do with oxidized cayenne pepper. "Thanks, guys."

"Welcome," Basic said with a smile.

"What should we do with them?" Hilary asked.

I shook my head. "Nothing. At least not yet. You two have got to get back. We don't have much time before—"

Fireworks sounded in the distance, cutting me off as green confetti streamers burst into the air, their emerald bodies dancing across the wind even as the marching band began to play.

"Before the parade begins," I said.

St Patrick's Day Parade. March 17th 1301hrs

THE ROAR OF THE crowd echoed through the streets, thousands of voices coming together in celebration, echoing past me in a wavy cadence that left me feeling cold and scared.

On some level, I refused to believe that we were the only ones who'd worked out what was going to happen. Who believed that the leprechaun gold, which had lured so many, contained a poisoned sting.

Deep down, people had to have suspected what could happen, and yet, they still came. Because they couldn't resist. Because they had to see it for themselves. Because the whispered hint of gold was just too appealing to pass up. Even if it cost them their lives.

"Get back to your positions," I said. "Hurry."

"What about you?" Hilary asked.

"I'll be fine," I said. "Now, go!"

The boys traded one last glance, then they took off, racing back toward the crowds and the parade route. I watched them go, then I took a minute to clear my head. The castoffs of pepper spray had burned my hands and face, similar to what you might receive from a bad sunburn, but I forced myself to ignore them, and set off at a quick jog.

The air had grown thinner, colder somehow, or else it was just my imagination playing tricks on me. Which, given the circumstances, was understandable. I was battered, tired, and hurt, but I refused to quit. The consequences of doing so were too grave to even consider, so I forced myself to keep moving, placing one foot in front of the other, over and over again. It was strenuous work, and I was huffing and puffing pretty hard by the time I finally reached my destination.

One block south of the parade route sat an old, triple decker duplex with wide bay windows on every floor but the top. In year's past, it would have housed six separate families, but a mortgage brokerage company had bought out the building years ago, and now used it for their business operations. As I came to a halt beside it, I paused, gulping air as I surveyed the home.

Someone had kicked in the front door, and I could hear sounds coming from the darkness. I drew my pistol from the holster, an act which should have been automatic, but one that took me two tries because my hand was shaking so badly.

It wasn't exhaustion, although that played a part. It was fear. Plain and simple. I was afraid.

I hadn't gone into law enforcement because I wanted to hurt someone. I knew it was a possibility, but I'd never yearned for action and gunplay the way some officers do. I'd joined because, at the end of the day, I'd wanted to help people. To be of service, both to my city and to the residents who called it home. Even now, my work in Blue Moon was about helping to set people's minds at ease. It wasn't about violence, or retribution. I didn't want to hurt anyone.

But I didn't have a choice.

Halfcrown was inside, and he was preparing to rain death down upon the citizens of Boston. To cast his darkness into the very soul of the city, and I couldn't just stand back and allow that to happen.

So I forced myself to take a breath and put on my big-girl britches, metaphorically speaking of course, and tightened my grip on my pistol until my hand stopped shaking.

I was convinced by now that Tempest had the right of it, that the world of the paranormal was just a fantasy playground for people's minds to explore. But I'd be lying if I said that the house didn't contain one heck of a nasty aura. The temperature dropped as I made my way up the trio of steps, and the cold stabbed at my exposed hands and face, even as the darkness beckoned.

The front door stood broken, indented and shattered wood revealing where someone had kicked it in. I took a deep breath, then I slipped inside, keeping my pistol at the ready. The front door led into a long hallway, with rooms on either side. The mortgage company that had purchased the property had removed the separating walls, transforming family rooms into conference rooms and bedrooms into offices. I went room by room, clearing quick and quiet. As I reached the rear of the house, I stepped into a nicely furnished kitchen with a coffee machine the size of an engine block sitting on the counter. I cleared it, and moved on, hesitating at the entryway.

Footsteps sounded above my head, heavy boots causing the wood to creak as the perpetrator made his way across the floor. I listened for several seconds, then turned and made my way through the halls, coming to the base of the staircase and slowly ascending.

The second floor had more of a working office layout, computers and cubicle desks in abundance for the agents. There were large stacks of paper and messy whiteboards covered in monthly call lists that made me think the clients likely didn't see this area often.

As I came around the corner, I spotted movement in the far office, and ducked down, crouching behind the cubicle wall as a man moved past the doorway. I only glimpsed him, but it was enough to see that he was dressed in dark tactical clothing, with a wrap-around hockey mask and a heavy Mossberg shotgun in his hands. A shiver went through me at the memory of Red Sammy's corpse, crashing down to the cold cement. Just another body in a long line that could be laid at Mack's fee t.

I felt my anger rise.

Now that I knew the identity of the other two assailants, it was easy to see that the third gunman was a match for Mack in terms of height and weight. He was moving fast, with no need of a cane, suggesting that he'd been duping me and everyone else in the department for some time, making us think he was more injured than he actually was in order to alleviate suspicion. It was a dirty, sneaky, underhanded move, and it fit what I knew about him perfectly.

Bastard.

As I crouched, I could feel my ire rising. I'd never spoken it aloud, but Mack was one of the officers I'd looked up to when I was rising through the ranks. I'd liked him. Not only for his quick, if sardonic, wit, but because he believed in getting the job done, no matter what. I thought he was like me, dedicated to the city and eager to be of service. But I'd been wrong.

Mack wasn't in this for the city. He was in it for himself, plain and simple. He liked kicking in doors and dragging drug dealers out by their thumbs because, at the end of the day, he liked hurting people. And his badge gave him the ability to do that without consequence. In some ways, he was as much a junkie as the people he arrested, except in his case, he craved the adrenaline, and the feeling you got after pummeling a suspect into submission. The thrill from turning them, remolding them into informants, then discarding them once they were no longer useful.

It was as close to playing God as someone could reasonably hope to get, and it sickened me in a way that few things ever had.

And it made me angry. Really, *really* angry.

Angry enough that all my compunctions about causing violence melted away. Angry enough to make me leave my hiding spot and sneak across the floor, pressing myself up against the wall and lying in wait until the moment he passed by. Most importantly, angry enough to leap out at the last second and slam the butt of my pistol against his head hard enough to crack his hockey helmet and, hopefully, his skull beneath.

Mack screamed, and stumbled back, his broken helmet dangling loose, blinding him as I drove my fist into his side. The air went out of him in a giant *whoosh*, that only served to fan the fires of my anger. Had I been thinking clearly, I would have disarmed him, then backed off and held him at gunpoint. But I wasn't thinking clearly. I was seeing red, and all I could hear was the sound of my own blood pumping in my ears.

I wanted to hurt Mack.

I wanted him to suffer for what he'd done. For what he'd tried to do to me. For every sleepless night and moment of fear he'd inflicted with only a word. For every whisper that made me feel like I was less than I should be. I wanted payback for all of it.

I slammed my hand into the side of his head, pistol whipping his head back and forth. At some point, he tried to bring his shotgun to bear, but I slammed my knee into his chest and grasped the barrel with my other hand, ripping it free of his grip and sending it spinning across the floor.

I didn't look to see where it landed. I couldn't. Anger and rage were my driving forces now, the fires of hate spurring me on as I smashed the butt of my pistol into his face again and again. Unfortunately, in my fury, I forgot one very important thing.

Mack had a rage all his own. And while mine might have been born of righteousness, his was born of self-interest, and cultivated over a career spanning decades. I could rely on my anger in moments of desperation, but Mack practically lived on his.

I drew back my arm for another swing, and he jerked forward, smashing the top of his broken helmet into my face.

My head snapped back, and I stumbled, feeling the floor tilt beneath me. He shot forward, seized my legs behind the knees and jerked my feet out from under me. I hit the ground, my head bouncing off the wooden floor, and a desperate cry escaped my lips as pain threatened to overwhelm me. I tried to bring my arm around, but he was faster, and he ripped his helmet from his head, swinging it around in a wide circular arc and catching my hand as it came toward him. Pain exploded, and my gun flew across the room, torn from my numb finger s.

Red streaks flashed across my vision, and a low groan escaped my mouth as I brought my hand to my chest. The red gave way to dark stars, dancing their way across my sight, eventually fading and leaving me staring at the unmasked gunman above me. The one who I'd, mistakenly, believed to be Everett Mackleroy.

"Jerry?" I heard myself say.

"Hi, Chloe," he said.

Jerry Gantenbein, lead forensic investigator for the city of Boston, wiped at his face, clearing the blood out of his eyes as he peered around. He searched for a moment, but when he didn't see his shotgun, he settled instead for one of the office rolling chairs, lifting it into the air and swinging it around to test the weight. It couldn't have been more than fifteen pounds, but it was enough to crush someone, i.e., me, if he swung it hard enough.

"It wasn't supposed to be like this," he said. "I imagine you're a little surprised to see me."

"That's an understatement," I said, slowly rising to a sitting position. "Please God, tell me this is not about your balls."

Jerry's face scrunched. "What? No. Of course not. Well, actually, it kind of is, but not like you're thinking."

"Jesus Christ, Jerry."

"It's about the money."

"What do you need money for?"

"What do you think?" he asked. "My brother has nine children. My sister has eleven. We're Irish Catholic in the truest sense."

"So what?"

"So, I have three!" he said. "Do you know how embarrassing that is? For a Gantenbein to only have three children? It's not even enough to field a hockey team. I wanted a house full of kids, Chloe. For as long as I can remember. Girls that looked just like my Rosie, and maybe a couple Jerry juniors in there too."

"So have more."

"*We don't have time*!" he practically roared. "Rosie and I, we're not as young as we used to be, and all the statistics say the same thing. Once you hit forty, the risk of pregnancy skyrockets. You can end up with all sorts of developmental problems. I'm almost fifty! And even if we wanted to risk it, we can't afford it." His voice got very quiet, and his eyes took on a faraway glaze. "I did everything right. I graduated from a well-respected school. I had a perfect GPA, and I busted my ass afterwards to pay off my student loans. I got hired by one of the largest departments in the new England area, and for twenty-five years I've been a model employee. I show up on time, I do my work well, and it all means nothing. There's nowhere for me to go. No more promotions to strive for. This is it." He glared at me. "Do you have any idea what daycare for three kids costs these days?"

"Jerry..."

"I could clone myself three times over and still not make enough to pay for it. That's how bad it is." He shook his head. "I spent my whole life striving for the American dream. The wife, the kids, the white picket fence and the dog. And you know how I can best provide for my family? By dying. True story. My death benefits will pay out more than I ever could. Now you tell me, where's the justice in that?"

"Jerry, this has to stop."

342

"You tell me, Chloe. What's a guy to do?"

"I'm pretty sure masked vigilantism isn't the way to go."

"No? well, maybe you're right, but it seemed like a good idea at the time."

"Isn't this all a moot point?" I asked. "You've already gotten snipped."

"There is a reversal procedure. It's expensive. Worst case, they can always extract it right from the source. But, again, that takes money." He sighed. "It always comes down to money, Chloe."

"Scutt and Thompson are dead."

His face turned dour. "That's unfortunate. Can't say I ever cared for either of them, but still."

"They're going to trace it back to you, Jerry," I said. "People are going to know what you did."

"That's unlikely," he said. "Especially since I'll be the one leading the forensic team. I can claim that any DNA evidence that shows up was just me being sloppy. Blame it on the painkillers from my balls. It'll be embarrassing, but I suspect I'll be taking early retirement soon anyway."

"Hope you have another job lined up," I said. "Because in case you haven't been paying attention, that gold is gone."

"Not all of it," he said. "Twelve and a half million spent means twelve and a half million is left. And I don't need that much. Four or five should be enough." He looked at me for a moment, and his face turned sad. "I'm sorry it has to be this way, Chloe. If I thought I could buy your silence, I would happily do so, but I think we both know I can't." He raised the chair up over his head, preparing to smash it down over my skull. "If it helps, I'll make it look like you died bravely in the line of duty. For what that's worth."

He swept his arms down, the chair streaking right for my skull, and I turned away, raising my arms and bracing for the impact that would end my life.

A loud boom rang out, and the impact never came. I glanced up, noting the scent of gunpowder in the air and found Jerry two steps back from where I'd last seen him. He was staring down at his chest, noting the blood leaking out from behind his vest.

A second boom rang out, and his face disappeared in a haze of blood and gore. I screamed and turned away, instinctively crawling back as his corpse toppled to the floor.

Footsteps sounded as someone crossed the floor, and I peered up just as Agent Gordan came to kneel beside me.

"Are you okay?" he asked.

He took my arm, and helped me to my feet, brushing the dirt and blood off my face and shoulders.

"Chloe?"

"Alex," I said. It came out as more of a choked whisper, but I forced myself to swallow and try again. "I'm fine. It was Jerry. He..."

"I heard," Agent Gordan said. "I'm just glad you're okay."

"It was his balls," I said.

Agent Gordan hesitated. "I don't understand what that means, but we need to get you out of here before—"

"No!" I snapped and seized his arm, forcing him to hold. "Halfcrown."

Agent Gordan frowned, then realization dawned. "Wait, he's here?"

I nodded and glanced up toward the third floor.

Agent Gordan followed my gaze, and he swallowed. "What do we do?"

"Gun," I said.

He nodded and briefly stepped away, returning a moment later with my pistol in his hand. I checked the magazine while he did the same with the shotgun. Both appeared to be in working order, and I made my way across the room, pausing at the base of the stairway.

"You coming?"

He nodded, and brought Jerry's shotgun up to his shoulder, steeling himself. "Yeah."

"Okay then," I said. "Time to end this."

Halfcrown.
March 17th
1312hrs

I DON'T REMEMBER WHAT the interior of the third floor looked like. I'm pretty sure it was mainly storage, but I wasn't paying attention. I led the way through the doorway, Agent Gordan covering my back, and immediately drew a bead on Halfcrown standing beside the window.

The leader of the leprechauns stood with his hands clasped behind his back, peering out toward Broadway Street, and the St. Patrick's Day Parade. Dressed in a tailored suit, he wore his mask comfortably, seemingly unbothered.

"Hands!" I snapped instinctively, aligning my pistol on him. "Show me your hands!"

Halfcrown tilted his head but otherwise didn't move. "Sergeant Mayfield. How lovely to see you again."

"The rest of the floor is clear," Agent Gordan said. "He's alone."

I nodded, and drew my handcuffs with my opposite hand, my barrel never leaving Halfcrown's form. "Gerome Reed," I said, my voice loud and clear. "You are under arrest for the robbery of the Federal Reserve. Turn around and put your hands above your head."

Halfcrown, Gerome, didn't move, but I could hear the smile in his voice when he spoke. "That won't be necessary, Sergeant."

"Like hell it isn't," I said. "Do it or I'll shoot you."

"Shoot me if you must," he said and shrugged. "But be aware that doing so could cause a premature detonation. It would be such a shame if now, in the final moments, we were to jump the gun."

A tremor of fear ran through me. "What are you talking about?"

Halfcrown reached up and peeled the mask from his face, allowing his dark wavy hair to be free. He still wore his heavy dark shades, explaining why I'd been unable to see his eyes back in the ironworks facility. "Come and see for yourself. I'm sure Agent Gordan can keep me sufficiently covered for the purposes of one conversation."

I glanced at Agent Gordan who shook his head. He didn't like it, and neither did I, but I couldn't risk it, not if it meant people might die as a result. I grimaced and holstered my pistol, but kept my handcuffs ready as I moved up beside him.

"What am I looking at?"

"Right there," Halfcrown said, and motioned with his hand.

I followed his outstretched finger to where the parade was taking place. Being situated atop the third floor allowed us to see over the Broadway Street storefronts, allowing us a first-rate view of the street.

"Guess you're not as blind as you pretend," I said.

Halfcrown smiled. "Light sensitivity. An accident involving phosphorus in my youth."

"Isn't phosphorus used in bombs?"

"I believe it is. Look now, or you'll miss it."

I looked, and from my vantage point, I could see the parade as it moved. A teenage marching band passed, batons twirling even as they played. Next came a trio of horses, big Clydesdales with their riders waving large flags. They were followed by a large parade float, and I felt Halfcrown shift beside me.

From a distance, there was nothing overly sinister about the float. It was situated on the back of a truck, one of the big ones, used for cargo hauling. The base was made of emerald Astro-turf, and there were wrought iron archways covered in paper mâché decorations, with leprechaun puppets along the side. In the middle stood two large columns. They looked like roman marble, covered with green streamers and clover decorations, but if someone looked closely, you could see they were shaking, trembling really, and the reason behind it became clear a moment later, when the driver, presumably Halfcrown's last remaining accomplice, pressed a button, and the columns fell away, their plastic bodies shredding apart as the floor of the truck shifted, revealing circular openings through which pots of gold rose.

There were nine of them, in homage to the Irish's lucky number. They gleamed on the floats, catching the sunlight in a blinding display that couldn't help but demand attention. For all their dizzying glamour, though, I wasn't looking at the gold. I was staring at the two figures who'd been hidden inside the plastic columns.

I recognized the woman on the left as Maura Youngman, Chief Financial Officer of the Federal Reserve. Beside her was Walter Crosier, head of Avant-Garde Financial Securities, who'd been stripped to the waist with his hands bound above his head, the chains attached to the curved archway. He'd been beaten, his eyes and face swelled nearly shut, with bloody spittle forming dried stains on his chin.

"Here it comes," Halfcrown said. "Any moment now."

"What are you hoping to accomplish by this?" I asked.

"Isn't it obvious?" he asked.

"Humor me."

"The city has lost its soul, Sergeant. You must have seen the signs."

"The city has problems," I said. "But so does everywhere else."

"Problems can be dealt with, but true rot must be cut out or else it will crumple the entire organism. That's what a city is, you know. A collection of parts forming one organism. I'm doing what is necessary, Sergeant. It pains me that you can't see that."

"I'm not sure how taking two men hostage qualifies as returning a soul."

He snorted. "You call them men. I disagree."

"What would you call them?"

"A virus," he said. "One that had blinded its host."

"And you're going to help them to see clearly?"

"No," he said. "I'm going to force them to see clearly. For the first time in their lives, I'm going to pull away the blindfold, to let them see their own corruption. And then—"

"Devil!"

The voice rang out from the hallway, followed by the sound of a sword being drawn from its scabbard. Vermont Wensdale stepped into the room, flipping his cape over his shoulder as he brandished his silver sword. "At last, I have you now, demon. Prepare to answer to the Almighty God, you bastion of Hell!"

"Stand down, Vermont," I said. "He's not a demon. He's just a man."

"With all due respect, Sergeant. These devils are known to be tricksome. Step away, and I will happily smite him."

"I've seen his birth certificate, Vermont. And the reports following his placement into the Department of Children and Families. He's as human as you or I."

Vermont's face faltered, just for an instant. Then his look turned stubborn. "We shall see."

"Alex," I said.

Agent Gordan turned, brandishing the shotgun toward Vermont. "That's close enough."

"You would stand in the way of God's divine justice?"

"Regular justice will do just fine today," I said. "Besides, I can prove it to you."

"How so?" Vermont asked.

I glanced at Gerome. "Would you like to explain, or should I?"

He motioned me with one hand. "By all means, Sergeant."

"Gerome Reed," I said. "Born in the city of Boston, raised in Southie, in this very building in fact." My voice got quiet. "You lived right here in this room, didn't you?"

"You already know the answer to that," Gerome said. "How else would you have known where to find me?"

"None of this proves anything," Vermont said.

"Keep listening," I said, keeping my attention fixed on Gerome. "Your mother passed away of a drug overdose when you were six. Methamphetamines, as it were. Your father was nowhere to be found, and none of the neighbors bothered to check on you. They were used to the screaming, used to the shouting and the loud music. As a result, you spent weeks up here, alone with her corpse, before the smell finally forced them to look in on you."

"Water wasn't hard to find, once I figured out the tub. Food was more of a problem, but I worked around that."

I recalled what I'd read in the report regarding the canine bones and shuddered, swallowing twice before I spoke again.

"You got passed around from foster home to foster home, never really fitting in. When you were eighteen, you scored a near perfect on the SAT's, and received a full ride to Boston University, where you majored in finance and accounting. After graduation, you got a job with Avant-Garde, where you've remained ever since."

"You've certainly done your homework, Sergeant."

"I try," I said. "But I still don't understand why."

"Why what?"

"All of it," I said. "If you wanted payback, you could have just built a bomb. There was no reason to steal."

"I considered it. But others have tried that approach. The marathon bombing, for example. But it was unsuccessful. Do you know why?"

"Tell me."

"Because it was an act of outside violence. Even insects will bind together to stop foreign invaders, but once the threat is dealt with, people are quick to return to their old habits. Real change can only come from within. I'm going to give the good people of Boston a chance to wake up. To recognize the parasites among them and purge themselves of their sickness."

"By detonating a bomb in the middle of the parade?"

"By showing them how shallow they've become," he snapped.

He turned suddenly and raised his hand, revealing the cellphone in his grip. I could see the screen already had the numbers typed, and would only require one touch in order to send its signal. "Look at them, Sergeant. Look down at them and tell me I am wrong."

I didn't want to but I couldn't help it. As the marble columns fell away, the crowd's cheers had turned to gasps, and then... chaos.

Some people screamed and turned away. Others grabbed their children and loved ones, desperately trying to make their way through the throng without being trampled. While others... God help me, others raced toward the float. More than I cared to admit. They leapt over the safety barriers and pushed past the police officers, climbing onto the float and utterly ignoring both Maura Youngman and Walter Crosier as they reached for the gold.

"You see?" Halfcrown said, his voice soft. "They don't even see them. Too obsessed with their own desires."

"You still haven't told me why you needed the gold," I said.

"Because, Sergeant," he said. "It was theirs in the first place."

"What is he talking about?" Agent Gordan asked.

I was quiet for a long moment, allowing the pieces to form together before I spoke. "He's talking about Fidelitycoin," I said.

"What is that?" Vermont asked.

"It's the latest cryptocurrency story," Agent Gordan said. "It went bust, taking untold millions with it."

"Not untold," Gerome said. "Twenty-five million."

"I don't understand how that fits in here," Agent Gordan said.

"It was Avant-Garde, wasn't it," I said. "They were the ones behind Fidelitycoin."

Gerome nodded. "I'm surprised you made the connection, Sergeant."

"Technically, I didn't," I said, thinking back to the papers Hilary had given me. "I've got some friends who have experience selling made-up products."

"Well, this would certainly qualify," Halfcrown said. "It's scary how easy it was. When Mr. Crosier first pitched the idea, I didn't believe it could work. How could you sell a product that never even existed?" he shrugged. "But we pretended it did, and we marketed it, and the money came rolling in. Like a hose leading down into the city, sucking the life from its citizens, stealing pensions, mortgage payments, college tuitions and life savings. We bled this city for all we could, then we just turned it off. Dropped the value to zero and disappeared. And you want to know the worst part? No one even cared, Sergeant. No one even came looking, or asking questions. We ruined lives, stole homes and dreams, and no one even bothered to ask us why."

"That doesn't give you the right to kill anyone," I said.

"Doesn't it?" he asked. "You would seek half-measures, but that will only delay the inevitable. We have to wake people up, to make them realize that their survival is intertwined with one another. And the only way to do that is to take what they thought they valued most, and detonate it before their very eyes. To show them the remains of their own, torn apart by the very gold they craved, and ask them which they would prefer to have returned to them. No, Sergeant. I will not deal in half measures. This is the way it has to be."

My pistol came free from my holster as he raised his hand, hesitating with his finger over the green *send* button.

"Don't do this."

"You're a good officer, Sergeant Mayfield," Halfcrown said. "But you're just as blind as the rest of them."

He tapped the *send* button, and the screen flashed, and out by the parade grounds... nothing happened.

Inside the house, silence reigned for several seconds, and then Halfcrown looked at his phone, noting the *No Signal* message flashing across the screen.

"I assume this is your work?" he asked as he lowered his hand.

"Actually, it came from a really inventive little virgin, if you can believe it," I said. "Kids today are scary. All it took was some know-how and a few hundred dollars to knock out every cell phone in the South End."

"Jammers are notoriously fickle. I'm surprised you were willing to trust it."

"Desperate times," I said. "Plus, I wasn't trusting to one jammer. I was trusting to four."

That part was true. Basic, Hilary, Robbie and Lieutenant Kermit were all spread throughout the parade, each with jammers inside their backpacks.

"Extraordinary," Halfcrown said and sighed. "What happens next?"

I drew my cuffs from my pocket. "Turn around and put your hands behind your back. Gerome Reed, you are under arrest for... a lot."

"A lot will do for now," he said.

He turned around, and the cuffs went on without complaint. I patted him down, but found no other weapons, and we all departed the attic, making our way down the stairs to the street. I suddenly realized that my car was crushed a few blocks away, but Agent Gordan's loaner car was pulled up along the curb. He'd gotten my message late, and rushed here as soon as he could.

"I'll take him," he said, motioning toward Halfcrown. "This is still a federal investigation, but I'll be sure Blue Moon receives all the credit.

Agents have already been dispatched to apprehend the leprechaun driving the float. I give them even odds."

"We can hope," I said.

Agent Gordan took Halfcrown and lowered him into the back of the car. The leprechaun leader went in without complaint. A thought occurred to me, and I stepped forward before Agent Gordan could shut the door.

"Ask you one last question?"

"By all means," Halfcrown said.

"Why the leprechaun motif?"

"Ah, that." He gave a sad little smile. "Because, Sergeant, people aren't interested in other people anymore. They're interest in brands. Consumers want to be able to connect to something. They want trademarked names and familiar emblems. A business can't simply be a business anymore. It must have a greater goal, a purpose beyond merely providing its goods. And since we no longer trust our politicians, sports stars, news anchors, or scientists—"

"You gave them a mascot, an idea."

"Precisely," he said.

"Well, I've got to hand it to you. You really thought it through."

"Not well enough, evidently." He hesitated a moment, then turned to me. "You won't be able to forget it, you know. The sight of all those people, tearing into one another to retrieve the gold. It will stay with you, lingering in the back of your mind. Always making you wonder."

"It's not pretty," I admitted. "But we'll get it worked out."

"This isn't the end you know. People will come. Others, like me, to finish what I've started."

"Maybe," I said. "Or maybe they'll find a better way."

"There is no better way," he said. "I would think you of all people would understand that."

"Me?"

"You upheld your vows, did your duty to the best of your ability and what did you get for it? Cast aside like a stray dog, thrown to the periphery so that your superiors didn't have to look at you."

"I prefer to think of it another way."

"How is that?"

"I was assigned to a division that I'd never even heard of before. Maybe it wasn't what I wanted, but I've made the best of it, and I found a purpose. And right now, I'm thinking I wouldn't trade it for anything."

"They'll turn on you at the first sign of weakness."

There was no need to ask which they he meant. "They've already tried. But I'm still here. At least for one day more."

"Is that enough?"

"It will have to be," I said.

Aftermath.
March 24th
1700hrs

THE SIGHT OF HALFCROWN'S parade float, as well as the kidnapping and imprisonment of Maura Youngman and Walter Crosier, not to mention the presence of multiple explosive devices in close proximity to the St Patrick's Day parade crowd, went over about as well as you might expect.

Deputy Bulwark as well as the chief of police were called to give statements, which were then followed by the mayor, as well as several other city officials, who all read *their* statements. The words might have differed, but the sentiment was the same. Crime would not be tolerated, and everyone seemed to agree that heads would roll.

For once though, my head wasn't on the chopping block. Agent Gordan made sure of that when he outlined Blue Moon division's contributions in his official report. As a result, I got to sit back and watch politics in action. It was kind of fun, actually.

Halfcrown disappeared into the corrections system. No bail was given, for obvious reasons, and he would need to cool his heels while the FBI prepared to go to trial. They never found his last man, although all implications seem to be that it was August Varice, who has since disappeared into parts unknown. The FBI issued a warrant for his arrest, and Agent Gordan seemed convinced it was only a matter of time before he ended up in custody.

Vermont Wensdale and his partners disappeared shortly after Halfcrown was arrested. Off into parts unknown. Wherever they ended up, I hoped they stayed there.

The Swan-Sisters were long gone by the time officers arrived at the scene, and there's been no word of them since. I still didn't know for certain who they'd been working for, but something told me I hadn't seen the last of them yet. Not every mystery gets solved at the time we might wish, and I decided not to push too hard.

Hilary and Basic flew back to England a few days later, proudly toting their battle scars as I dropped them off at the airport. It's entirely possible that, in the wake of the events, we all went out celebrating, drank too much and ended up with matching tattoos, but that's a story for another time.

The news of Jerry, Scutt, and Thompson rocked the upper brass, who took steps to sweep it under the rug as quickly and quietly as possible. The official story was that three officers had gone rogue searching for the gold. No one was eager to push any harder than necessary to close the report, and their funerals were somber affairs.

Mack's name was never brought up or associated with them, slippery bastard, and it was about a week later, once he'd finally closed the Ricky Brannon case, when I finally caught up to him in the men's locker room.

I was leaning against the wall with my arms crossed when he emerged from the shower. I was certain he noticed me, but he pretended he hadn't, dropping his towel to the floor and rolling his shoulders before he turned around.

"Chloe," he said feigning surprise. "You sneak in here to try and see me naked?"

"Sure did," I said. "I had no idea you preferred cold showers."

"Very funny," he said. "Help you with something?"

"Wanted to see if you had dinner plans," I said. "Thought you might be getting lonely, what with all your friends dead."

Mack's face darkened, but he shook it off fast. "Thanks, but I'll pass."

"I also wanted to deliver a warning. Back off me, or else this gets ugly."

He snorted. "You think you can scare me?"

"I think I know you, Mack. Or at least I understand enough to expose you for what you really are."

"What's that?"

"A real tough guy."

"Flattery won't save you, Chloe."

"It wasn't meant as a compliment," I said. "Tough guys don't like being pushed around, and they sure as hell don't like being taken advantage of."

"What are you talking about?"

I reached behind my back and drew out a manilla envelope. Inside were three photographs, depicting the elder leprechaun, the one with the machete, and the ex-military junkie. I drew them from the envelope and tossed them down on the floor. "Ernest Harris, Amelia Brackwater, and Frankie Crispin. All part of Halfcrown's crew. All dead."

"So? What's this got to do with me?"

"I'll get to that," I said. "In the meantime, it makes you wonder, doesn't it? How Halfcrown went about recruiting these individuals. I mean, he wasn't exactly an intimidating figure, and I haven't been able to find any ties to organized crime or the black market. Really makes you think, doesn't it?"

"You're still grasping at straws."

"Maybe," I said. "Course, if I was Halfcrown, I know what I would do. I'd find someone to help me out. A middleman, such as it were. Someone who knew the underworld like the back of his hand. Someone who could point me in the right direction, help me to recruit people with the right skills but also sense enough to keep their mouth shut. Any of this ringing a bell?"

"Can't say it is."

"I'm glad to hear that. Because if I was wrong, or if you were lying, well that would mean you played an integral part in the robbery of the Federal Reserve."

"You done rambling yet?"

"I checked, Mack. All three of those people have priors, and all three of them were made confidential informants per your request."

Mack's face had taken on a deadly sheen, and there was a hardness in his eyes that sent warning bells ringing in my head.

"You share this little theory with anyone yet?"

"No need," I said. "It's enough that you and I know."

I could have kept going, but honestly, there was no need. We both knew I'd figured it out.

To Mack's credit, he probably didn't actually know what he was getting into. Trying to rob the Federal Reserve was beyond the scope of most people to imagine, and likely Mack had no clue what they were doing until it was too late. Halfcrown wouldn't have shared the target with him, and Mack would have assumed it was a local bank, or possibly Gerome's own company. He would never have gotten involved had he known the truth.

Some crimes you can get away with, but not this one. Robbing the Federal Reserve was too big, and if any of them got caught, now or down the line, they were almost certain to leverage what they knew into a reduced sentence. In short, Mack had been duped, and now his ass was on the line. Which is why he brought in Ruscutt, Thompson, and Jerry. Only problem was he didn't know where to find Halfcrown. He likely assumed they'd fled the state, but once the bags of coins started showing up, he knew they were back.

He couldn't hunt himself, not while still recovering, so he put his people on the trail, set them to scouring the city in search of Halfcrown and his minions. Jerry might have thought it was about the money, but I was willing to bet Ruscutt and Thompson knew the truth. They wouldn't be safe unless Halfcrown and his people were in the ground. The gold could be dealt with, in time, but not until all the loose ends were tied up.

Mack is nothing if not efficient.

"People are dead, Mack," I said.

"This is Boston," he said. "Men have always died for it. Today or tomorrow, that will never change. You've been on the street for a few years and you think you know what's what, but take it from someone who's really been there. I've seen into the dark soul of this city, and no one who goes looking for trouble stays innocent for long."

"I guess we'll find out," I said. "Be seeing you, Mack."

I left the locker room and went home, arriving to find a message on my cell phone. It was from Agent Gordan. He called to tell me he was going to be staying in Boston for a bit and asked me out to dinner. I was pretty sure it was a date, and I would be lying if I said I wasn't excited. Time will tell how that goes.

I never bothered to see how much of the gold was recovered. In the end, I didn't care.

There are plenty of other things more important than money.

The End

Author's Note

Dear Readers,

I've always loved a good heist story. The gathering of roguish professionals, each boasting their own area of expertise, the casing of the target, the plan, the heist, the inevitable setback, and finally, victory through the narrowest of margins. All too often though, the story fails to address what happens after. Is it all beachfront resorts and little umbrella drinks? How do you *actually* exchange millions of dollars' worth of gold? Such questions bounced around in my mind as I began to work on Massacre Site.

Halfcrown was an interesting, if slightly dark, character for me to write, in that he made me ponder what would need to happen to cause someone to not only steal such a large amount of gold, but then to turn around and give it back, albeit in unexpected ways. He's certainly a complex character, and I can't promise that he won't reappear again at some point.

Regarding Fidelitycoin. I am not, nor will I ever claim to be, an expert on cryptocurrency. I will, however, say that even a cursory online search will reveal several celebrity or influencer-endorsed cryptocurrency investments that seemingly disappeared overnight, taking untold amounts of wealth with them. Make of that what you will.

Some of you may have noticed that I racked up the tension between Detective Everett Mackleroy and Chloe in this one. While still a work of fiction, interdepartmental disagreements do occur in real-world law enforcement departments, and putting on a badge does not magically bestow upon one the ability to peaceably work through disagreements with their fellow officers. Coups, blackmail, and betrayals do happen, and oftentimes, carry heavy and unforeseen consequences.

My choice to include the St Patrick's Day Parade in this tale was not an accident. I had the good fortune to witness multiple parades during my time in Boston, and there truly is nothing quite like it. Green beer, green blessings, and good energy abound. In many ways, such celebrations form the very the heart of the city.

It is my sincere hope, dear reader, that you have enjoyed Chloe's adventures up to now. I know I have enjoyed writing them, and being able to bring Hilary and Basic into this book in such a profound way had me giggling with glee on more than one occasion. Likewise with Vermont Wensdale. I believe that his parking garage sword-fight with the Swan-Sisters may be one of my favorite scenes so far.

What's next? Book 3 will follow Chloe and Blue Moon division as they come up against their most dangerous, and most renowned, enemy to date. Legends of Sleepy Hollow are in rich supply, catching the attention of the supernatural world, including those of the Sisters of Salem, as Chloe sets out to solve the mystery of the Headless Horseman.

Until next time, thank you all so much for your continued support. It means the world to me.

Justin Herzog

What's Next for Chloe?

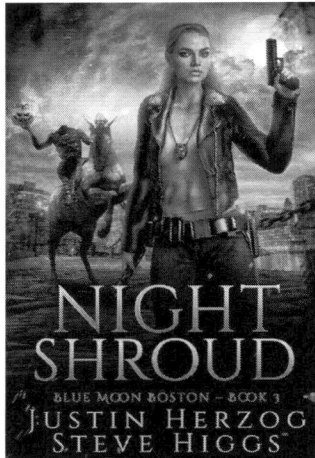

The Headless Horseman. Everyone knows the legend. That's all it is, right?

MASSACRE SITE

When a third headless victim is found on Boston's streets, Chloe Mayfield is tasked with finding the person behind the crime spree – no one else wants a case this weird. It would be easy to dismiss the murders as nothing more than the random acts of a madman with a cosplay fetish, but when her investigations lead her to the morgue, she comes face to face with an apparition she cannot explain.

Throw in the stalker-like attentions of a deranged clown, dangerous interactions with the Salem witches, and an enemy within her own police department who intends to see her fail, and Chloe is in for an uphill battle. Not only to solve the case but to get through it alive.

Mess this up and she's either out of a job, dead, or both.

Other Series in the Blue Moon Universe

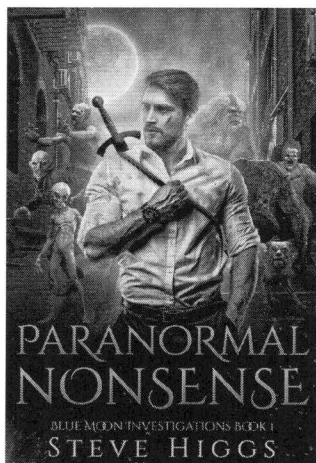

Fight a demon, investigate a werewolf biker gang, have tea with mum ... it's all in a day's work for England's #1 paranormal P.I.

When a master vampire starts killing people in his hometown, paranormal investigator, Tempest Michaels, takes it personally ...

... and soon a race against time turns into a battle for his life. He doesn't believe in the paranormal but has a steady stream of clients with cases too weird for the police.

Mostly it's all nonsense, but when a third victim turns up with bite marks in her lifeless throat, can he really dismiss the possibility that this time the monster is real?

Joined by an ex-army buddy, a disillusioned cop, his friends from the pub, his dogs, and his mother (why are there no grandchildren, Tempest?), our paranormal investigator is going to stop the murders if it kills him ...

... but when his probing draws the creature's attention, his family and friends become the hunted.

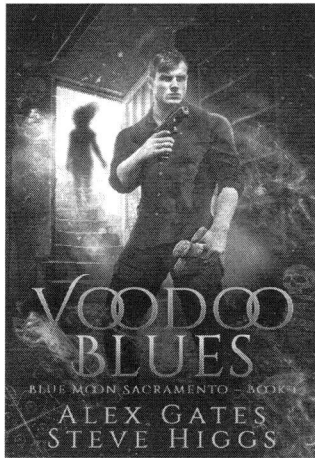

Curiosity. It's going to get more than just the cat killed.

Sacramento has its share of spooky, crazy, and unexplained, just like everywhere else, but most other places don't have a self-appointed paranormal investigator to really stir things up.

There are good reasons to fear the night. August Watson is about to kick them in the pants.

With an oversized sidekick, a school-skipping apprentice, and too many bad habits to count, August aims to drag the truth into the light. Kicking and screaming if necessary.

More Books by Justin Herzog

Fairy tale legend Goldilocks is all grown up and working for the US Forest Service.

The newest member of the agency, she spends her days patrolling the

Divide, guarding the bridgepoints that separate our world from The Land and the descendants of the Native American tribesmen who reside there.

When a daughter of the Thunder Song Tribe is killed on our side of the forest, Goldilocks sets out to learn the truth. The chiefs want answers, not to mention her boss, and Goldilocks means to find them, preferably before the tribesman declare the Cabot Accords void and cross The Divide themselves.

When the evidence names her oldest friend as the murderer, she finds herself in a race against time, searching to find the truth and catch a killer whose murderous actions could set the whole forest ablaze and see her burned along with it.

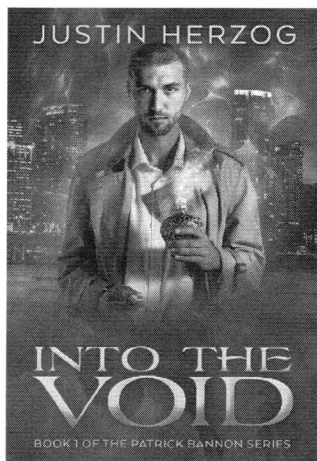

MASSACRE SITE

My name is Patrick Bannon, and I'm a demonologist.

Most people would agree that the study of demons isn't a practical area of research. Lucky for me, Miami has never been a practical kind of city.

With more reported cases of demonic possession than any other two cities combined, the jewel of South Florida can be a dangerous place for those who don't respect it, and when trouble strikes, it falls to me to set it right.

Now a renowned Catholic reverend is dead, and the church wants to know if it was suicide or murder.

Simple, except when it isn't.

To make matters worse, word on the street is that Tiberius, the demon responsible for my brother's suicide, is trying to claw his way back up from the Void.

One guess who sent him there.

Free Books and More

Want to see what else I have written? Go to my website.

https://stevehiggsbooks.com/

Or sign up to my newsletter where you will get sneak peaks, exclusive giveaways, behind the scenes content, and more. Plus, you'll be notified of Fan Pricing events when they occur and get exclusive offers from other authors because all UF writers are automatically friends.

Copy the link carefully into your web browser.

https://stevehiggsbooks.com/newsletter/

Prefer social media? Join my thriving Facebook community.

Want to join the inner circle where you can keep up to date with everything? This is a free group on Facebook where you can hang out with likeminded individuals and enjoy discussing my books. There is cake too (but only if you bring it).

https://www.facebook.com/groups/1151907108277718

Printed in Dunstable, United Kingdom

65474206R00220